CONQUER
ME

THE ROYALS SAGA

Alexander & Clara

Command Me

Conquer Me

Crown Me

Smith & Belle

Crave Me

Covet Me

Capture Me

A Holiday Novella

Complete Me

Alexander & Clara

Cross Me

Claim Me

Consume Me

Smith & Belle

Breathe Me

Break Me

Anders & Lola

Handle Me

X: Command Me Retold

MORE BY GENEVA LEE

CONTEMPORARY ROMANCE

THE RIVALS SAGA

Blacklist

Backlash

Bombshell

THE DYNASTIES SAGA

London Dynasty

Cruel Dynasty

Secret Dynasty

FANTASY & PARANORMAL ROMANCE

FILTHY RICH VAMPIRES

Filthy Rich Vampire

Second Rite

Three Queens

THE ROYALS SAGA: TWO

CONQUER ME

GENEVA LEE

ESTATE

CONQUER ME

Estate Publishing + Entertainment

www.GenevaLee.com

First published, 2014, fourth ed.

Cover design © vitaly tiagunov/adobestock.com

To Lindsey,
your attitude inspires me

CHAPTER ONE

Portobello Road hummed with early morning activity. Vendors set up cluttered tables as shopkeepers swept their steps. All around me the familiar, cozy neighborhood came to life, waking to a new day. But I was trapped in a nightmare. The world still spun, but I couldn't process the mundane, daily rituals of normal life any more than I could comprehend what had happened. My chest ached with the stabbing pressure of a shattered heart. I'd come here yesterday expecting only one thing: closure. I'd gotten it. At least, I thought I had. But with each step I took away from Alexander, it became harder to breathe. My lungs had turned to lead, unable to inhale the warm summer air. My knees went weak, barely able to support my weight.

I couldn't be Alexander's secret. I refused to be. But cutting him out of my life felt like I was carving out my own heart and leaving it behind me. Life without Alexander seemed an impossibility. Living a lie with him was too dangerous. Shouldn't I choose a clean break now rather than be systematically shattered by secrets and lies and gossip? I'd done what I had to do, but that fact was cold consolation.

And beyond that, I'd abandoned him. What he'd offered me wasn't a life—not a real one. Could he even see that? All it proved to me was that he felt as deeply for me as I did for him. Instead of showing him I loved him, I'd left. How could I do anything else when he denied me even the reassurance of words? He was expected to marry politically. He was expected to rule this country.

Neither of us had expected to fall in love.

Now we'd destroyed each other.

The realization crashed into me, and I stumbled, falling against an old brick storefront. How would I survive Alexander?

The numb ache that permeated my body shifted to powerful grief. The rawness in my throat burst into a torrent of angry tears that rolled uncontrollably down my face. I didn't bother to wipe them away even as the evidence of sadness pooled on my lashes and blurred my vision.

It didn't matter. Nothing mattered.

I had dared to love him despite the risk. He'd warned me. I had warned myself. I hadn't gone to his bed blindly, but I hadn't expected more than a fling. I'd been reckless, and the price had been my heart.

I had given him my body, and he had taken my soul.

And then he was there, standing before me with the same pain shining from his beautiful blue eyes. Every inch of me longed to go to him, to ease away the ache I felt in his arms. I sensed that he needed to be comforted, and I knew I was the only person who could give him peace. I held back even as my tears fell freely.

"Clara, you can't leave. Come back with me," he commanded, but uncertainty colored the demand, the question lurking in it foreign to his perfect lips. Alexander was not a tentative man. He took what he wanted without argument. Partially because he was the Crown Prince of England, but partially because he exuded a raw, almost primal, authority. He was not a man to be questioned, and he wasn't a man to question. But now he was standing before me doing the one thing I couldn't have imagined.

I blinked against the sea of tears obstructing my vision and drank him in. My breath hitched in my throat at the intensity blazing in his eyes, blue as the tip of a flame. His nearly black hair was still tousled from my fingers clutching it as he'd fucked me relentlessly hours before. Had his chiseled, full lips been on mine so recently? It felt like an eternity since I'd felt their soft, but firm touch—since they'd slipped between my legs and left kisses that promised so much more pleasure. But what had stolen my breath wasn't his godlike face or the edge of vulnerability hidden in his command.

He stood in sandals and worn jeans that hung low on his hips, but in his haste to reach me, he hadn't bothered to find a shirt. The body he had kept from me for so long—the body that I found indescribably beautiful—was on full display, *including* the ugly scars of his past. He had hidden out of shame until I'd pushed him to reveal himself to me in a night that had taken us both over the edge. Now he was here, demanding more from me. Despite his tone, I knew the truth. He was as unguarded as I was, bleeding out before me as he risked everything to bring me back.

I loved him even more for it. That didn't change anything. I couldn't allow it to.

"I can't, Alexander." My words were hollow, as dull on my lips as an empty promise. Each time I refused him, I broke more, my heart shattering into millions of fragments with each denial, and I couldn't imagine that it would ever heal again.

"I don't accept that." He moved toward me so quickly that my head spun. With him even closer, it became harder to think as my body betrayed me, drawn to his mere presence before I could fight my baser instincts. His arms circled tightly around my waist as he pulled me roughly against him. My nipples beaded under my shirt as they brushed against his bare chest, and my sex pulsed, still filled with him. My body submitted without a word, desperate for him to take me. Alexander was my drug, and I was powerless to deny myself. I craved him—his tireless tongue, his thick cock and more than anything the liberation of being under his control. "You're mine, Clara. You can't fight that. You belong to me."

Even as he laid his claim, and even as my thighs clenched at the knowledge of what it meant to be Alexander's, I couldn't ignore the truth. "But you don't belong to me."

"Like hell, I don't," he growled. "You have me by the balls, Clara. All I can think about is being inside of you. It's taking every ounce of restraint that I have not to put you over my shoulder, carry you home, and fuck you until you're too sore to walk away. Fuck you until you understand that I won't let you go—not without a fight."

I shook my head, wrenching away from him. My sadness turning to white-hot rage. "Tell me that I won't be your secret. Tell me that I'm more than a good fuck, Alexander. Tell me that no matter what happens—no matter what your father thinks or what your birthright demands—that you belong to me."

Alexander shoved a hand roughly through his hair, tension rippling across his tensed jaw. "It's more complicated than that."

"It's as simple as that," I spat back, crossing my arms protectively against my chest as though to erect a barrier between us. Still I struggled to keep my body under my own command. "It's only as complicated as you make it."

"I told you the Royals were fucked up," he said, the words spoken with distaste. "And I'm the most fucked up of all."

"Choose to be your own man." My words were harsh, but I couldn't quite hide the plea in my voice. "Can't you see that you have a choice?"

He laughed, but there was no trace of amusement on his face. "Can't you see that I don't?"

I steeled myself, knowing what he needed to hear—what he needed to face—and knowing that saying those words again would hurt worse than before, especially while my wounded heart was still raw. "I love you, Alexander."

The fire in his eyes cooled and he stepped back. I'd expected the reaction, but it stung all the same. It was a lot to ask him to say it. Hell, it was a lot to ask him to return my love. I knew he did, I felt it with as much certainty as my own feelings. Watching him recoil was enough to show me that would never be enough though.

"I can't, Clara," he said. His tone wasn't sad, it was cold.

My lips trembled as sadness pricked my eyes. "You won't."

He regarded me for a long moment, a muscle twitching in his neck before he opened his mouth. "I won't."

"Then I can't come back with you." I didn't fight the fresh

tears as they came. We'd both acknowledged the truth. Now there was no choice but to move on.

The thought left me numb, frozen to the spot, as though I'd been cursed. When Alexander wrapped an arm around my waist and drew me slowly to him, I didn't resist. I couldn't find it in me. The pain gave way to an emptiness that echoed inside me. It felt like that abyss would stretch across the hours into the days into the months into the years and fill my life with oblivion. I scarcely registered it as Alexander brushed a strand of loose hair from my face and tucked it behind my ear.

"Impossible to control," he murmured, and this time there was sadness in his words.

"Stop trying," I whispered.

A faint grin tugged at his lips, but it was gone in an instant. "I already miss you."

My eyes squeezed shut, the hot tears leaking through. There was no point in pretending this was okay. It was not going to be okay. My life wasn't a fairytale, and there was no happily ever after. I knew that even as his mouth captured mine.

Our mouths crushed together, betraying the urgency coursing through each of us. There was so much that would never be said, and I opened my mouth to his, allowing his tongue to take mine—allowing him to dominate me one more time. His kiss burned through my blood until I was on fire. Passion mixed with fear, and even as I clung to him the flames of desire slowly engulfed me as though I'd found myself ignited on a pyre. Gasping against him, I clutched his shoulders, my fingernails digging into his hard flesh, terrified to let go. Terrified of what waited for me on the other side of that kiss. But he didn't release me, even as our lips broke free, and we struggled for air.

We understood what would happen if we let go.

Alexander brushed a kiss across my forehead and I closed my eyes, searching for one last burst of strength to see this through. It was there, and the sad thing was, it was there because of him. Him. Us. I'd found that strength in what we shared. He'd given it to me.

He gave me the strength to pull away.

His head dropped as I stepped back and when he finally lifted it again, he only said two words.

"Goodbye, Clara."

Alexander raised his hand in the air and a second later a sleek Rolls-Royce pulled to the curb beside us. He opened the door and gestured for me to get in. I didn't question him. The fight was gone from me, the strength ebbing away.

I slid into the backseat without a word. He gave a quiet smile, so different than the cocky grin I'd fallen in love with, and shut the door.

Norris didn't speak. He understood without instructions what was expected of him, and as he pulled away, Alexander turned in the direction of the house that could have been ours. There was no hesitation. He strode toward it as though there was no other choice. He'd made it clear there was none. So I wept for my broken heart and my broken man as he walked back toward a future that we would never share—as he walked back out of my life.

The door clicked shut softly behind me. Morning light streamed through the slit where the curtains met, but I was going back to bed. The thought of facing today was too much. I needed to be unconscious, but even sleep wouldn't be an escape. Alexander would follow me into my dreams.

Something stirred on the sofa as I passed it, and a sleepy Belle sat up, rubbing her eyes. Judging from her tousled hair and yoga pants, she'd fallen asleep waiting for me to come home. She opened her mouth but shut it again when she saw my face. I didn't need a mirror to know that my eyes were rimmed with red and my nose was running.

"You went to see him." It wasn't a question, it was a statement of fact. There was no judgment in her voice. She'd made her fair share of mistakes in her love life as well, which was probably why she sprung into action without another word. Within seconds, a blanket, still warm from her body, was wrapped around my shoulders.

I sat, numb from shock, as she wrenched open and slammed kitchen cupboards. She found the coffee, took one look, and threw the bag back onto the shelf. "Screw that. We need something stronger."

It wasn't even nine o'clock in the morning, but I didn't argue with her. I didn't have the strength. She poured a glass of white wine and held it out to me. I took it and sipped absently.

I could sense Belle's barely contained curiosity. She wanted to know what happened, and if I knew my best friend, she was doing a lot to contain the questions that must be bursting out of her. That was why she was my best friend. Anyone else, my mother included, wouldn't have been able to control themselves. Belle understood what I needed: time.

Time to process what had happened. Time to get used to the idea that Alexander was no longer a part of my life—that he would never be a part of my life. Right now...right now, that seemed impossible. Right now I couldn't fathom how the world was still spinning.

Belle led me into the bathroom and began to fill the tub. I didn't protest. I kept watching until she pried my wine glass from my fingers. It slipped from my hand and a sob wrenched through me. What else would be taken from me? It was an irrational thought and I didn't care. Nothing made sense anymore. Why fight it? My life—the life that only a few weeks ago felt like it was just beginning—was over. Tomorrow I would have to start over. Tomorrow I'd have to face a reality without Alexander.

"Today, you cry," Belle said softly, as though she had read my mind.

Today I will cry, I agreed silently. I would slip into the warm bath she had run and let my tears fall into the water until I was raw and new—until I had washed away the pain. But even as I lowered myself into the tub, I knew I'd never purge Alexander from my memory. He was in my blood. His touch was branded into my skin. I belonged to him even if I could never belong with him.

"Tomorrow will be easier." Belle perched on the side of the tub. She didn't pressure me to talk to her. Instead, we sat there in silence.

Belle was wrong about tomorrow. It would never be easier. I'd had my heart broken before, but not like this. Losing Alexander had fractured something deep inside of me —he'd broken my soul and spirit. I had never given myself to anyone like I had given myself to him. I never would again. It wasn't possible. Love as beautiful and brutal as ours didn't come twice in a lifetime. A human might be able to survive its loss once, but our survival instinct would never allow us to be that vulnerable again.

"I'm here when you're ready to talk." Belle slipped from the room, but she would be right around the corner. I had no doubt that she'd give me the space I needed to cope while sticking as close to me as possible.

For now, I was alone, and I released my grief fully, allowing myself to truly feel it. It ripped through me, splintering and shattering my heart until there was nothing left. All that remained was a hollow ache that sat in my chest and made it hard to breathe. Even at that moment, I wouldn't have changed anything. The only thing more impossible than imagining life without Alexander was imagining that he'd never been a part of my life at all. I would live on memories. I would subsist on remembrance because before he came into my life I was starving and hadn't known it. I'd made the right decision. Any longer and I might not have lived through it when he inevitably left me. Today wasn't about what my heart wanted; it was about survival. I'd had him for a fleeting moment. Our time together had been too short, but I knew it had to be enough.

CHAPTER TWO

I breezed past the man holding the door for me with a genuine thank you, moving quickly when I realized he wanted to chat with me. He didn't look like a reporter, but I'd learned the hard way to distrust any seemingly random interest shown by strangers. Besides that, there was no time this morning. Belle, my well-meaning but nosy best friend, had delayed me twenty minutes at the flat we shared. Now I had less than half an hour to prep for a meeting with one of our most important clients.

Peters & Clarkwell was still relatively quiet this early on a Tuesday morning, but that wouldn't last for long. Ever since we'd officially landed the Isaac Blue campaign, the atmosphere in the office had shifted from relaxed to insanely hectic—and I loved it. Whereas many of my co-workers hated the new work pace, I thrived on it. The workload distracted me from my mess of a personal life and left me little time to think about Alexander. For two and a half months, I'd practically lived here, the first one in and the last one home. I didn't stop working until my eyes refused to stay open, making my dreams the only time Alexander invaded my thoughts. I couldn't stop him from finding me there.

Tori waved at me from her cubicle, surprising me a little. The vivacious redhead actually had a life—one she'd been pressuring me to be a part of—and she had never once beaten me into work. I paused at her desk, bracing myself for the usual entreaties to go out for dinner or to grab a drink. "You're here early."

I forced a smile onto my lips. I liked Tori, someday we might even be friends. Right now all I could think of was work. Fun wasn't in my vocabulary. I'd tried to go out to dinner with Belle and a few friends a couple of times over the course of the summer, only to be acutely reminded of Alexander's absence. Now I knew better.

Tori grimaced and tugged her jacket together to hide a glittery halter top.

Smudged eyeliner and questionable work attire? "Rough morning?" I asked.

Or rough night? I added silently.

She leaned forward and lowered her voice even though we were the only ones in the office this early. "Can you tell that I haven't slept? Four in the morning is not the time to remember you forgot to get the last numbers run for the Blue campaign, especially if you're at Brimstone."

I laughed weakly, hoping I appeared sympathetic. Inside I reeled over her innocuous confession, feelings and thoughts swarming my brain too quickly to process. I'd been to that club before, and the flash of jealousy that ripped through me at its mention startled me. Had he been there last night, too? Had she been close to him without even knowing it? It wasn't only that. Just the term *brimstone* meant so much more to me than Tori could possibly know. I hadn't had to face it before now. Brimstone wasn't exactly a word used in everyday conversation. That was one of the reasons I'd chosen it as my safe word. Brimstone was supposed to be the word that protected me when Alexander pushed things too far—when he demanded more than I could give him.

I'd only used it once, and I'd never use it again.

Tori coughed politely and I shook my head, trying to free myself from the painful memories. "Sorry," I murmured. "I have to finish up a few things before Isaac arrives, too. My head's in two places at once."

"I completely understand," she sympathized. "We should get lunch when we wrap this up."

I hesitated, immediately searching for an excuse. "This week is terrible for me. I have a hundred reports to follow up on with Isaac's publicity team."

Tori dismissed my excuse with a shrug. "Maybe some other time."

"Absolutely," I said. *Maybe* was the only commitment I could give people these days. Glancing at the office clock, I realized my conversation with Tori had effectively wasted five precious minutes.

Slinging my bag into my desk drawer, I pulled out my Blue Foundation campaign file to prep for today's meeting.

"You ready?" Bennett asked. His usually friendly smile had grown tired.

I paused and studied my boss. The circles under his eyes were darker and his curly brown hair seriously needed a comb. "How about you?"

"I look that bad, huh?" He dropped into the chair next to

mine and tugged on his tie. "Why do kids get summer holiday when their parents have to work?"

"It's cruel," I agreed. Bennett was raising twin six-year-old girls, which would have been difficult even if his wife hadn't died unexpectedly last year. I couldn't imagine how overwhelmed he felt, although he did his best not to show it. "Why don't you let me watch them Friday night for a few hours?"

"I could never ask you to stop working!" Bennett widened his eyes in mock-horror.

"The Blue Foundation campaign is winding down," I said casually, ignoring his obvious sarcasm. I didn't add that until our next big project came along I was desperate to fill my time with anything that would distract me from Alexander's absence from my life.

"Maybe you're right." Bennett rubbed his temples, sighing loudly. "Would it be sad if you watched them while I slept?"

I studied Bennett's haggard appearance for a moment before I raised an eyebrow. "I think I have to insist that you sleep."

"You're a lifesaver, Clara." He paused, rummaging through the scattered notes in his bag. "Someone called here asking about you. I thought I wrote down his phone number."

The color in the room drained away. There was only one person that would call and ask about me. Only one person who wouldn't contact me directly. One person who hadn't contacted me directly for months.

"Hey, you aren't interviewing for another job, are you?" Bennett asked, studying my stricken face.

I shook my head and forced myself to answer. "Nope."

"Good, because you look a little panicked." Realization

dawned on him, lighting across his face. “I don’t think it was him, Clara.”

I wasn’t sure if that made me feel better or feel worse. Actually, I wasn’t feeling much of anything. I pushed away the questions I wanted to ask Bennett. Did he ask for me by name? What did his voice sound like? Had he really left a number? Because Alexander wasn’t the type to call. “It was probably just a reporter.”

But I couldn’t quite shake my uneasiness.

“Do you want some tea before we head in?" he asked, standing to leave.

"Coffee for me, please. I'm almost done reviewing the report." I motioned to the open file on my computer screen. I’d spent every waking moment preparing for today. I decided that I wasn’t going to be derailed now.

"Sometimes I forget you're American, and then you ask for coffee," Bennett teased.

I wagged a finger at him, turning back to my work. "I am not the only person in this office who drinks coffee, and I'm not American."

"You're more American than you'll admit, but perhaps if I ply you with enough tea and biscuits, you'll embrace your Brit."

"Not bloody likely," I said in my worst Cockney accent.

Bennett's laughter faded away as he walked toward the break room. It was good to see him lighten up. He might joke about me working too hard, but I couldn't help being worried about his stress level. He was all his girls had left.

Thankfully everything looked in order for the Blue Foundation presentation. With any luck, Bennett would be back with my coffee in time for a quick swig before we needed to head downstairs to the conference room. I turned on my phone to check the time and saw a missed call from my mother.

They're attacking on all sides.

Madeline Bishop didn't know how to take a hint. I had been avoiding her calls for weeks. The truth was that I couldn't stomach her particular brand of bluntness. As far as she was concerned, Alexander and I were still together. Once she knew we had split up, she'd have no problem identifying exactly where things had gone wrong for us and how I could fix it. If curiosity killed the cat, proactiveness brought it back after a couple of rounds of CPR. Situations could be fixed, according to my mother. I didn't have the heart to tell her there was no fixing us.

I'd told Alexander that I wouldn't be his secret, but here I was still guarding the truth about our relationship. Maybe I'd never been as strong as I thought I was—as he thought I was.

Bennett appeared back at my desk and handed me a steaming mug. "Are you ready to wow?"

I sipped my coffee. Pretending to be okay was becoming second nature, pretending I had my shit together was another thing entirely. I could be honest with him. Instead, I plastered a smile on my face. "Lead the way, boss."

I COULDN'T HELP but admire our client's transformation. In the few months since I'd met the famous actor, he'd gone from troubled movie star to a thoughtful leader, taking on more and more responsibility with the campaign. I had no doubt that his blonde publicist, Sophia King, who hovered near him at all times, had a lot to do with it. There had been speculation about Isaac Blue's relationship with her, but today when I caught him drop his hand protectively on the small of her back as we adjourned the meeting, my suspicions were confirmed. He removed it too quickly for anyone else to see, but her eyes flashed to him, smoldering with an intensity shared only between lovers.

Pressure tightened in my chest, pain squeezing my heart. I'd never share that look with anyone again. I longed for Alexander's hand to touch me protectively once more. Sophia's gaze shifted to meet mine, and I turned away, embarrassed to be caught staring.

"Thank you for all your work," Isaac said, extending his hand to Bennett. "The Blue Foundation is off to a solid start thanks to Peters & Clarkwell."

Bennett took his hand but shook his head. "This is who you need to be thanking."

Despite all the work I'd put in on the campaign, I cringed at being given credit. I wanted to move upward in the company, but I also wanted to do so after the tabloid interest in my personal life had finally faded from recent memory. Isaac turned to thank me, but stopped when he caught sight of me. With his cropped brown hair, dimpled cheeks, and ripped physique, most women would kill to have his attention. I wasn't most women. Isaac was sexy as hell, but he wasn't Alexander.

The star, perhaps due to years of acting, recovered quickly and offered his hand. "Thank you, Miss...?"

"Bishop," I said, playing along. There was no doubt he'd recognized me. Anonymity wasn't one of the perks of being on the cover of *People* magazine. We exchanged a few more pleasantries, and even with the awkward introduction, I couldn't help but be charmed by Blue.

Sofia lingered at the door, shooing her client and lover out with the rest of the group. Once they were out of the conference room, her hand fell across the door frame, blocking me from leaving.

"Can I help you with something?" I asked.

"It's interesting," she said. "You sound like an American, but you act like you're British. You're too fucking polite, Clara."

At least she wasn't going to play games. "I can be rude. Maybe even as rude as you."

She laughed at this, crossing her thin arms elegantly over her fitted red sheath. "I doubt it. I don't mean to offend you, but I saw you staring."

"Isaac has that effect on women," I said lightly.

"He does. But let's not pretend I'm talking about him. I imagine that you understand the desire for discretion and privacy in a relationship better than most." Sophia shifted so that she was no longer blocking the door, but neither of us moved to leave.

"I suppose that I do," I admitted. "I won't say anything."

"It's not a secret, but we aren't advertising it either," she confessed. "My relationship with Isaac isn't why I stopped you. I think you could use someone in your corner, Clara."

She drew an ivory business card out of her Birkin bag and handed it to me.

"What do you do exactly?" I asked, my curiosity getting the better of me.

"I turn things around."

I smirked at this. "I think it's a little late for that now."

Sophia glanced toward the hall Isaac had disappeared down. When she glanced back at me, her eyes blazed as she shook her head. "It's never too late."

Her words echoed in my head as I stowed the card in my desk drawer. Clearly, Sophia King was gifted at her job, but I wasn't looking for someone to fix things for me. That was impossible. I'd spent the last few months clawing my way out of despair. It had been a hard won battle, and I was still fighting it. The only thing I could do was move on as best as I could. Taking a deep breath, I walked slowly over to Tori's desk and waited for her to get off the phone.

"How about next week?" I asked as soon as she was free—before I could talk myself out of it. "I've been buried in work all summer. It's time I unearth myself."

"Excellent!" Tori clapped her hands together. "I'm holding you to it."

"You better," I said as a genuine smile crept onto my lips.

Small steps.

Dropping my bag on the granite countertop, I rifled through the day's mail, suppressing a surge of disappointment when all I discovered was bills and sales flyers. So much for small steps, a small voice taunted from inside my own head.

Belle entered the room clad in a turquoise maxi dress that flowed over her elegant figure. She fanned herself as she brushed a few sticky strands of blond hair off the back of her neck. Her aunt let us our flat, and while I loved the pre-war architecture and monthly rent, it lacked some modern amenities like air conditioning. "Let's take a summer holiday," she suggested, "Majorca or Seychelles?"

"I think it's likely to be even hotter there, and I have a job."

"Beach hot is different." Belle sighed and grabbed an ice cube from the freezer. "It's miserable to be hot in a city with all the people. Can't you get off for a couple of days or a long weekend?"

"Is this all?" I held up the stack of mail, ignoring her question.

"As far as I know." She studied my face for a minute. "How was your meeting?"

"Fantastic," I said, hoping she wouldn't ask for details. I still wasn't sure how to respond to Sophia King's offer.

"You worked hard on that campaign. We should celebrate," she suggested. "Grab a pint."

"I need to get in a run." Exercise was my fallback excuse when I didn't have work to occupy me.

"Bollocks," Belle said. "You're avoiding me."

"I'm not avoiding you." I sighed, searching for a way to explain without getting into the painful subject of Alexander. "I just don't feel like going out."

"You never feel like going out," she accused. "I love you, darling, but you can't hide from life forever. When are you going to move on?"

"I'm going on a run. Don't read so much into it." I grabbed my purse and flew past her before she could press me further.

Belle didn't come out of her room when I emerged fifteen minutes later ready to run. I tugged my ponytail into submission and headed out of the flat. Despite the evening's mugginess, the air felt good on my sweaty skin as I quickened my pace. Running cleared my head to the point of blankness, which was almost as good as being completely occupied with work.

I jogged to a stop at the corner, waiting for the light to change. A sleek black Rolls across the street made my heart jump. Sucking in a deep breath, I stepped closer, realizing with disappointment that it wasn't Alexander's.

Get a grip, my inner critic chastised.

This time I needed to listen to her. I took off at a full run, arms pumping, blood pounding through me, as I forced myself to speed up until I forgot everything. I was running away from my problems. I knew that. But what other choice did I have when I had no one left to run to?

The thought vanished from my head as the physical demands of my pace took precedence over thought. Half an hour later my head was clear as I bounded up the front steps of my flat. I was completely blissed out from running. If only the feeling could last forever.

"Clara!" Aunt Jane called from her doorway.

"Hi Jane," I panted.

"Come in and have some water. You look like you just ran a marathon."

I felt like I had, too, but I shook my head despite my dry throat. "I'm gross. I should shower, but thank you."

"Nonsense." Jane glided into the hallway and pointed to her flat. "Inside now."

There was no arguing with Jane when she got like this, so I trudged inside. Belle's Aunt Jane looked more like a pixie than someone her age had a right to, complete with spiky gray hair and a slight figure. What she lacked in size, she made up for in spirit. I held my hands up in surrender and followed her inside.

I gulped the water she gave me gratefully.

"Thanks," I said when I was done.

"You're doing a little more than working out," Jane noted. "You look like a girl who's running away from something."

I shrugged, but my eyes avoided hers. I didn't want to see myself reflected in Jane's penetrating gaze. "I'm just moving on."

"Why?"

Whatever I'd expected her to say, I hadn't expected her to question me on this point. It wasn't typical post-breakup advice. I should know. I'd heard it all. I fumbled around looking for a response, but in the end, all I could do was stare blankly at her.

"You're in love with him, Clara," Jane said, reaching out to take my hand. She patted it. "It's obvious, my dear. So why aren't you with him, then?"

I closed my eyes, gathering my strength before I answered, "Sometimes love isn't enough."

"Is anything?" Jane scoffed. "Clara, there is a season to all relationships. Some loves are meant to last a lifetime and others are not."

"I know," I whispered.

"Is your season with Alexander over?" she pressed.

I turned away from her to stare out the window. The Rolls was still parked at the corner, and my heart leapt again. I guess that answered her question. "I still love him," I admitted. "But staying together isn't possible. Our season is over."

"Be sure of that. Forcing love to end, forcing the season to change, doesn't mean it goes away. Not when the end is false. When you destroy a relationship, it only leads to regret," she advised. "Regret poisons lives, and there is no greater regret than abandoned love."

I guessed from the edge of her voice that she had some personal experience with this type of regret. I didn't ask her to share it with me.

I wasn't as old as Aunt Jane, but I'd learned a few hard lessons regarding love already. It was comforting to believe that time healed all wounds, but that was a lie. Time could never fully erase the anguish of a broken heart. It was always there, plucking at you no matter how deep down you buried the past.

"I'm afraid I don't have any choice," I told her, "and he doesn't want me anyway."

It stung to admit this aloud. I hadn't told anyone—not even Belle—that I hadn't heard a word from Alexander in over eight weeks. He'd reached out only once since I left him in Notting Hill—then nothing. Even if Jane were right, it wouldn't matter. Alexander had moved on with his life.

"How do you know that?"

"I just know."

Belle had been careful to keep tabloids out of our house, but she couldn't stop me from seeing them at corner stands. I'd seen the photographic proof—Alexander had been spotted at clubs and bars. I'd recognized some of his friends in the photographs, including Jonathan Thompson, his school friend and Belle's biggest mistake. If Alexander was spending time with him, I could only imagine what the gossip rags weren't reporting. To my knowledge, Alexander hadn't been caught with another woman yet, but it was only a matter of time. Meanwhile, I was still on the paparazzi's radar showing up under headlines that questioned the status of our relationship like *We're Unclear—Where's Clara?*

Jane pursed her lips, searching my face for a moment. "Wait here."

There was an ominous undertone to her words and I stood in her kitchen, frozen with dread. The heat of anger melted my coldness when she returned with a stack of envelopes. I recognized the creamy linen, even before I spotted the thick, red wax seal that sent my heart racing.

"Where did you get these?" I asked as she released Alexander's letters to me.

"We thought we should give you some time," Jane said in a soft voice.

"*We*?" I repeated. "You mean *Belle*."

Jane squinted at me sternly. "Don't be cross with her. She thought she was helping you."

I snorted at this and clutched the stack to my chest. How could my best friend keep something this important from me? Belle had been pushing for me to move on. Now it seemed she wasn't above sabotaging any chance Alexander and I had at reconciliation. "That's funny, because I've never been so hurt."

But even as I spoke the words, I knew I was lying.

I'd been more hurt before. Hurt by the man who wrote these letters. So why was I so desperate to read them?

CHAPTER THREE

I skipped the shower and closed myself in my room. My hands shook as I counted the envelopes. There were dozens of them. I didn't know where to start—did it even matter? I traced my name, written in Alexander's hand. He had touched this paper, and now separated for months, the thought filled me with a longing so intense that my breath caught.

Sliding a finger under the red wax seal, I withdrew the first letter, dated late June. It had only been a few weeks since he sent it—weeks that had felt like an eternity. I wasn't sure what I would find in these notes. I slowly released the breath trapped in my lungs as I read:

Clara,

How has it only been days since I touched you? My nights are no longer filled with nightmares. Instead, I dream of you—your skin pressed against mine, your taste on my tongue as I devour your cunt, your lips wrapped around my cock. Sleep is becoming my haven. The day is my nightmare because when I wake you're gone.

X

An unfamiliar surge of desire swelled inside me, but it quickly shifted into a pang that ached through my chest. How could he turn me on and make me want to cry at the same time?

My X. I brushed a kiss across his signature. He came to me in my dreams, too, but in those dreams he always left me. Sometimes for another woman. Sometimes for no reason at all. The nightmares jarred me awake and I would lie unblinking, knowing that the fear and despair I felt in my dreams wouldn't vanish with the dawn. If my dreams were like Alexander's, would I feel the same way he did? Would I fight to stay awake if Alexander made love to me while I slept? I wasn't certain. It seemed dangerous to even fantasize about his touch.

The hunger grew in me until I couldn't contain myself and I began ripping open letter after letter, discovering an odd mix of emotion in their pages. Many were as primal and brutally sexual as Alexander himself. I had no problem imagining the things he described. Alexander kneeling before me, my fingers fisting in his silky, black hair as he fucked me with his mouth. Or taking his thick cock between my lips, licking and sucking until he spilled over my tongue.

The pulse in my clit roared through my blood, and I slid a hand down my shorts, finding relief as I pressed my middle finger to the throbbing beacon. I couldn't recall the last time I'd touched myself. It had been before the first time I slept with Alexander. I'd had no compulsion to when we were together. He was the only thing that would satisfy me. After him, I'd had no desire. Only he could release me. Now his words were doing just that.

I clutched another letter as my finger massaged circles across my clit. Still when I read this one tears welled in my eyes, even as my muscles tightened expectantly. The tears rolled down my cheeks even as I arched with pleasure. I drank in his words, allowing them to wash through me with waves of ecstatic release.

Poppet,

I can't sleep. You've slipped from my dreams just as you've slipped from my life. I'm writing to you from our home in Notting Hill. It's curious that even months later, I can't let it go. It was the last place I filled you. The last place I kissed your lips. The last place you cried my name followed by those precious words.

I know you aren't reading these letters. You would be here if you were. How long will you fight it, Clara?

You belong to me. Only you. Always,

X

I gasped his name as I came and the world shattered around me, breaking me along with it. As my body shook from the powerful orgasm, I collapsed against the pillow. I clutched his letter to my chest as I trembled. How would I put myself back together after this? He'd bared his soul to me in letter after letter; the truth hid amongst his fantasies. My body yearned for his—for the promise of his words.

Completion.

Release.

Safety.

Despite my arousal, I couldn't ignore what was missing from his messages. There were no direct admissions. He'd said how he felt about me in a hundred different ways but never in the way I needed to hear.

I was still his secret, and we were still separated by a wall that grew higher with each day we spent apart.

There was a knock on my door, and I scrambled to hide the letters before I realized what I was doing.

He can't be your guilty little secret either, Clara.

I left the letters open on my bed and crossed to open the door. Belle pushed past me, whirling around as soon as she saw the letters.

"Clara—" she began, but I held up a warning finger.

"I'm guessing from your dramatic entrance that Jane told you she gave those to me." She started to speak, but I shook my head. "I'm not interested in your opinion on this."

Belle's mouth fell open, but she recovered quickly. "You're going to hear it anyway!"

"How could you?" I demanded.

"How could I what?" she cried. "How could I protect my best friend from being repeatedly hurt?"

"I've spent the last two months thinking he'd moved on." My rage was already simmering at a low boil and any minute it was going to bubble over.

"You didn't tell me what happened between the two of you. What was I supposed to think?"

"That's not true—" I started.

This time she stopped me with one manicured finger. "You told me some of it, but there was more. I know there was more, Clara. He *broke you*—I saw it. I couldn't let him do it again."

"You have no idea what happened between us!"

"Then tell me!" she pleaded. "Tell me how you can love him and fear him. Tell me why you ran! Because I can't understand it, Clara. He had to have done something to you. I've watched you become a shell, and I don't like it."

"I am not a shell!" But her accusation stung.

"Bloody hell you're not. Go to work. Bring home work. Run until you're near collapse. Sleep. Repeat. Answer me this, when was the last time you ate a meal without an alarm reminding you to do it?"

I balked at her question, but she didn't need me to respond. She already knew the answer. "Can you blame me?" I asked, angry tears falling hot on my face. "You don't get it. The only person that has ever made me feel alive is killing me. When I'm with him, he consumes me. When he's gone, I'm lost. So tell me what to do, Belle, because you have all the answers!"

She didn't respond. Instead, she took a tentative step in my direction, pausing a moment before she wrapped her arms around my shoulders. I crumpled against her, and she held me as I sobbed, no longer demanding information. I hadn't told her what had happened with Alexander past the drama surrounding his family and their disapproval of me. She knew there was more. She knew me too well not to see that he'd possessed me fully—mind, body, soul.

"I wanted to protect you," she whispered, and this time there was an apology in her tone.

"Why does everyone say that right before they stab me through the heart?" I croaked.

"Oh Clara." Belle stroked my hair soothingly. "I thought it would make it easier if you didn't know..."

I pulled away from her, wiping tears from my face. "If I didn't know what?"

"That he loves you," she said in a quiet voice.

"He's never said it," I admitted to her, my voice breaking along with my heart.

"Clara," she said my name gently, "he has written to you every single day since you left him. Most men's memories last as long as the lipstick around their cocks. Trust me on this."

"It's not enough." My words were merely a reminder to myself. I couldn't let it be. Could I?

Thoughts muddled into a confused mess in my head. Belle had been the one keeping this a secret from me, but now she was pushing me to face the one thing that made me want to run. It was just another sign of how fucked up our relationship truly was that it had even twisted Belle's feelings.

"I can't make that determination for you." Belle wrapped an arm around my waist. "But while you decide—now that you know—you've got to live a little. Not just for me and not just for him. For you. I miss you. I love you, and I'm not the only one who's worried."

I dropped my head to her shoulder. "I thought if I just pretended I was okay for a while, I would be okay."

"Life doesn't work that way, especially when love is involved." She stepped away from me, twisting her ring around her finger. "I pretty much already know the answer to this question, but you want to get cleaned up and grab a pint?"

I glanced to the pile of letters on my bed. They would still be here in a few hours. Alexander would still be out there in a few hours. I'd spent the last few months clouding my life with work and exercise so that I wouldn't have to live without him. Maybe I wouldn't know what I wanted until I actually faced life without him—until I lived my life.

My mouth tugged into a small smile. "Can I take a shower first?"

"Yes!" Belle's eyes lit up. "I'm not taking you out smelling like that! But I'm holding you to this, Clara Bishop. You have thirty minutes before I come in after you."

"I'll make it quick," I promised her. A weight I hadn't known I was carrying lifted from my shoulders. Maybe it was just a possibility and nothing more. Maybe tomorrow no letter would come. Maybe trying would hurt even more.

But suddenly I couldn't wait to get my life started.

THE PUB down the street was packed with the late night crowd. As soon as we were through the door, Belle grabbed my arm and dragged me to two barstools that had just opened up. We slid onto them seconds before a group reached them. One of the girls glared at us, but Belle raised an eyebrow and smiled smugly.

"You're such a shark," I called to her over the crowded room.

Belle winked at me as she waved for the bartender. "I take what I want."

"It reminds me of Alexander," I admitted, tapping my fingers on a coaster. He took what he wanted as well. Although he'd shown surprising restraint the last few months. I, on the other hand, was always hesitating. Could I take what I wanted, too?

Of course, I would have to figure out what I wanted first.

"Uh-uh." Belle wagged a finger at me and slid a cocktail in front of me. "No thinking. Not for the next few hours. I demand you have a good night."

I didn't bother to tell her that reminded me of Alexander, too. Instead, I raised my tumbler and tapped it to hers before taking a long swig. It burned down my throat and I coughed, caught off-guard by its strength. "What is this?"

"Bourbon." Belle's lips curved wickedly behind her glass.

"And?"

"And what?" she asked. "It's bourbon. I knew that the only way to get you to let go is with a high alcohol content."

"In me or the liquor?" I sipped tentatively at the amber-colored liquid.

"Both." She finished off hers with one long swallow, grimacing for a split second before slamming the glass back down on the bar. "Damn!"

I followed her lead, barely managing to down mine. I shook my head, feeling as if I were breathing fire. "Which one is going to be the responsible one tonight?"

She winked at me. "With any luck, neither of us!"

I watched as she ordered two more shots, wondering if I would be calling in sick to work tomorrow. At the rate she had us going, I would be. "I'm not sure Philip will appreciate it if I let you get trashed in a pub."

"Getting pissed in a pub is a long and proud English tradition," she reminded me, shoving another drink in my hands, "and Philip is all about tradition. Drink up!"

I held up my free hand as I took another swig. "Are we in a hurry?"

"I want to dance, and by my calculations you need to

finish that and one more before you become pliable enough for my liking."

"Scandalous!" I clutched my hand to my chest, laughter bubbling into my throat. "Are you trying to get me drunk?"

"That is exactly what I'm trying to do," she said, gesturing for one more round. "I want to dance."

"This doesn't exactly seem like a dancing crowd," I pointed out as I drained my cup. The bourbon was already working its magic, loosening my limbs and heating my belly.

"Not here," she said in exasperation. "We'll have to go to a club."

The thought of going to a club made my head spin, and I gripped her wrist. "Anywhere but Brimstone."

Belle raised an eyebrow and waited expectantly.

"Bad memories," I said. I left it at that. Surely Belle remembered that the only time I'd been there had been with Alexander.

"That's exactly where we should go then. Sod him! Let's go take it back. I don't care who he is, he doesn't own that club and you look hot tonight."

I narrowed my eyes at her, shaking my head. I should have known this was about more than grabbing a quick pint when she'd tossed a tiny, red dress on my bed. "Is this why you insisted I look runway ready?"

"I won't let you reclaim your life in trainers and gym shorts."

I knew Belle well enough to know this wasn't the only reason. "As long as you aren't trying to get me to hook up with someone."

"You never know when the right one will come along," she said with a shrug and a knowing gleam in her eyes.

I thought of the day I'd met Alexander, of the unexpected kiss we'd shared as we both hid during the festivities at the Oxford-Cambridge Club, of the undeniable connection I'd felt for him the first time we'd gone to bed together. Raising my glass, I tapped it against hers. "I'll drink to that."

The fear I'd expected wasn't there. Maybe it was the considerable amount of alcohol coursing through my veins courtesy of Belle or maybe it was something more than that—a hunger that had been gnawing through me since I'd read Alexander's words earlier this evening. I wasn't here to see him. Not exactly. Going to Brimstone was about confronting myself. The club held a special significance for me. It had been the first place that Alexander warned me away. I'd seen the darkness flashing in his eyes that night. It was also the place that had brought us together—and the place where I'd walked away from him. I hadn't chosen the club's name as my safe word lightly. Now it felt dangerous to be here, but after weeks of longing for Alexander, I craved the risk.

The line of hopefuls wrapped around the building. From the outside, it was hard to tell it was London's hottest nightclub. I looped my arm through Belle's and walked past the line, receiving a fair number of dirty looks in the process. We looked hot tonight—me in my short red dress and Belle in a shimmery silver slip dress—but that wasn't what was going to get us in.

"Maybe we should go somewhere else." Belle's gaze flickered toward the line.

"This is where I want to go." I peered ahead, pushing my shoulders back as we drew closer to the bouncer.

"An hour ago you didn't want to go here," she reminded me.

"That was before I had three doubles." Right now I felt like I could face anything. Maybe tonight I would get lucky and run into Pepper Lockwood, Alexander's childhood friend and my wannabe rival. My mouth twisted at the thought.

"Exactly," Belle said, pulling me from my fantasy. "You're drunk."

"And whose fault is that?"

"I just wanted you to loosen up, but I'm not sure—"

"I am," I interrupted her as we stepped to the front of the line. Behind us, I heard a mix of groans and cursing.

"Miss?" The bouncer crossed his arms, straining the seams of his already strained shirt. He tipped his head to the back of the line. Belle tugged at my arm while a few people whistled behind us.

I searched the man's face for a moment with a raised eyebrow. He was definitely the one that had opened the door for me when I fled from Alexander the night of our formal introduction. "I suppose you don't remember me. It's not wash day."

I smoothed my dress down suggestively and bit my lip for good measure. He studied me for a moment before slowly asking, "A guest of Mr. X?"

"You could say that." I fluttered my lashes, waiting for him to finally place me.

His eyes widened as he reached for the velvet rope that barred entrance to the club. "Of course. I'm sorry. Any guest of Mr. X—"

"I assumed," I purred. Sashaying past him, my hips

swaying with my newly found confidence, I paused. "Is he here this evening?"

"I don't think so, Miss..."

"Clara," I corrected him. "Don't forget this time."

"I won't," he promised. His gaze traveled down my form one more time before he sighed and turned back to the line.

Belle grabbed my arm and spun me toward her, staring at me like I was an alien. "What the hell was that?"

"I've been here before," I reminded her.

She continued to gawk at me, but I saw the smirk playing at her lips. "You've never pulled that card before."

"What card?" I asked innocently.

"Don't be coy with me. The Alexander card. Or should I call it the X card?"

I shrugged. "Why shouldn't I pull it? I've had half of my life dug up and printed on the covers of magazines. I might as well skip the line."

"I'm not sure what to think of this new Clara Bishop," Belle said slowly. "Where did she come from?"

"Probably from half a bottle of bourbon," I said truthfully.

"Then let's get you another drink before she disappears." Belle laughed as she dragged me toward the bar. "I think I rather like her."

So did I. I hadn't felt this confident for a long time, but tonight I knew I was sexy and powerful and I wasn't afraid to show it. It could be the liquid courage, but the truth plucked at me from deep in my chest. I'd spent the last ten weeks believing that I'd been wrong about everything that had happened between Alexander and me. That it was all a lie. It wasn't reading his letters that made the difference now. It was knowing the truth. He wanted me. What happened between us had been real—might still be real. I wasn't still that stupid girl falling for a guy like Daniel, who had never cared about me. Although I wasn't sure my taste in men was getting any better.

Of course, Alexander's feelings were still up for debate. Maybe it was the bourbon heating my blood or the subliminal messages in his letters, but I had no doubt that he cared for me.

None of that meant that we could work things out. It just meant that I wasn't crazy. At least, I hoped it did.

Belle handed me a shot and I laughed to see her hair was already sticky on her scalp and her eyeshadow smudged. I probably didn't look much better actually.

"To the new Clara!" she shouted over the pulsing music of the club. I nodded and threw back the shot.

Belle grabbed my shooter and slammed it on the bar before pulling me out to the dance floor.

Brimstone took its name from hell, and it was nearly as hot in here. The floor was packed with a cluster of sweaty bodies fighting to the music, and every few seconds someone would crash into me. I didn't care. Belle and I danced closely together, drawing the attention of more than a few men around us. When a handsome blond pressed against me, circling hips into my backside, I grinded against him, lost to the music. It infected my blood and took control of my body. Belle stayed close, wrapping an arm protectively around my neck. I knew she wanted to let me know she was there if I needed an out, but that was the last thing on my mind. All I wanted to do was dance. I wanted to slip away into the pulsing storm of the music.

I wanted to be free.

How long would that last? I pushed the thought out of my head, refusing to let it affect my mood. The only thing that mattered was this moment, and it was nearly perfect.

It was only missing one thing.

I turned away from Belle and met the eyes of the stranger we were dancing with and waved to him, pushing back against Belle so that we could disappear into the crowd. He raised his hands, giving me a pitiful face, but I shook my head. He wasn't bad looking, but there was no way to pretend anyone could fill the hollow part of me. Suddenly, a hand yanked the man back.

Belle's fingers closed over my arm as Alexander stepped forward and shoved the stranger into the crowd. Before a fight broke out, a suited man appeared and guided the man I'd been dancing with toward the bar. The stranger threw glares over his shoulders but didn't resist.

If it weren't for Belle's fingers digging into my arm, I would have thought I was dreaming. I tugged away from her but didn't move toward him. Alexander and I stood there, separated by barely a breath, and stared each other down. His gaze pierced through me, igniting my already heated blood. Around us, strangers continued to dance and music pounded, but there was only him.

I glanced behind me, breaking eye contact for a precious second to allow myself a clear head. Belle raised her eyebrows and I gave her a reassuring smile. When I turned, he was still there. He wasn't a dream. He was flesh and bone. Blood and heat. Protector and tormentor.

My beautifully flawed X.

I was frozen to the spot. All he had to do was sweep me

off my feet and throw me over his shoulder. I wouldn't resist him.

He didn't move. Instead, he extended his hand—a small gesture, but one laced with meaning. He was giving me a choice. I could accept his hand and walk out of here with him. Or I could turn away. But staring into his eyes, his hand outstretched and waiting, I knew the truth.

There was never a choice.

CHAPTER FOUR

As soon as the door slid shut behind us, Alexander was on me. I barely had time to register the familiar surroundings before he shoved up my skirt, crushing his lips against mine as we tangled together. I'd been in this room before, fighting my attraction to him. I'd come for an explanation and discovered something dark lurking behind his sexy, brooding facade. He had fascinated me then. He still fascinated me, but now my head spun from the bourbon and from the change of circumstance.

And from him. Oh god, from him.

My fingers clutched his hair as he pressed me to the wall, and I didn't resist when he gripped my panties and tore them away. My sex reacted, swelling under his dominance, knowing exactly what came next. Everything about Alexander—his scent, the brush of the next-day stubble on his jaw, the firm grip of his fingers kneading into my hips—made me wet, as though my body had been conditioned to prepare for his cock.

But even as my body responded willingly, the tiny voice

in my head tried to control me, too, reminding me of the risk I was taking. Alexander was fire—white-hot and blazing. His touch smoldered, igniting my body until my arousal couldn't be contained. I would let him take me anywhere. Anytime. But playing with fire also meant getting burned, and Alexander had burned me before. There was no way I would walk out of here unscathed.

I wasn't thinking clearly. I *couldn't* think clearly—not with him around. Still one question kept peeking through the haze that clouded my judgment: why was he here? But with his lips on me, trailing down my neck until his teeth bit hungrily into my shoulder, I didn't care. I was here with him, and for the first time in months, I felt complete.

I felt alive.

My skin even responded sensitively to his more chaste touches. The back of his hand caressing the length of my arm sent desire pooling between my legs. A brush of his lips across my cheek made me moan. We were as in tune as ever, but our connection was on overload. Too long had passed since we'd touched, and no lingering doubt or fear seemed capable of checking my body. I was drawn to him out of pure instinct and primal lust. I couldn't say no to him now.

Because I couldn't say no to myself.

"Do you remember the last time we were here, poppet?" The low rasp of his voice sent a tremor of anticipation running through me. "I wanted to pin you against the wall and fuck you until you begged me to stop."

I whimpered as his hand slipped between my legs. I wanted him to fuck me now. Fuck me before I could talk myself out of it. Fuck me until I couldn't remember how to beg. Fuck me hard until I forgot my objections.

Alexander's finger traced my seam and my sex clenched involuntarily, aching for contact. "Tell me what you need, Clara. Do you want me to fuck you with my fingers? Or my mouth? Or my cock?" His mouth dropped to nibble on my ear. "Give me your order of preference, because I plan to do all three."

Yes, please.

"I want to feel you inside me," I whispered, my voice barely a breath as I struggled to produce words. All I could think of was him touching me. How had I survived without his touch?

His breath hitched and his eyes found mine. They blazed with unrepressed carnality, piercing me through the heart. Neither of us spoke as he freed his cock. Instead we stared at each other, questions mixing with passion in our gazes. But when his hard length nudged against my swollen cleft, my eyes closed involuntarily, savoring the moment.

"Wait." The word was a plea on my lips. It had been too long.

"You're so tight. There's been no one to look after your beautiful cunt," he murmured, stroking the crest of his cock along my seam. "Have you been touching yourself?"

I shook my head, which only made the world spin faster. I couldn't think. Had I? Only this afternoon. Only when I read his letters. I paused, considering this, and nodded.

"Your pleasure is mine," he growled. He pulled away. My desperate whimper turned to a gasp when his hand pushed against my sex, gripping it possessively. "This is mine."

I nodded again, even as tears of frustration pricked at my eyes. My eyes opened, searching his. If I was his, why hadn't he come after me? Why had he sent me letter after letter?

Letters that had aroused me. His words had twisted me. His words had unraveled me–unraveled my resistance.

"Say it," he demanded. "Tell me you're mine."

He didn't need to hear it. He already knew the truth. No matter what he did. No matter the pain or loss I experienced because of him, I would always be his. He had invaded me –*infected* me–the moment we met, and I couldn't get him out of my blood. "I have always been yours."

Alexander dropped his forehead to mine, abnormally silent. Usually he wanted to hear more. Usually he commanded me to say his name, to repeat his possessive promises–he craved the control. He'd had so little of it in his life. He'd been young when his mother died, and he'd been there the night of his sister's death. He'd had no power to stop either. Just as he had no power to change who he was born to be and the role he was destined to play as the King of England. His desire to dominate came from a need for control. Control over me. Control over our relationship. Control over his feelings.

It was up to me to show him that he couldn't control love. My body submitted readily to him, but I wasn't ready to allow him to dominate me completely. I shoved his hand off my cunt, pushing him away as I did so. His head tilted to the side, watching me with a calculating look. He was a predator and I was his prey.

But this prey wasn't about to lie back and wait to be pounced upon.

I slid my hand down my navel in a slow, deliberate motion before dipping my index finger between my legs. Finding my clit, I rubbed small circles over the aching bud. Alexander's eyes hooded as he watched me and I let a moan escape my lips, as aroused by the precious contact as I was by putting on a show for him. Frustrated pleasure built in my core. I wanted to spill over. I wanted to show him that I could take myself to the edge without him. I wanted to show him that I was still in control. Maybe I needed to prove that I was to myself.

But even as my limbs tightened, I wanted him more. My sex ached to be spread and stretched by his cock.

"I love watching you touch yourself, poppet," he rasped in a low voice that sent a shiver racing down my spine. His hand fisted his thick shaft as his mouth curved into the smug grin that drove me wild. "Two can play this game."

He stroked his shaft violently, drawing a thick bead of pre-cum to its magnificent crown. I groaned at the sight, my pleasure building to its apex and crashing through me. My legs trembled, buckling involuntarily as I fucked myself for him. It was delicious and wanton to feel his gaze fixed on me as I came in front of him.

Without touching me, he'd taken me—with his eyes, with his brutal sensuality, with his mere presence. It made me want him even more. Despite my release, my sex throbbed, aching to be filled.

"Not enough," he said, edging closer to me. He pushed my legs back apart and slid a finger along my slit. My body responded defensively. My thighs clamped together, trapping his hand. "You're all wet from teasing me. Slippery and ready. Do you want more?"

My ability to speak vanished along with my resistance. His fingers delved inside my cleft. One. Two. Three. He fucked me slowly, plunging in and out as his thumb circled around my tender clit. It was too much. It was always too much with him.

"Do you want more?" he repeated in a soft voice, but there was an edge to it. He was back in control, and when my eyes found his I saw a familiar darkness creeping into them. It thrilled me as much as it terrified me. My desire to control the situation—to prove something—evaporated, lost to the darkness reflected in his crystal blue irises. "That's better, isn't it? Losing yourself to me?"

I nodded, my mouth going dry. Everything made sense when he took charge. I felt alive, wanted, and more than anything, safe. It was the rest of the time–when we had to be fully clothed—that made me doubt our relationship. Not that we had a relationship. Not anymore.

"I want to rip off this pathetic excuse for a dress," he said, drawing me back to the moment. His fingers stroked and twisted, pushing deeper than I thought possible.

"What will I wear out of here? The paparazzi will have a field day," I breathed, but I knew that I wouldn't stop him if he tried. My muscles constricted, winding tight as wire, as he leisurely fingered me. Then he was gone and my eyes flew open with panic.

"*Shh*, poppet." He brushed a strand of hair out of my eyes as his other hand guided the head of his cock to my slick entrance. My sex throbbed as he pushed the tip in, but he held it there. "Such a greedy cunt. I can feel it trying to milk me. It wants to be fucked, doesn't it? Tell me how much you need to be fucked."

I shook my head, unable to speak. My teeth sank into my lower lip, my eyes pleading with him.

"Do you *want* to be fucked?" he asked.

"Yes," I whimpered.

"That wasn't so hard. You only have to ask, Clara, and I'll give it to you. I'm going to fuck you and watch my cum drip down your thighs as I take you home." Alexander brushed his lips behind my ear, leaning in to whisper, "And when I get you home, I'm going to strip this off and fuck your tits and your mouth. I'm going to cover your body with me."

His words sank in through the drug-like haze permeating my brain. I couldn't go home with him. Not until we talked. Not until I knew things would be different. "We have to talk, X," I forced myself to say. "I can't go home with you until we talk."

He stilled but didn't withdraw. "But you want me to fuck you now?"

"Yes," I said too quickly.

Alexander's head dropped, breaking eye contact, but his cock slid further in. "You want this?"

"Yes," I breathed.

"I have to know you're mine, Clara," he demanded.

The desire pooling in my core ratcheted into a frenzy. My body eager to do anything he asked. My lips ready to say what he needed to hear. But I clung to my resolve. It couldn't be that simple. Once I was in his bed, there would be no turning back. "You hurt me."

"And you left," he reminded me harshly.

With the little bit of self-command I had remaining, I pushed him gently away. Alexander's hands caught my wrists in one fluid motion and pinned them to the wall behind me. My resolve faded more as he dominated me, but I fought the urge to submit.

"I still can't be your secret," I told him in a soft voice.

"You aren't my secret, Clara," he said. "You are my treasure. The one good, beautiful light I have in my life."

"And you want to hide me away?" I guessed.

"I want to protect you." He pressed closer, bringing his rock hard chest into contact with my overly-excited body. The effect was electric. My skin crackled and sang where it met his. My nipples hardened to sensitive points while the rest of my body softened and molded to his athletic form. His tip pushed a little further in, but not enough to satisfy the fire smoldering through me. "Come home."

"We don't have a home." A pang shot through my chest as I said it. Didn't I want to be with him? I'd spent the last two months dying a little each day. Now I was pushing him away again.

Because you have to.

"We could, and I can't fuck you until you agree to come home," he said, but he didn't withdraw. He left his cock inside my pulsing sex, torturing me.

"For how long, X? Until your family marries you off?"

Alexander froze. Then he exhaled raggedly and released his hold on my wrists.

I was still pinned to the wall. My body and my mind warred with each other. Each certain that the other was wrong. "It was a mistake to come here."

Why had I come here? Because I'd had too much to drink—or because I was desperate to see him. I knew now how this was going to end. All I wanted now was to return to my flat and cry away the pain of losing him again.

"You've barely left your flat in weeks," he said, dropping his lips to my neck. He cruised along the delicate skin, sending flutters of desire swirling through my belly and annihilating my resistance. "You can't make this go away by working or hiding from life. You can't make us go away."

My mouth fell open. I hadn't seen Alexander in months except when he graced the cover of a tabloid or popped up on a gossip blog. But he had seen me. How often? "You've been following me," I accused.

"I had Norris assign a detail to you—for your protection," he added, but it didn't make his confession any easier to swallow. He backed away from me then, leaving me empty and unsatisfied as he shoved his rock hard erection into his slacks.

I missed his touch immediately, want coursing through me. Alexander was like an addiction that I couldn't kick even as he proved, once again, how unhealthy our relationship was. "I don't need to be protected. I don't need to be followed."

"What do you need then, Clara?" he roared.

His sudden burst of anger scared me and I stumbled toward the door. "I need you."

"And you have me." He took a step closer to me but stopped himself. "So why can't I need you? Why won't you let me need you?"

"Because you can't," I said flatly. We could pretend we lived in a world where titles and money and politics didn't matter. Maybe they didn't for most people. But Alexander was not most people. That was part of what made him so extraordinary, but it was also what made him untouchable.

I smoothed my dress down and slid open the door behind me. Giving Alexander a small smile, I stepped through it. I couldn't say goodbye to him again. It had shredded me before. It might kill me now.

But he followed me, pausing in the doorway. "What will it take, Clara?"

"A different world," I murmured before adding, "Bye, X."

Who was I kidding? I wasn't going to survive this anyway.

CHAPTER FIVE

Curiosity got the better of me. Maybe it was my run-in with Alexander. Maybe it was a need for some empathy. Maybe it was that I couldn't decide if nearly sleeping with Alexander had been a mistake or a step in the right direction. But I suspected there was one person in my life who would be able to empathize. Alexander's younger brother had been a friend to me when I needed it the most, and I'd spent the last few weeks avoiding him. Besides, I was curious to catch up with him. Still in the closet Edward and his secret boyfriend David had broken up following the disastrous trip to the country that had also ended my relationship with Alexander.

What happened to that damn cat? I chided myself. Curiosity had prompted me to open those letters. Curiosity had given Alexander a window back into my life. Curiosity was going to kill me.

And that was how I found myself sitting in a quiet corner table waiting for the more emotionally stable son of Cambridge. We'd arranged to meet late in the afternoon—

well past tea or lunchtime—in a pub on Kensington High Street. No one in the office had batted an eye when I left for the afternoon. I guessed Bennett was secretly pleased to see me going out, although he'd simply joked that he owed me an afternoon since I would be spending the evening watching his twins.

As I'd suspected would be the case, the place was deserted save for a few regulars in residence at the bar. Edward swept into the pub with an air of authority that matched his birthright. He didn't look snobbish or out of place as he crossed the well-worn plank floor and took a seat in a rickety chair across from mine. This was his country after all and he fit here, like a benevolent lord come to visit his patrons. His demeanor reminded me of Alexander. It didn't help that he had the same striking blue eyes and thick black hair. But Edward's hair was curly and his figure lean. With stylish, horn-rimmed glasses perched over his nose, he seemed boyish in comparison to his brother. Maybe that's why I'd felt comfortable around him from the moment we met. He didn't intimidate me the way the rest of his family did—the way that Alexander did—even with his obviously royal air.

"Clara." A lazy smile spread across his handsome face. "It's good to have the band back together."

I raised an eyebrow.

"The lonely hearts club, of course." He perused the menu as he spoke.

"I take it that one is the loneliest number then?" I'd expected as much, but I couldn't deny that I'd secretly hoped Edward and David had worked things out. If they'd been able to...but it was stupid to even entertain the possibility. Being with a royal came with demands and expectations that mere mortals couldn't live up to.

"At least today two can be as sad as one."

The waiter delivered us from our lyrical pity party and we ordered the house fish and chips and some pints.

"Very British menu choices." Edward lounged back in his chair, folding his long arms behind his head. "Are you sure you don't want something more American?"

I sighed dramatically and took a sip of my beer. My dual citizenship was definitely a topic of controversy in the tabloids—and behind closed doors in the palace. Not that it mattered since Alexander and I weren't together anymore. Or were we? Our whole relationship felt as confused as my citizenship. "Haven't you heard that I'm vying to be the next Queen of England?"

"But I've had my heart set on it for years." He clutched his chest dramatically, feigning pain.

"I think you stand as much of a chance as I do," I said dryly. "Not that it will stop any reporters from dissecting my chances."

The tabloids had been following me less, but I was still a hot topic. Was Alexander hiding me away? Had we broken up? Was he seeing someone else? The irrational side of me hated that rumor the most. My thoughts drifted to our stolen moment in the club. I was being paranoid. I'd read his letters and I'd felt his touch. There was no one else.

Not yet.

"If you're going to take a mind trip, can I go along next time?" Edward asked, calling me from my thoughts. "Preferably somewhere sunny."

"England's pretty sunny in August."

"Okay, anywhere *but* England."

If only that was a real possibility for either of us. Alexander wasn't the only Royal harboring secrets. Edward's sexual preferences were closely guarded by the palace as well. No wonder the whole lot was so screwed up.

"Actually," he said thoughtfully, "it will probably boost both of our images to be seen together. I can see the headlines now: *Betrayed by His Brother*."

I chuckled humorlessly. "Your father would love that one. Both of his sons linked to a terrible American."

"Father loves any news piece that insinuates I'm heterosexual."

Our conversation died down as the waiter delivered our food. Neither of us were eager to be overheard, lest our private discussion turn into actual tabloid fodder. It was one thing to joke about it, and totally another thing to fend off the rumors that I was bouncing between two royal beds. As soon as we were alone again, I lowered my voice and returned the topic to a more serious subject. "When was the last time you spoke to David?"

"When was the last time I spoke to him?" Edward dabbed the corners of his mouth with his napkin. "Or when did I last try?"

"At least you're trying," I murmured. Staring down at my fish, a wave of empathy rolled through my body. I knew what it was like to be caught, publicly fried, and tossed onto a plate for public display. Suddenly I wasn't very hungry.

"Alexander hasn't attempted a reconciliation?"

I hesitated, uncertain how to answer. It was impossible to explain Alexander's behavior. I hadn't known about the letters until a few days ago. If I'd just read them, I might believe

Alexander wanted to get back together. But his behavior at Brimstone had only confused me. Alexander didn't want me back, he wanted me under his control. "I suppose he has."

"Let me guess." Edward leaned back in his seat and eyed me appraisingly. "He made promises that things would be okay, but you didn't believe him."

"It sounds like you're familiar with this situation." I'd given up on lunch entirely now.

"I suppose I am. Except that I'm in the opposite position, making all the promises and knowing I don't have a hope in hell of living up to them."

"Then why make them at all?" The question exploded from me, earning a censorious look from my companion.

"Because we want to believe in fairy tales, Clara," he said in a quiet voice. "That we'll find our one true love and live happily ever after."

"Then allow me to speak for David for a moment. We don't expect magic or glass slippers or fairy godmothers. We just want to love you."

"Clara, Alexander and I have lived our whole lives under the scrutiny of the world. Asking someone we love to endure the paparazzi and endless tabloid attacks is the last thing either of us want to do."

I sucked in a breath to steady myself. I already had a fair share of tabloid headlines to my name. What was a few more? "Try again."

"I suppose—" he paused, folding his hands on the table — "we're scared. Scared that we can't protect you. That we'll break you. That you'll see how broken we are."

"You aren't broken," I told him softly.

His answering laugh was hollow. "I live a lie. And Alexander currently vacillates between drinking alone at home and drinking in the private room at Brimstone."

This was news to me. I'd seen Alexander at Brimstone, of course, but learning that he'd taken to drinking alone came as more of a surprise than it should.

"For what it's worth," Edward continued, "Alexander loves you."

"Then why did he push me away?" The words whispered across my lips.

It was impossible that Edward heard them, but he answered anyway. Perhaps he was asking himself the same thing. "Because that proves how much he loves you. Enough to give you up and walk away."

"Like you love David?" I asked.

"I don't have the strength that Alexander has." Edward slipped his glasses off and rubbed his temples. When he looked up, his smile was brittle at the edges. "I didn't give David up. He left me, remember? I'm afraid I'm too selfish. David won't even return my calls."

Something about his words recalled the old proverb drilled into our heads as children. "Actions speak louder than words. Find him and show him. Don't give him a chance to run from you."

Edward's head cocked to one side, considering my advice. "Perhaps you're right. Maybe it's time for action."

I gave him an encouraging smile as I tried to avoid the jealousy that churned through me. I was hopeful for David and Edward, but I couldn't help but wish that Alexander would fight for me. He'd made plenty of promises, written in letters and spoken with honeyed lips, but without action, promises were only wishes.

"I LET them have water before bed, but god help you if you give them candy." Bennett piled another sheet of emergency numbers into my waiting hands and I tried not to giggle at the sight of my self-possessed boss acting like a nervous parent. He could handle presentations for movie stars and politicians, but his daughters had him frantic.

"I've got this," I said soothingly. "You've already wasted half an hour making sure that I knew how to call the police, the fire department and the ambulance. I have your mobile number. Get out of here before you're late for the play." It felt good to get away from my rigid schedule and do something for someone else. Besides that, I knew the girls would keep me so busy I wouldn't have time to think about Alexander. It was a win-win.

"Okay." Bennett checked his back pocket for his wallet and straightened his shirt, but he was still anxious. I didn't have the heart to ask him if this was the first time he'd gone out socially since his wife had died, but I suspected it was. "I'll be back by ten."

"Take your time," I encouraged him. It wasn't as if I had any plans.

"I think it's better if I ease back into the world of the living."

I didn't miss the subtle hint, but I ignored it, pushing him toward the door. By the time I finally locked it behind him, he'd managed to give me two more phone numbers I could call if I needed help.

Abby and Amy were balls of energy. They shared their fathers bouncy curls, but their eyes were wide and curious and trimmed with thick lashes. Their mother's eyes, I guessed. We had a tea party on the floor of the flat. I was the guest of honor. It was the most civilized party I'd been to in months—including the one I'd had with the queen.

They also ran on what appeared to be an inexhaustible supply of energy. By the time I plopped down on the sofa, I was pretty sure I was going to fall asleep. It had taken over an hour to calm them down enough to put to bed. Now the flat was silent and for the first time in a long time, I welcomed the peace and quiet.

The shrill ring of my mobile interrupted the moment. I checked the screen, sighed, and slid accept. "Hi Mom."

"Clara, you answered." There was a note of disbelief in her voice. In all fairness, I'd been avoiding her for the past few weeks. I hadn't been able to do so entirely, but I had managed to only see and speak with her during public outings where I was certain she wouldn't ask me about what was happening between Alexander and me.

The problem was that I couldn't avoid her forever.

"I had a free minute," I explained, glancing toward the door to the twins' room and lowering my voice. "What's up?"

"You're quiet," she accused. "Where are you?"

There was no doubt she was expecting a juicy answer. "Actually, I'm babysitting."

"Babysitting?" she repeated.

"For my boss. His wife passed away last—"

"Well, I suppose Alexander is with you."

It was a trick and I knew it. When I said no, she would launch her interrogation. She'd seen the tabloid headlines for weeks—the ones speculating on the state of our relationship—although she had a different perspective than the average gossip rag reader. She'd met Alexander. She'd seen us together.

She knew I loved him.

But Mom and I had never had an open relationship. We didn't discuss things and I didn't confide in her. We'd confronted my illness together in the past, but it hadn't made us any closer. Sometimes I wished it had, because right now I could use some unconditional love.

"He's not, actually." I kept my response simple, hoping to avoid further questions.

"I don't know what's going on with you two, but you have a life outside of him, Clara." Mom paused, but I didn't speak immediately.

She was right. I did have a life outside of Alexander—I'd just been avoiding it. But seeing him at Brimstone had changed something. Maybe it had only been a few stolen moments, but they had breathed life into me. "I know that. Work has been crazy. I've been handling a large campaign."

"We should get together and do lunch soon."

I couldn't dodge her phone calls and requests much longer and we both knew it. "That would be nice."

"*Soon.* I have something I need to speak with you about." Her voice caught as she spoke and a shiver ran up my spine.

"Is everything okay?"

"Everything is fine."

But I knew my mother well enough to know that *fine* was code for trouble. It was likely that trouble had something to do with my father's late nights and her fragile emotional state. She didn't understand why he insisted on chasing new projects, but I did. Keeping a woman like Madeline Bishop happy was no small feat. She oozed anxiety on the best of days.

"Clara," she continued, "you would tell me if something was wrong? If you were slipping up?"

My throat hitched and I swallowed. "Of course."

"Because I saw on TMI that—"

"Don't believe what you see on TMI," I cut her off. I'd tried to avoid the stories they posted about me, but I was only human. No matter how many times they speculated about my weight or my nonexistent relationship or Alexander's late night activities, I couldn't stop myself from looking at their so-called reports. But I knew they weren't true.

"Clara," she began in her shrill, *I-am-your-mother* voice, but a beep interrupted her.

"I have another call. I need to take it. It could be my boss."

"Of course. I'll speak with you this week." Her voice was flat with annoyance, but I said a quick goodbye and answered the waiting call.

"Saved by the Belle," I quipped as I answered my best friend's call. Once again I found myself grateful for Belle's almost preternatural timing. It was as if she could sense when she needed to save me from my mother.

"Are the children in bed?" Belle asked.

"Yes. *Finally*. I never thought they would sleep."

"Good," she said quietly. Something was up by the sound of her voice. "You should turn on Entertainment Today."

My stomach bottomed out and I couldn't bring myself to respond as I fumbled for the remote and flipped on the telly.

"You're sitting down, right?" she pressed.

Frustration and fear got the better of me. "For fuck's sake, Belle, what's going on?"

"Alexander gave a rather interesting interview at the Global Aid fundraiser tonight."

Had he done so with a certain gorgeous, but bitchy blonde on his arm? Is that what she wanted me to see? Proof that he was the good-for-nothing she believed him to be. This time my stomach turned over and I fought the urge to run for the loo. It was bound to happen sooner or later, but I'd stupidly let myself believe that the other night at Brimstone had meant something to him.

"He couldn't wait around forever," I mumbled into my mobile.

There was a pause on the other end that lasted so long that I checked the screen to make sure we hadn't been cut off. "Just watch. They teased the clip a few minutes ago and they should be playing the whole bit here in a minute."

"You aren't making me feel any better."

"This might," she said. "Oh! It's on."

I found the right channel just as Alexander's handsome face flashed on screen. His eyes were even bluer on camera and a pang twisted my heart. "Found it."

We lapsed into silence as the Entertainment Today host introduced the story with speculation on Alexander's lack of a date. Relief flashed through me, but it didn't last for long. I twisted a loose lock of hair around my finger and tried to stay calm as they aired the interview. He looked amazing in a classic black tuxedo that was precisely tailored to show off his muscular body. I wasn't sure if it was the same one he'd worn to the gala we attended together, but regardless my body responded to the sight as if it remembered the things he had done to me while wearing it.

A buxom redhead reporter sauntered close to him with mic in hand. I hated her simply for being near him. "Alexander, where's your date this evening?"

She was American. Her accent and the almost rude directness of her question gave it away, but Alexander simply flashed her a dazzling smile.

"Clara is at home tonight," Alexander responded fluidly. Nothing in his face betrayed the truth—that he had no clue where I was this evening and that he hadn't for quite some time.

"She's been spotted coming and going to her flat lately, but not with you. You two haven't been seeing much of each other these days."

"My girlfriend has a career," he reminded her and my heart leapt involuntarily. "She's tired and I told her I would see her at home tonight. As I'm sure you know, we recently moved in together."

My mouth fell open, mirroring the reporter's. She didn't know that. No one knew that. Because it was a lie.

The woman recovered and gave a half-hearted look of sympathy. "We hope she's feeling better soon."

"I'll tell her that," he said smoothly, "when I speak with her tonight." His eyes pierced through the camera. How could he know I was watching?

"So..." Belle trailed off as the show went to commercial.

I clicked off the television and tried to find the words. There were plenty of them rushing through my mind at the moment. I cursed and fell back on the sofa with an exasperated sigh.

“You have to talk to him.”

“Do you think?” I snapped, closing my eyes and trying to center myself. She was right, and I was being bitchy. “I know.”

“I won’t wait up,” Belle said. “But try to call me sometime this weekend.”

“I’m not going to just disappear,” I promised her. “It’s over between us.”

“Why?” she asked. It was such a simple question, but it shredded me. Probably because I’d been asking myself the same thing.

“Because it has to be,” I whispered.

She didn’t say anything. We both knew I was lying to myself, but the wonderful thing about best friends is that they know when to push and they know when to shut up. “Call me.”

“No promises,” I warned her before ending the call. Talking to Alexander meant walking into the lion’s den. Who knew what would happen once I was inside?

I sat in silence. Twenty minutes ago I’d wanted peace and quiet. Now I could almost swear I heard each second tick by, counting down to the inevitable.

CHAPTER SIX

My hands shook as I unlatched the gate and made my way to the front door. I'd only been here once before, and I hadn't thought I'd return again. But I knew he'd returned to this house this evening. Waiting for Bennett to come home had nearly killed me, but now I was back at the one place I'd never wanted to be. The paving stones under my feet felt uneven as though any moment they might flip and turn my world upside down. Of course, that had already happened.

I should have been surprised that he'd called my bluff in such a public way, or at least shocked by his audacity, but I wasn't. Had I been stupid enough to think Alexander would take no for an answer? But if he thought he could lie and pretend nothing was wrong between us, he had another thing coming. I'd walked out of here for a reason. It was the same reason that I'd managed to avoid him for nearly two months.

There was a deadline on our relationship—a ticking time bomb that lust, or even love, couldn't defuse. His family had expectations for his marriage, and I'd grown up in the twenty-first century. I wasn't about to become his mistress.

The door swung open before I'd climbed the final step, and there he was, still dressed in his evening attire. His bow tie hung loose around his unbuttoned collar, revealing the neck that I longed to run my lips down. I pushed the thought down into the darkest recesses of my mind and willed myself to maintain control. This wouldn't be like the night at Brimstone. It couldn't be—not after what he'd said and done.

"Expecting me?" I asked dryly, crossing my arms protectively over my chest and doing my best to ignore how my nipples stiffened at the slight contact. My body was a traitor in his midst, always responding to him.

Always ready for him.

Alexander stepped to the side, motioning for me to enter, but I froze on the stoop as his eyes raked down my body. The long, purposeful look, as though he was planning how to devour me, heated my blood until flames of desire licked across my skin. I knew this look, and I knew the second I stepped through the door I would be at his mercy.

And Alexander was not a merciful man.

"I'd hoped you would come." He slipped his tux jacket off his shoulders and stepped forward to wrap it around me, but I backed away, nearly stumbling as my heel came too close to the edge of the step. Was this his plan? To kill me with kindness? To wrap a warm jacket around my shoulders and blanket me in the heady scent of him until I fell back into his arms? Because I knew it would work if I let him enact it. Alexander was a wolf in gentleman's clothing, and I wasn't a stupid sheep. I wouldn't be such easy prey this time.

"You must have known I was coming. I didn't even have

to knock," I said, each word more biting than the last. "Did you have someone follow me?"

"Clara." His tone was filled with warning, but I raised my eyebrow, forcing him to add, "What I do is for your protection."

"What you do is a cry for help! Has anyone told you that you have control issues?"

His lips twitched, but he kept the smile off his face. "Many times. But we've had this argument before. Tell me why you're angry now."

"Saying something in front of a camera doesn't make it true. I don't live here." Though even as I spoke, my heart twisted. I could live here—with him. I shook my head, trying to keep my thoughts clear even in his intoxicating presence.

"You needed a commitment," he reminded me in a low voice that dripped with sex, "and I want to give you what you need."

"Christ, X!" I threw my hands up in the air and stomped into the house, telling myself I wouldn't go past the foyer. "I needed you to be honest with me. That's all I've needed from the beginning, but it's been one lie after another."

"Secrets are not lies." His eyes flashed and he turned away, closing the door behind him. My heart jumped as the lock clicked into place. I'd stepped over the threshold into his domain and now he had me caged.

"And what was tonight?" I demanded. "What was the point of telling those leeches that I live here?"

"You wanted a commitment," he repeated, "and I gave it to you."

"Can you for one fucking second not be such a politician?

I know you were bred to be one, but I'm sick of the spin, Your Majesty. You can't sell telling a lie as doing me a favor."

Alexander whirled toward me, grabbing my wrists and clasping them behind my back. His body pressed against mine, unleashing a torrent of longing that surged through my core. "This is not about who I am or who I will become. This is about you and me. Right here. Right now."

A moan escaped my lips as his hips ground his erection against my belly. Even through our clothes I felt the heat of it. "You and me. Clara and Alexander. Who cares what the outside world thinks?"

"You do," I breathed.

He released his grip on me, stepping back as though I had slapped him.

"You do," I repeated more firmly. Now that he wasn't touching me, I could almost think clearly again. *Almost.*

"I care what *you* think," he said flatly, his words daring me to contradict him.

"If you cared what I thought, we wouldn't be standing here having this argument." But where would we be? Would I be here with him tonight? In his bed and living a lie? Or would things have ever gotten this far between us? Maybe it was naive to believe things could be different between us, but I couldn't help thinking that if he did care, we would either be blissfully happy or long over.

Alexander moved toward me and I retreated until my back made contact with the wall. If he noticed that he'd cornered me, he didn't show it. His blue eyes blazed like the edge of an inferno, and if I let him get much closer, I would be consumed by the fire burning through him. "I warned you away. I warned you about me."

"And you took me anyway," I accused. The indictment was pitiful at best. He had warned me and I'd chosen to take the risk. I'd plunged into this relationship with eyes wide open. That certainly meant I had no one to blame but myself.

"I took what you gave, poppet." His thumb trailed over my lower lip, pushing between my teeth and opening my mouth. "You gave me this mouth. Don't you remember?"

I swallowed instinctively—protectively—and my mouth closed over his finger for a moment. He seized the opportunity, plunging his thumb against my tongue as though urging me to suck it, and I gasped at the familiar taste of him.

"You gave me this pretty little mouth to fuck," he said as he pulled his thumb from it. "Your mouth remembers that. It remembers my cock pumping inside of it."

I wanted to tell him he was wrong, but he'd seen the proof. I hadn't been able to control my response—my desire. If he'd shoved me down on my knees and thrust his crown to my lips, I would have taken it and sucked him off. It was instinct—uncontrollable, animalistic instinct. But although Alexander might be a wolf, he wasn't about to take advantage of that. We were playing a dangerous game. He was betting he could seduce me back into his bed and I was gambling that he couldn't. Someone was going to walk away a loser.

Alexander shifted closer, his hand slipping under the hem of my shirt, but he didn't stray past my navel. "Feel how your body responds to my touch," he instructed me, "and then look me in the eye and tell me you don't want me to take you upstairs to fuck you."

I set my jaw and raised my gaze to his, forcing the words past my lips. "I don't want you to fuck me."

"You're a terrible liar, Clara." He laughed as his hand slid down and past my waistband, his fingers massaging through the lace of my panties. "You're so fucking wet for me. Drenched. Are you always this wet when you don't want to fuck?"

He knew the answer to that, because he knew my body well. Too well. He knew that all he needed was to run one finger over my skin and I'd respond. Alexander removed his hand from my panties and trailed his wet fingers down my bare throat. "*That's what* you want. Now tell me. Which one of us is lying?"

"Maybe you're right," I admitted with a whimper. "Maybe I want you to fuck me, but I don't *need* you to."

His eyes closed and he dropped his forehead against mine. Our skin was slick from the subtle tug-of-war we were engaged in, and with him this close, I breathed in his scent, lost in his brutal, unadulterated sexuality. "You don't need to fuck me. You never have," he whispered, sending goose bumps tickling across my skin. "But I need to fuck you. I need to be inside you. I don't know how to show you any other way. I don't know any other way to show you that I need you."

My lips crashed into his, my control obliterated by his confession. I'd spent months telling myself no and going through the motions, and I couldn't do it any longer. Maybe I didn't need Alexander, but I couldn't deny I wanted him. His body. His words. His heart. I'd fooled myself into believing that if he couldn't say it, he didn't feel it. But had he been showing me all along?

Alexander shoved my pants down, lifting me up and out of them before I'd even entirely processed that we were kissing. I broke away, my chest heaving as I shook my head. "This doesn't change the fact that I don't live here."

"I think you'll find I can persuade you." His lips slanted over mine before I could protest further. He dropped me back to my feet and pulled away. I watched, mesmerized, as he unbuckled his pants and pushed them to the floor. Running his fingers across the low neckline of my shirt, he paused with deliberation, then wrenched the fabric with his hands, ripping through the thin garment to reveal my bra. Without hesitation, his thumbs scooped under my breasts and popped them free of the restrictive lace. The rough pads of his fingers circled across the sensitive tips. My nipples hardened under his caress, stirring an ache that tightened in my chest.

"Has anyone touched you like this?" he asked. His breath was hot on my neck as he caught my earlobe between his teeth. Nibbling teasingly, he sucked it as he continued to fondle my breasts. The world around me swam, making it impossible to think, but I still knew my answer.

"No." No one had touched me like this since I left him here. No one had ever touched me like this.

"Because you are mine," he growled, his hands capturing my hips and lifting me against the wall. "And I am yours."

He thrust inside me without warning, and despite the aching readiness of my sex, the rough entry tore through me as though he had cleaved me in two. I gasped and clung to him, allowing him to anchor me at my very core.

"You know what to say, and I'll stop." He rolled his hips, giving me the chance to utter my safe word. But I didn't want him to stop, and he knew it. Alexander's groin rocked into me, his shaft lodged snugly between my folds. Then he began to move, slowly at first. Each thrust was cautious and forceful at the same time. He was still waiting for my response.

"Alexander," I breathed in welcome, and he responded by pumping swiftly in and out of me, leaving me breathlessly dangling between reason and ecstasy.

"You're so tight," he grunted between gritted teeth as he held me against the wall and drove into me with relentless abandon. "So fucking wet and so fucking tight like you've been waiting for me."

"Oh god!" The cry spilled from my lips as he filled me. I had been waiting. Unable to move forward and desperate to not look back. I'd been hiding from him—from this—because it scared me, and as the pleasure ripped through my body, tightening and exploding through my limbs, the intensity mixed with that fear. I dug my fingernails into his back, clutching onto him as if he might vanish any second. My body spiraled into terrifying pleasure, lost in an abyss of reckless delirium. There was no hope. I was lost at sea and Alexander was pulling me under, luring me toward the dark, inescapable depths of our passion.

"Say it," he commanded as I struggled to breathe.

"I love you." The words were small, nearly lost in our frenzied lovemaking, but Alexander's head dropped to my shoulder as they fluttered from my mouth. He groaned as violent spurts lashed inside my velvet channel, draining his seed and the last of my resistance.

CHAPTER SEVEN

Alexander lowered my feet to the floor, one hand remaining on my back to steady me. It was a good thing, too, because after that orgasm my legs were shaking like a newborn colt's. He pressed his forehead to mine, sweeping a soft kiss over my lips, and I sensed the relief and fear in his touch. It mirrored my own. How was it possible that I couldn't live without him, even when our whole relationship was tainted by dishonesty and repression?

"Stop thinking, Clara," he commanded in a husky voice. His hand dropped lower, cupping my ass and hoisting me into the air. I wrapped my legs around his waist willingly. Desperately. This was how Alexander and I communicated best–through thrusts and sweat and moans. I needed the reassurance of his touch.

He carried me as far as the hardwood stairs before he lost patience. "I need to taste you."

Setting me gently down on a step, he was decidedly ungentle as he pushed my legs open. His lips trailed along my inner thigh, teasing me with slow, deliberate kisses. My head lolled back, his tongue erasing the conscious world. There was only this. Only him. Only his mouth closing over my sensitive clit, his tongue circling it with erotic precision. I was lost to him. I thought I could conquer my feelings for him, but he had conquered me.

My muscles tightened in expectation, but my body ached. Even with his mouth closed over my sex, I felt hollow and unfulfilled. It didn't matter that he'd been inside of me only moments ago, I was desperate for him to fuck me. Desperate for physical proof of our connection—the only proof I'd ever really had. I pushed against him, trying to stop him, but he ignored me. A moan escaped my mouth as I fought against the pleasure. This wasn't how I wanted to climax.

"Stop." My plea was nearly lost to another whimper as he sucked my clit hungrily. "I want you...I want you inside me."

Alexander stopped and his face appeared before mine, his eyes blazing. "I say how you will come, poppet." He dropped back between my legs, his hands wrapping possessively around my thighs.

I wanted to come, and I knew soon I wouldn't have a choice in the matter as another wave of pleasure coursed through me. There was only one way to show him I was serious—to show him that I needed more. I needed him. "Brimstone."

His response was immediate. Alexander drew away, sitting back on his heels. Pain glinted in his eyes. If he was angry that I'd used my safe word, he didn't show it. Instead he looked cautious, but under the veneer of control, I saw the wildness in his eyes. He was an animal—a mass of raw sensuality—and I had caged him.

Still he had stopped when I asked. Considering the delicate state of our trust, it comforted me to know he took the gift of my submission seriously. *Baby steps.*

No words passed between us, but I could hear the unspoken question in his eyes. Why had I stopped him?

Had he crossed the line?

My heart broke a little to see the anguish on his face. Alexander was scared to love. He was scared he would destroy me, and now I'd used what was supposed to be a last resort: my safe word. But I needed more than a quick screw on the stairs—we both needed more than that. I stood, my knees still shaky from our frenzied lovemaking, and held out my hand. I knew he would take it. Just as I had taken it the other night at Brimstone. We were powerless to one another. Control and dominance were merely a ruse to cover our feelings for each other. Neither of us could be certain what would happen if we let it slip away. I'd caught glimpses of the man behind the mask before. He was raw and broken, and in those moments he consumed me.

Alexander's eyes met mine as he gently took my hand.

"It's okay," I murmured, feeling the need to reassure him and perhaps to also reassure myself.

I'd stayed one night here weeks ago, but the memory of this house was seared into my brain. During particularly lonely nights, I replayed the moments I spent here until I was too numb to cry. I knew exactly where the bedroom was and I silently led him there. My heart pounded, sending blood roaring through my ears. This place—this house—had been my nightmare for so long, but it had also been my fantasy. Now that I was here with him I didn't know how to feel. Love and fear commingled in my blood. I had to trust my heart. I'd spent the last few months trying to ignore it.

Alexander pulled his hand from mine and with one smooth motion gathered me in his arms and carried me to the bedroom. I struggled to say something, to express my feelings. "I need this...I need us..."

"I know what you need, Clara." He brushed a soft kiss across my forehead before laying me across the bed. His hands swept my ruined shirt off my shoulders, then he removed my bra. I was spread before him—bare and vulnerable. Sensing that, he stood and unbuttoned his shirt slowly before stripping it off. We were both exposed now. Alexander carefully lowered himself over me, and I reached up to run my fingers across the wicked scars that marred his beautiful chest. He was built like a god, carved and chiseled to inhuman perfection, but the scars were visible proof that he was human. He was mortal. Alexander carried the deepest scars from the accident that claimed his sister's life inside of him, but these marks reminded me that he had almost died that night, too. Tears rolled down my cheeks and I blinked in surprise.

"It's okay, poppet," Alexander murmured. His lips dropped to the hollow between my breasts and moved outward until his tongue was circling my left nipple. He took it tenderly into his mouth, swirling and sucking the furl. Pleasure mixed with the emotions surging through me and I began to weep. Alexander moved in a flash, gathering me in his arms and cradling me to his chest.

I pressed my hand against his scars, wishing I could will them away. "I almost lost you."

"You've never lost me," he whispered, his arms tightening protectively.

"No," I said between sobs, "Then. That night. I never would have known—"

"*Shh*," he admonished me. "Let's not talk about our mistakes."

But there were so many of them, and all too often it felt as though they'd been layered and piled on top of one another, erecting a giant barrier between us. I knew what it was like to lose him. The thought that I'd almost never had him was unbearable.

"Show me," I demanded in a low voice. Alexander couldn't say he loved me, not after the night that gave him those scars. He demonstrated his feelings for me physically through a near obsessive and inexhaustible appetite for my body. It was a hunger I shared.

His mouth closed over mine, one hand skimming down my hips and urging my legs apart. Deepening the kiss, his finger traced my slit before spreading me open. His tongue licked across my teeth as his thumb settled over the throb of my sex, massaging it with light, teasing circles. He swallowed my moans, unwilling to break the kiss. Rolling my hips against his hand, I dropped my legs open wider, desperate for him to fill me. When he finally pulled away, we were both breathing heavily. Wildness blazed in his eyes, but he maintained his control. He usually employed that deliberate restraint on me, dominating every moment of my pleasure. Alexander decided when I would come and when I would hold on to the edge. But now he was holding himself at bay.

Sitting back on his heels, he continued to rub my sensitive bud. My hands clutched the white linen sheets frantically clinging to the edge, unwilling to go over it without him. When I hung over the precipice, Alexander positioned himself at my entrance, rubbing his cock teasingly up and down as I squirmed with anticipation. "Clara, I..." he trailed away, his eyes growing sad.

My breath caught in my throat, as though I was afraid I might spook him if I exhaled.

"I..." But he shook his head. "There's only you. There will only ever be you. You're mine, but never forget, I am yours—as much as I can give of me, you can have of me."

His words pushed me over the brink. I unraveled as I fell, crying out when he pushed inside of me and sent a second orgasm rolling through my body. His cock stroked slowly in and out of my sex, prolonging my pleasure until I lay trembling on the bed, but he didn't stop. His hands gripped my hips, coaxing me toward another. It was too much. Shivers broke across my skin, but I didn't ask him to stop. I wanted him there forever. Filling me. Completing me. Although I couldn't stop a whimper from escaping my lips.

"*Shh*, poppet," he soothed me, brushing his thumb across my lips. "I'll never have enough of you."

That was why I couldn't stay away from him. Leaving him had been a futile endeavor. What we had was primal, instinctive, consuming, and I craved it like oxygen. I couldn't survive without it—without him.

THE THING about dating a modern sex god was that I always woke up hungry. This morning was no exception. I slipped quietly from bed, hoping not to wake Alexander. A search of the closet yielded a silky, red robe that looked suspiciously like it had been purchased for me along with a number of other clothing items. Apparently he'd been quite certain I would stay. Either I was easily convinced or he'd had more faith in our ability to work this out.

My muscles were sore, my lady parts were sore, and my stomach was grumbling. That would teach me to sex on an empty stomach. Of course, I hadn't come over here last night with the intention of sleeping with him. Thankfully, the kitchen was fully stocked with fresh organic fruit, eggs, and bread. I pulled a quart of milk from the fridge, nudging it shut with my ass, and nearly dropped it when I caught Alexander watching me from the doorway, wearing only black silk pajama bottoms. They hung off his hips, accentuating the brutally chiseled V I loved. I also loved how much more comfortable he was showing me his body now.

He ran a hand through his tousled black hair and shook his head as if ridding himself of an unpleasant dream. Unfortunately, he had a lot of those.

"You okay?" I asked, abandoning my pursuit of a frying pan. "Nightmare?"

Alexander didn't like talking about the dreams that terrorized him or the memories his subconscious viciously dragged to the surface at night, but I knew that ignoring them each morning wasn't helping.

"You were gone," he said gruffly.

Oh. I'd unwittingly forced him to relive another bad memory. One that was painful for both of us: the morning that I'd walked out on him. "I'm sorry, X. I was hungry."

A grin played at his lips as he prowled toward me. So much for breakfast before our reunion tour continued. "So I'm X again...or do you mean ex-boyfriend?"

"Just X," I said, stretching onto my tiptoes to give him a quick kiss.

"That was...demure." Alexander arched an eyebrow.

"I don't want to give you impure thoughts. I'm hungry." I demonstrated the veracity of my claim by popping a grape in my mouth.

"Then you shouldn't wander around in this." He fingered the delicate material of my robe.

"If you didn't want me to wear it, you shouldn't have bought it for me."

Alexander popped the lid of the glass jug of milk and took a sip, then offered it to me. "I didn't. Norris stocked your closet."

I choked on my milk.

Alexander laughed and wiped a stray dribble from my chin. "Now you're really giving me ideas."

"Norris shopped for me?" I asked incredulously.

"I asked him to. Edward helped." He shrugged as if this was no big deal.

"Of course he did. Do you do anything for yourself?"

Taking the milk from me, he set it on the counter. Then he turned and circled me, pressing my ass against the granite counter. "There's lots of things I do for myself, and a lot of things I do for you. You know that, poppet."

"Uh-uh, Your Majesty." I wagged a finger at him. "You have to feed me if you're going to have your way with me all day."

"Actually, it's Saturday morning. I thought we could check out Portobello Road." He opened the cabinet behind my head and took out a frying pan. "I'll even make you breakfast."

My eyes narrowed. "Like a date?"

"Don't boyfriends do things like that?" he asked as he grabbed an egg from the carton.

"You're hardly a typical boyfriend," I pointed out. "And are you actually cooking me breakfast?"

Case in point: if Alexander was a typical guy, it might not be so shocking to watch him as he lit the burner on the hob.

"It's how I'm going to have my way with you," he reminded me, cocking an eyebrow suggestively.

"I thought we were going on a date."

"Breakfast. *Countertop*. Shower. Date," he said.

"Quite the schedule." I didn't bother to hide the amusement in my voice. "So I can't shower now?"

"I wouldn't recommend it." He cracked another egg into the pan. "You're going to need your strength today, and don't think I haven't noticed you lost more weight. Three eggs for you."

He spoke casually but there was an edge to his words that wasn't welcome this morning. This morning I wanted to be happy. "I've been running more."

"I know," he said quietly.

I decided to let that slide. It wasn't exactly news that he'd had a security team following me and even if I didn't like it—and I didn't—I wanted today to be about us and not all the drama. I swatted his ass as I sashayed by.

"I'll rearrange the schedule if you keep that up," he warned me.

Plopping onto a bar stool at the kitchen island, I feigned a swoon. "But I might starve!"

"Food, it is," he groaned. "You're going to fit in with the Royals so well. You definitely have the dramatic streak."

I did my best to ignore the way my heart leapt at those words. It didn't mean anything. Although I wasn't entirely sure what I wanted it to mean.

I didn't respond and we fell into a rhythm—laughing and teasing each other as he cooked and I offered pointers. But even as we ate breakfast together, anxious excitement swelled in my chest. It felt so normal. So happy. So *everything* Alexander and I had never had with one another. It felt too good to be true.

But then again maybe we'd had enough lies.

CHAPTER EIGHT

I fingered the spines of a well-worn, but still beautiful, edition of *Pride & Prejudice*, while mentally running through each room in the house. Did we have bookshelves? Pulling it from the table of rare books, I realized we could always get bookshelves. I flipped the page and froze. *We*. I'd never explicitly agreed that I was moving in with Alexander, but here I was thinking about what we could do in the house.

The vendor, scenting a sale, stepped next to me. "Very nice edition. Late nineteenth century. It's a bargain at two hundred pounds, my lady."

I blushed and placed the book back on the table, shaking my head. "I was just admiring it."

The man nodded vigorously and began to pluck other books that might interest me from the piles. It wasn't going to be easy to get out of here without buying something. Even as he piled another book into my hands, I couldn't shake the strange mix of emotions still churning in the pit of my stomach. My eyes instinctively found Alexander as I murmured absent an *thank-you* to the stall owner. He was partially turned away from me, studying a book. Dressed in a fitted t-shirt and jeans that showcased his sculpted frame, it would be harder for most people to immediately recognize him. Although there was no way they could ignore him. His dark hair had dried into a wild mess after our shower. He hadn't bothered to shave, leaving the slight scruff of next-day stubble across his jaw. Just thinking about how that would feel later on my thighs sent a thrill running through me from tip to toe. But it was the careful positioning of his body that reminded me of his possessive nature. One flick of his eyes and I would be back in his sight. A few steps and he would be at my side.

I had to give him credit for giving me space, especially since it was obvious from his body language that he was in a state of vigilance. We'd spent very little time publicly together. Alexander spent very little time in public period. Even the clubs he frequented gave him access to private rooms.

He glanced up and a slow smile spread over his face when he caught me looking at him. My heart sped up, sending blood roaring to my ears, and the world fell away, leaving only us. Alexander dazzled me. I knew then that there was no possibility of separation. Not for me. I'd tried and failed to walk away from him. I'd died each night I'd spent without him only to be reborn every morning to suffer the pain again.

Alexander crossed to me, wrapping his arms around my waist. Resting his chin on my shoulder, he studied the book I held. "You should buy it for our place. The library is sadly understocked."

"We have a library?" I blurted out, simultaneously

surprised at the information and overwhelmed to hear him say *our place*.

"Remind me to give you a proper tour this evening."

There was no doubting the suggestive undertone to his words. "I have a feeling I'm going to like this tour."

"You will, poppet." He planted a soft kiss behind my ear, sending a tingle of anticipation down my neck.

Alexander was serious about stocking the library. We left the rare book booth twenty minutes later with an order for all of the man's oldest and rarest volumes.

"You're in a generous mood," I noted as we strolled along the busy street, stopping occasionally to inspect another strange artifact.

"I am." His grip on my hand tightened as we maneuvered through the crowds of shoppers. More than a few people stopped and stared at us, but whether it was because they were uncertain or because they respected our privacy, no one had taken any pictures yet.

It was liberating. Thanks to Alexander's lie last night, the world believed we were living together. I was beginning to believe it myself. Twenty-four hours ago, I'd had no faith he could ever provide me with commitment. Now I had little doubt whether we were both fully committed to this relationship. There was still a tiny voice tucked deep inside me that warned me to protect myself. The problem was that I had Alexander protecting me now, and more than ever, I wanted to give myself fully to him—body and soul.

Stopping in a small shop with antique and rare fixtures, I pointed to a beautiful Tiffany reproduction lamp. "What about this for our place?"

His answering smile nearly blinded me. "Anything you want, poppet."

"No," I said, shaking my head, "this is our place."

"I can't describe what it's like to hear you say that," he admitted. He picked up the lamp and headed to the counter.

"I bet it feels like winning," I said dryly.

He chuckled softly as he passed the lamp to the cashier.

"£15,000," she informed him.

I gawked at her. After I recovered from the shock, I asked weakly, "This isn't a reproduction?"

"No, this is a Tiffany Studios lamp." She turned it over and showed me the stamp. "Dated 1896. It's a rare piece."

That I knew. Alexander handed her a thin, black credit card, seemingly unimpressed by the sum.

"Let's look for something else," I suggested under my breath.

"Nonsense." He waved off my concern. "You liked this lamp."

I had, but paying £15,000 for something I was going to be afraid to touch seemed a trifle extravagant. Watching the shopkeep wrap it for us, I imagined what would happen if I accidentally dropped it. Thanks in part to Alexander's nonchalant attitude regarding the piece, I knew that the only person who would be mad was me. When she handed me the carefully wrapped package, I immediately passed it to him.

Despite growing up wealthy, I'd never really spent money. My mother had replenished my closet and decorated the numerous homes we lived in over the years. In college, my tuition was paid and there was always enough in the account for food or books or other expenses. I had access to my trust fund now, but little occasion to use it save to write the rent check or to purchase new work clothes. I had furniture and belongings and such, but I'd never really had a proper grown-up residence before. The flat I shared with Belle was full of bits of our lives collected up to this point. I'd meant to decorate, but life—or rather Alexander—had distracted me before I got around to it. But even if I had, I seriously doubted I would have spent £15,000 on one lamp.

"You're quiet," Alexander pointed out as we left the shop. He tucked the package under his arm, slinging the other arm over my shoulder possessively.

"Thank you." I motioned to the lamp. "It's beautiful, but it feels a little extravagant, too."

"I wouldn't have royal blood in my veins, if my tastes didn't lend themselves to the lavish." He paused and turned to face me. "For example, my prized possession."

"Does that mean you'll take me to get falafel?" I bit my lip innocently.

"Anything you want, poppet." He tipped my chin up, studying my face for a moment before he kissed me. There was a time when I might have objected to being called his possession, but I understood what he meant now. I also knew that he belonged to me as much as I did to him. His lips lingered on mine, firm and hot, but the kiss didn't step over the bounds of polite public displays of affection. He broke away leading me onward, but I couldn't tear my eyes from him. I was vaguely aware of the bustle surrounding us, although I didn't care. When I was with him, there was only him.

My thigh bumped into a table and I was forced to look

away. Swiveling around to find the vendor and apologize for my clumsiness, my world came crashing to a halt. I stood frozen to the spot as my eyes locked on the man standing in the street behind us.

It was Daniel.

CHAPTER NINE

The numbness spread across my chest and up my neck as if I was going into shock. I wasn't certain how we made it back to the house, but in the afternoon light, it looked like a haven. Yesterday I would have been afraid to walk up and knock on the front door. I had been afraid. Today I wanted to run inside and hide. Alexander had remained level-headed even when I'd suddenly stumbled and panicked in the middle of the street. He hadn't asked questions. He'd acted out of instinct, bringing me here where he could protect me. But while he had guided me patiently through the maze of tourists and shoppers, the second we were through the gate, he scooped me up and carried me into the house.

Setting me on the counter, he grabbed a glass and filled it with water. Alexander waited a moment while I drank it out.

"Are you okay?" he finally asked.

"I saw—" But the buzz of my phone alarm caught me off. It was noon. Lunchtime.

It dawned on Alexander as I silenced my phone. "You need to eat."

"I'm fine." Eating was the last thing I felt like doing. Not while my stomach was a tangle of nerves and knots.

"This is non-negotiable," he informed me. "You wanted falafel. It will only take me a few minutes to run up the street and grab it."

"There's going to be a line, X," I said. It was Saturday at lunchtime. He wouldn't be back for an hour, and the thought of being separated from him that long scared me. Almost as much as being alone right now.

Alexander shook his head. "I can be very persuasive. Ten minutes. Or I could make more eggs?"

"Falafel sounds good." Our first day back together needed to be about us. It needed to be normal, not weighed down by the past. Telling him that I thought I saw my ex-boyfriend on the street was at best silly and at worst paranoid.

"Are you sure?" His gaze searched my face for a sign as to what had happened. "This is what happens when I give Norris the day off. I have to choose between taking care of you and feeding you."

"Feed me," I ordered, pushing him toward the door.

Thankfully I could occupy my time with exploring my new home. Over the last few months I'd become adept at distracting myself from things better left in the past. I could apply that skill to seeing Daniel—if I'd seen him at all. The fact that I'd agreed to live here with Alexander was definitely distracting.

The living room was spartan and comfortable at the same time. Once we got some more furniture and rugs in here it would be quite cozy to sit by the fireplace. There were other things we could do by the fireplace as well.

Upstairs I found two more bedrooms in addition to what would be our master bedroom. Someday we'd be able to invite guests over to stay, but for now I wanted to keep our love nest to ourselves. Alexander had procured this house as a place for us to escape the outside world. Maybe in its safety he would finally open himself to me in ways he still found too difficult. He wanted me here with him. He'd openly announced we were living together. This wasn't just a hideout. It was his way of giving me the commitment that he found so hard to offer me with words.

A creak from down the hall startled me and I clutched my chest. It was an older home. It was bound to make plenty of odd noises. I was just jumpy after seeing Daniel in the market. At least, I thought that was who I'd seen. It had been naive to think that London's dense population would protect me from him forever. Besides that, our relationship was long over. So what if he was in Notting Hill today? His geographical coordinates shouldn't affect me in the slightest.

But they did, because if I was being honest, I'd hoped to never see him again. Breaking up with Daniel had been difficult, and he hadn't made it any easier on me. Not that he'd tried to contact me since then. If he'd seen me today, he probably would have avoided me as well. Still I couldn't help but hope he wouldn't often find himself near here. Notting Hill was supposed to be my safe haven and I was desperate for its security.

When Alexander walked back in the door fifteen minutes later, I hadn't managed to calm myself down at all.

"You're late," I snapped.

Alexander set the take away on the kitchen counter and sauntered toward me. "Watch yourself, poppet."

But I wasn't in the mood to be teased. I was in the mood to fuck. I needed to feel something other than the anxiety clawing at my chest. There were too many reasons why this wouldn't work—too many people and too many variables that could mess this up. This morning I had been happy. I wanted to feel that again. I wanted the blissful oblivion of being screwed senseless. So instead of responding to his warning, I crashed into him. Our tongues tangled together as our bodies fought to free ourselves of our restrictive clothing. My hand slipped down the front of his jeans, gripping his hard length. If Alexander was confused at my sudden desire, his cock wasn't.

He took the cue, shoving my thin sun dress in a bunch around my hips as he lifted me onto the edge of the kitchen counter. With a snap, he ripped my thong off and pushed between my legs. In one swift motion, he freed me from my dress altogether. His kiss deepened as he removed my bra, his tongue plunging inside my mouth as my breasts spilled free. Pulling his lips away, he breathed heavy against my ear. "Do you trust me?"

Did I? But the moment I asked the question, I knew my answer. I trusted him—with my body and my heart. I didn't have any choice but to trust him. Our entire relationship was an act of faith. But I also had seen the shift in him. His desire for control had shifted to protectiveness. I was his as he was mine.

I nodded.

"Say the word and I stop," he reminded me. His body peeled away from mine and I fought the urge to reach out and drag him back to me. Bending down, he picked up the remnants of my panties. "I will not do anything to you that we haven't done before. At least in a sexual sense. What I'm asking is whether or not you trust me to be in control?"

Alexander had hinted about his desire to dominate me before, and more than once he'd blurred the boundaries I thought I had. This time I sensed it would be different. The resistance I'd expected to feel when he finally asked me to submit to him wasn't there. Alexander's blunt sexuality had governed me since the moment we met, winning out over reason and sense. But he'd always made sure I felt in control. Now he was asking me to relinquish that to him. Something that wasn't easy for me, given my past.

"I trust you." In some ways those words held more meaning than any others I'd spoken to him.

He knew it. Alexander brushed a kiss across my mouth. The sweet gesture only ratcheted up the pulse between my legs. "Put your hands behind your back."

I obeyed without protest. His arms slipped around me, pinning my wrists together before I felt lace wrapping slowly around them. He bound them together tightly enough that there was no chance I could pull an arm free but not so much that it hurt. A thrill raced from my stomach to my throat. A strange mixture of apprehension and elation swirled through my head. I bit my lip, trying to hold the dizzying effect he had on me at bay. For the first time, I didn't simply want this—I needed it. I needed him to take command and make me forget all the fear and anger I'd felt earlier.

He stepped back and regarded me—legs spread wide on the counter, hands bound behind my back—and smiled. The darkness that always flickered in the depths of his beautiful eyes flamed to life.

"Now you have me where you want me," I murmured, surprised at the sultry undertone of my own voice. I wasn't entirely certain who this vixen was, but I was eager for her to come out and play—eager to let go.

But Alexander held back, clearly not as restless as I was, and shook his head. "Not quite, poppet."

He slid open a drawer and removed a white kitchen towel. Shaking it open, he laid it on the counter and folded it longwise into precise thirds. When he lifted it to my face, there was a moment of hesitation. He didn't ask my permission again. He only waited for me to say no, but I was silent. Tying it around my eyes, he whispered, "You still have your voice."

Then he was gone. I sensed his presence and knew he was standing there surveying his prize. With my sight taken from me, I was aware of the sharp intake of his breath. The air felt cooler on my bare skin. Every inch of me felt alive.

"Beautiful," he said in appreciative voice. "First, you will eat."

I started to protest, but it was no use. There was no arguing with Alexander's protective side. Beside me a bag rustled and I heard the metallic crunch of foil being torn away. An exotic aroma flooded my nostrils and I breathed in, trying to guess what he'd brought home for me. I was an adventurous eater, but I'd always known what was going into my mouth.

"Open your mouth."

I did as he instructed and spice burst across my tongue. I chewed slowly, delicately. The flavors were Moroccan, I guessed, but although I'd had the cuisine before, I'd never savored it like this, deprived of my sight—deprived of even the ability to feed myself. When I was ready, he offered me another bite and another. Something about the act, so nurturing and yet so domineering, made the experience almost orgasmic. Each bite stole another moan of pleasure from me as the unexpected textures and flavors hit my palate.

"Are you ready for the next course?" he asked at last, and something in his tone sent anticipation fluttering through me.

I nodded, licking my lips.

His hands slid under my arms and he lifted me to my feet. "Kneel."

He guided me to the floor. The stone tile was cold on my knees as I waited, unsure what to expect next. Then I felt the warm crown of his cock nudge against my lips. They parted willingly, taking his length into my mouth. My tongue wrapped around his shaft as I began to suck, but his hand stilled my head.

"Relax," he ordered. "Take all of it."

I withdrew to take a deep breath and then closed my mouth over him once more. This time I was ready and he slid inside me, his crest bumping gently against my throat. "I'm going to fuck your mouth, Clara. Are you prepared for that?"

I moaned my readiness and he began to thrust inside me with slow, purposeful strokes. "Your lips look so pretty wrapped around my cock," he grunted and delight colored my cheeks. "Are you blushing, poppet, or are you turned on?"

I could almost imagine the hunger burning through his eyes as he spoke, and it made me want to reach out and urge his hips to a swifter pace. But I couldn't. I was at his mercy as he took his pleasure, and I'd never been so wildly turned on.

All I could do was show him by pressing my lips over him and sucking harder. He groaned his approval and deepened his strokes until I felt the first jet of his climax hit the back of my throat.

When he pulled out, I expected him to take off my blindfold, but instead he ushered me to my feet. Turning my body, he pressed a hand against my shoulder blades. Instinctively I bent until my breasts met the granite counter. I shivered as the delicate skin of my nipples beaded at the cool contact. *He isn't done with me yet.* It was the only thought blaring through my head as Alexander pushed my legs open wider. The tip of a finger trailed along my throbbing sex, and I cried out, torn between frustration and agonizing expectation. It stilled and I followed suit, realizing that he was waiting for me to prove I was ready for him—for his touch. When I was quiet, his finger delved between my folds and caressed my clit. The touch was too gentle to provide the satisfaction I desperately craved. Instead, the sensitive spot switched on like a beacon, pulsing with increasing demand as it waited for its relief. I squirmed, encouraging his hand to find it again, and the action was met with an unexpected, firm smack to my ass.

Alexander had spanked me before, but this took me by surprise and I gasped even as my body went limp against him.

"Let go," he demanded again. Molding his body to mine, he lowered his voice, "You will always come, poppet. That is not a question. The only question is *when*? Do you know the answer?"

"When you say," I guessed in a near breathless voice.

"Very good." He brushed his free hand down my hair. "I've told you before that you may ask, but not today. Today I want you to come freely but only by my hand—or whatever part of me I choose. Do you understand?"

"Yes," I moaned, not quite able to stop myself from wondering exactly how long that would be.

"It won't be long. I won't make you wait," he promised in a soothing voice. His thumb settled over my clit as he spoke while his fingers eased inside my slit. He massaged inside and out, and my limbs began to tense. I fought it, but then his words came back to me.

Let go.

I did as he commanded, releasing myself to him until I'd forgotten my bound wrists and covered eyes. Until I'd forgotten the problems awaiting us outside this house. I allowed the bliss to carry me away, sweeping me along with its powerful current as I surrendered the last of my control. It roared through me and I sobbed with agonizing relief as the waves crashed over me.

The binding over my wrists loosened and Alexander rubbed along the indentations left behind. He removed the blindfold next and the world came rushing back to me in vivid colors. For a moment, I sagged against the counter, too weak-kneed to move, but Alexander's hand on my back signaled for me to face him. When I finally lifted my eyes to meet his, the wildness that usually flamed in them had cooled. He cupped my chin and drew my lips to his.

"Thank you," he told me in a soft voice. "For your trust."

My eyes fluttered against the residue of tears recently fallen, and I shook my head. He shouldn't be the one thanking me. I should be thanking him, for finally giving me true release. For freeing me.

"Was it too much? If you aren't—" His now placid eyes filled with concern.

I raised a single finger to his lips to stop him mid-sentence. He was worried about how I felt. I'd given him plenty of cause for concern before. But he needed to know that everything was different now. He needed to know what I truly wanted and there was only one word he needed to hear. "More."

CHAPTER TEN

ALEXANDER

Clara was back in my bed. After months of trying to let her go or draw her back, she was here. There'd been no resistance when I had carried her upstairs, despite showing her the dominance hidden inside of me. I'd taken her again without warning when we reached our bedroom. She did not complain, although I was certain I hurt her—that I'd been too rough, too excited after tying her delicate wrists behind her. I needed to explain myself—my compulsions—before I scared her. She wouldn't be allowed to run away again, but I could not stomach the idea of her fearing me. Running a finger down the soft curve of her hip, I marveled at her presence—at the sense of wholeness I only felt when she was near.

But even as we lay here, rediscovering each other now with gentle caresses and stolen kisses, the future weighed on me. Being with me would destroy her. I was a one-man wrecking ball and no matter how much I tried to deny my feelings for her, I couldn't let her go. I couldn't save her. A life with me meant a life of pressure and more scrutiny that any one person should bear. I'd watched it poison my father, making him into a man I could no longer look to with respect. My brother was forced to live a lie. What would Clara be forced to endure to be with me?

"Stop it," she demanded in a low voice. "Here and now, remember?"

How did she know what I was thinking? How did she always know?

Because she loved me.

I pushed the thought away, but it was too late. The momentary lightness of the realization evaporated and my body constricted as though someone was strangling me. Loving me was dangerous. It was the one thing I couldn't prevent. I'd tried to stop her. I'd tried to hurt her.

And here she was.

I wasn't a weak man, but I was powerless to deny myself. My eyes swept over her lips and my cock twitched, already ready to fill her again. But I had to show her she was more to me than that. How could I, though, knowing I would inevitably fuck this up?

Reaching out, I gently guided her onto her stomach. The only way to stop the constant onslaught of confusion coursing through me was to give in to my baser instincts. The sight of her ass—shapely and inviting—did the trick. I couldn't tell her how I felt, because I didn't understand it myself. But I could show her. Lowering my lips to the nape of her neck, I pressed a kiss to her flesh. Clara released a soft sigh, and the vise-grip around my heart relaxed. This was what I needed—to hear the soft moans of her pleasure, to lose myself in the little noises she made as I took her. Her pleasure freed me, giving me a sense of purpose I thought I'd lost forever. Sweeping her hair off her shoulders, I ran my fingers through the loose strands. Another tiny whimper escaped her.

Resisting the urge to plunge inside her so quickly after our last rough encounter, I parted her hair and began to slowly braid it. "I love your hair. I love watching it fall across your face as I fuck you. I love when it brushes across my cock the moment before I'm in your mouth."

"X." Caution coloured her voice, as if she was afraid to be pleased by my confession. She wriggled closer to me, pushing her ass against my groin in invitation. "Please, X."

My chest constricted again, but this time with pleasure over her pet name for me. It was too soon for her body, although I couldn't ignore her plea. "*Shh*, poppet. *Soon*. I'll fuck you soon, but your body needs longer. I took you without making sure you were ready last time. I couldn't help myself."

It wasn't an apology exactly. I couldn't apologize for giving us what we both needed, but now there was no need to rush. I folded a section of her hair over another.

"I'm fine." But her words were forced. She needed the contact as much as I did. Something had happened earlier in the market. Something had spooked her. I wasn't inclined to push her for answers. Not this early in our reconciliation and not after she'd been so angry over my possessiveness. But even if she didn't understand the necessity of my vigilance, she would learn to live with it. I made a mental note to ask Norris to look into the matter.

Her body curved into a graceful arc as she pushed up and turned to look at me. Pert, pink nipples brushed across her upper arm as she knelt on the bed. She was original sin incarnate—my temptation and my redemption.

"I thought I didn't have to ask today."

"Don't argue. When your cunt is soft and wet—" I tightened my hold on her braid and leaned down to brush my lips across her shoulder—"then. When you're ready."

"I'm always ready for you," she reminded me in a whisper.

It took every ounce of self-control I had not to take her on the spot. Instead, I wrapped her hair slowly around her neck like a collar. Clara stilled but didn't object, although her hands fisted into the sheets. Did she anticipate what I wanted to do to her? It seemed impossible that she invited it. She had been clear that she wasn't interested in more than playful submission. Not that I required more, but...I enjoyed it. My past relationships had come on my terms. Women were eager to fuck me however I wanted to fuck, and I'd certainly taken advantage of their flexibility. But my desire for Clara ran deeper. I didn't want to break her. I wanted to conquer her and the fears that held her captive to the past. I understood all too well what that was like. The more she relinquished control to me, the more I could liberate her while showing her that my protective nature stemmed from a primal urge I couldn't deny.

"Do you want to tie me up?" she offered in a small, hopeful voice.

I groaned and sank my teeth into her shoulder in an effort to restrain myself. She craned her neck, offering more of her delicate flesh as though she longed for the pleasure tinged with pain. The image of her elegant body bound in silk rope flashed through my mind. I craved her however I could take her, but the idea of having her at my mercy—at being able to give her more pleasure than she thought she could handle—tormented me.

"Yes, poppet," I murmured against her ear, catching its shell momentarily between my teeth. "But our situation has changed and I need to be certain that we understand each other."

"I...I...want you to dominate me," she stammered. Her words came in a flurry of nervousness and expectation.

My free hand slid around her waist to cup her breasts. I allowed my fingers to skim across the fragile tissue of her nipples, which responded immediately to my touch. "Your body is so responsive. It longs for my touch as if it's just waiting for me. For my hands. Or my mouth—" my lips dipped once more to the hollow behind her ear. "But there are things we need to be clear about. First, I have to ask you. Did you enjoy it when I tied your wrists?"

Her eyes closed in reverence and she bobbed her head. My cock throbbed, and I forced myself to ignore its demands even as her supple ass brushed against it.

"Do you want me to tie you up? Do you want to give me control?"

"Yes," she breathed. Under the hand that covered her breast, I felt her heartbeat speed up.

"Do you understand what you're asking for?" I hated to force a serious topic at this moment, but I couldn't stomach the possibility of crossing the line with her. Not after what she'd endured before we met.

Finally there was hesitation. She didn't know how to answer me. "I trust you, X."

"And I will not betray that trust," I assured her in a

soothing voice. "But I want to be clear about something. We are not a dominant and submissive. Not truly."

"But you want to tie me...and s-s-spank me," she stuttered as she tried to articulate her confusion.

This is what I couldn't explain to her before when I'd glimpsed her fear, but now that lines were being crossed, I wanted both of us to understand what we needed from each other. It was a talk I'd planned to have with her after I'd taken the riding crop to her, and it was long overdue. "Clara, there are many things I want to do to you. I want to feel my palm vibrate against your ass as I spank you. I want to tie you up and leave you to the mercy of my tongue or cock or fingers. I want you to trust me with your pleasure. Sexually my appetite varies. Many times all I need is to be inside you, but since I've met you, I've sensed there was something different about you—a fearlessness."

"I'm far from fearless," she said with a soft snort.

"You are brave, Clara. Strong." I tugged the hair still wrapped around her throat, drawing her closer to me. "You see my need for control and you aren't afraid. It's almost as if you—"

"Like it," she finished for me in a breathless voice.

"Do you?" I attempted to keep my voice steady. Everything hinged on her answer.

"I don't fear it." She paused, considering the question. "I do like it. I yearn for it."

"Why?"

"Because in it, we're free." She spoke so softly that I almost thought I'd imagined her words.

She understood. The revelation hit me with the force of a sudden storm. She understood the delicate dance between the light and the dark that consumed me and that coloured my passion for her. At that moment, the fragile handle I had over my desires broke.

"I need to be inside you," I grunted. My hand dropped to spread her milky thighs.

"*Yes, please.*"

My cock spasmed at the familiar words. As always her eyes were closed and her voice distant as though she wasn't even aware she had spoken. But the urgency of them was always there. It was how I'd known it was okay to cross the lines she'd claimed to have earlier in our relationship. It was how I knew she needed to feel me now as much as I needed her.

I kept a hold of her hair, relishing the ability to pull her closer to me as I positioned myself behind her.

"Hold onto the headboard," I ordered her.

Her fingers stretched over her head, grasping the slats of the wooden frame firmly. Then I pressed my hand to her taut belly and drew her ass down to my waiting hips. My cock slid inside her cunt, meeting with no resistance. A strangled cry of pleasure slipped from her mouth as my shaft speared her, piercing her to the core. Clara settled over me, and even though she didn't circle her hips, her hunger radiated off of her, drawing me in and urging me on. I yanked the hair collaring her neck, tightening it so that she gasped and her breath shifted to quick, shallow pants.

"You know what to say if it's too much," I reminded her softly.

She nodded, but the only word she uttered was "more."

I was lost to the request, slamming into her until there was nothing but the slap of skin against skin and her near-breathless cries. My hand slipped from her belly to massage her clit as I quickened my thrusts. I was rewarded as the first of her pleasure clenched my cock. Her passage clamped against me, hungrily drawing forth my climax. I jerked her head back so that I could watch her face as she came undone.

"Say it," I whispered in her ear as pressure weighted my balls.

Her lips parted obediently, but the taut hold I had on her throat restricted her speech. She mouthed the words.

"I love you."

My pleasure erupted, spilling into her. At that moment, she freed me with her words, with her body. I allowed myself to feel her love and it washed over me as I hammered her toward another release. I didn't want this moment to slip away but as she shattered against me once more, her body crumpled, supported only by her white-knuckled grip on the headboard. Releasing her hair, I gathered her in my arms and lowered us to the bed, still filling her.

I couldn't give her what she needed, even as she gave me everything. I couldn't risk her life by being selfish.

"I will never have my fill of you." My whispered promise wasn't what she deserved, but it would have to be enough.

WE STAYED like that for somewhere between a minute and eternity. Time had ceased to hold sway over us. Clara drew herself from my arms, turning over to face me. Our eyes locked and lightness tightened my chest. It was always the same. Happiness followed so rapidly by self-loathing that I could not separate the two from one another.

Her fingers tangled in my hair, drawing my lips to hers.

The taste of her was honey on my tongue. When we broke apart, she glanced at me, an unusual shyness settling over her lovely features. "What did you mean when you said I wasn't truly a submissive? Am I—" she paused—"doing something wrong?"

I tightened my hold on her, pressing her close to my chest. "No, poppet. It's more complicated than that."

There were things Clara didn't know about my past. I couldn't imagine she wanted the torture of knowing about every woman I'd been intimate with. Still the only way to explain what I'd meant earlier was to reveal something that might hurt her or, at best, scare her.

"The dominant and submissive lifestyle is not something that one simply turns on and off." I paused, preparing myself for her reaction.

"You were in one?" she guessed in a quiet voice.

There was my Clara, always reading my mind. "Yes."

She stiffened but didn't pull away. It was a better reaction than I could have hoped for, so I continued. "It was brief and it occurred not long after Sarah's death."

"Did you love her?"

"No." My denial was harsh, but I understood what Clara was truly asking. Had I been capable of love before her? "I've never loved a woman romantically. As I told you, I loved my mother and sister. That's all."

It pained me to say it, knowing it hurt her. Clara drew in a sharp breath as though she'd been physically wounded, but she didn't speak.

"The girl who was chosen as my submissive was no one to me but a willing partner hand-picked by my friend."

"This friend picked a girl for you? You can hardly run to

the corner shop and pick up a submissive." There was an edge to her words that pained me.

"It was a friend of my father's who is a lifestyle dominant. I had heard the whispers, so I approached him. He understood the need for discretion and found a girl who could meet that need." Perhaps the more cut and dried I made it sound, the less doubt it would give her.

"What did you do to her?" she asked, but I heard the true question: what will you do to me?

Answering this question was like walking a tight rope. "She helped me discover that while there were aspects of the lifestyle I craved, others did not suit me."

"What did you do to her?" her voice broke as she repeated the question more insistently.

"I tied her up," I admitted slowly. "Sometimes I took a cane to her or a paddle. Other times a whip. She craved pain —nearly unbearable pain. It was more satisfying to her than pleasure."

I felt her withdraw from me even though she didn't move.

"Clara," I said her name as if I could catch her before she slipped away. "I was angry and confused. My body was still healing from the accident or I would have chosen self-punishment. But you must understand this was a mutual arrangement. She wasn't a slave or a victim. She was a willing participant."

"Do you...do you..." she trailed away, unable to find the words.

"Not anymore. It was a dark period in my life. I don't feel the same compulsion to punish now, although it did show me that pleasure can be drawn out. That it can be mixed with the edge of pain, and that dominance and submission can be liberating." I brushed back a lock of chestnut hair that had fallen over her forehead. It seemed a good sign that she didn't flinch. "What other questions do you have? I don't want you to feel there are secrets between us."

She hesitated, her eyes darting away from mine. "Why did you stop?"

"My father found out." My lips curled ruefully at the memory. Apparently I'd only needed to look to him for punishment if I'd wanted to feel pain. "I'd recovered from the accident, and he wouldn't stand for any more bad press, as he put it. So he shipped me off to Afghanistan."

We lapsed into silence. Clara to think, and I to allow her time to process. It wasn't the whole truth. I didn't need her to feel any more pity for me—or fear. Finally, she buried her face into my shoulder.

"The two of us are pretty fucked up," she said in a muffled voice.

I laughed humorlessly.

Clara pulled away, her eyes searching my face. Perhaps for the darkness she'd seen before. For the first time, I hoped she didn't see it.

"I only want to give you pleasure, Clara. If this scares you, I'm happy to take you to bed or up against a wall or in an elevator."

I was rewarded with a tentative smile. "So average boring sex?"

"Sex with you could never be average." The thought was ludicrous. "It's not a coincidence that I've been perpetually hard since we met."

"You have a similar effect on me. I still think—" she hesitated—"that I'd like to explore."

It was a perfect term to describe our mutual desire. Clara had once again surprised me, proving her strength as she opened herself to the unknown.

"Do you want to try?" she asked in a small voice.

"No." I shook my head and then rolled her onto her back. "Not now. All I want is to worship you."

She didn't object as I lowered my hips between her thighs and joined her. We moved together, lips lingering on skin and hands holding tightly to one another. Both determined to not let the other one slip away.

CHAPTER ELEVEN

It took considerable effort to pry myself out of Alexander's arms—and bed—to go to my flat for a few hours. After the whirlwind of the last thirty hours, I needed to clear my head. Tomorrow I had to be at the office and there were presentations to prepare. Besides that I hadn't spoken to Belle since she called me on Friday night. I owed her an explanation before she called Scotland Yard to report me missing. Pausing at the door, I took a deep breath before I unlocked it.

"I'm sorry!" I flew into the room. Dropping my pocket book on the counter, I hugged a startled Belle. "My phone died."

"I assumed as much when it went to voice mail for the last twenty-four hours." If my best friend was upset, she didn't show it. I could almost spot the twitch of a smile on her lips, but she raised her teacup to cover it. She was dressed in a rose-colored dressing gown that made her look every bit the vintage ingénue, but it wasn't Philip taking tea with her this morning. It was Aunt Jane. The older woman, already wearing today's flowing garb and assortment of funky jewelry, stretched her arms wide to hug me.

"She was worried," Jane said, earning a reproachful look from her niece. But Aunt Jane was far past caring what anyone, family included, thought of what she said. "I told her to stick a cork in it."

My eyes flashed from hers to Belle's, trying to keep a straight face but I failed miserably. To my surprise, they both joined in with my laughter. The atmosphere of the flat felt lighter than it had in weeks, and it seemed to be affecting all of us.

"You're in an excellent mood," Belle noted.

"She got shagged." Jane wasn't the type to tiptoe around the tulips. If the fastest path was to walk straight through, she'd mow them down. When it came to my love life, she didn't make exceptions to this rule. Still, I had to appreciate her frankness when it came to my recent romantic entanglements, even if she had a tendency to make me blush. After all, it had been her interference that had opened the door to allowing Alexander back into my life.

"It's the weekend. Who isn't shagging?" Belle asked.

Now it was my turn to raise an eyebrow. "I thought you were handling this well."

"Don't rub it in, girls," Jane said in a mournful tone.

"You see more action than both of us," Belle scoffed.

"Fernando moved to Spain," she informed us. "I suppose I'm, what do you young people say, back in the game?"

This time I didn't even try to smother my laughter. What would it be like to be a free spirit like Belle's aunt—saying what I liked and bedding men with exotic names? Of course, she wasn't married. I wasn't sure if she ever had been. From everything she'd said to me, there had been a long string of lovers in her life. But she'd hinted at one doomed relationship when she advised me to take a chance with Alexander. "Were you ever married, Aunt Jane?"

Her eyes widened a bit and I remembered that despite how forthright Jane could be, she was still English.

"Sorry," I murmured. "I was only curious."

"It's fine." She waved off my apology, the sleeve of her turquoise kaftan swirling in the air. "No, not really."

"I didn't mean to pry." I felt terrible for letting curiosity get the better of me, and her answer only left me more curious.

"Will I be seeing a lot more of you in the tabloids?" Belle asked, breaking the palpable tension in the air. No. Not tension. Sadness.

I forced a tight-lipped smile, appreciative for the change in topic. Although I hadn't quite decided how to broach the subject of Alexander yet. "I suppose so."

This was going to be the hard part, telling Belle that Alexander's red carpet fib was no longer a figment of his imagination. We'd barely even lived together for the summer and I was abandoning her. It hardly seemed important that in a year she would be married herself and moving into Philip's house, but partially because neither of us had anticipated how Alexander would change my life.

"I agreed to move in with him." It was better to just be over and done with it than to drag it out longer than necessary.

"You what?" Belle's scream was an odd mixture of laughter and horror.

"I'm going to live with Alexander." It felt odd to say it out loud. Even stranger than it had to call it 'our place' with him in Notting Hill. I felt at home with Alexander as though I was where I belonged after a lifelong wait. But facing the reality of my decision outside his presence forced me to consider what I was choosing.

"I got that part," Belle snapped. Abandoning her tea on the counter, she rummaged through the cabinets until she found a bottle of scotch.

"It's not even noon," I said as she poured a shot in a rocks glass and handed it to me.

"It's Sunday and we're English."

That was apparently the final word on the matter. Aunt Jane took her glass without protest and swallowed it swiftly. She stood and gave me another hug. "I suppose I need to go check my partner.com profile. Maybe my next Fernando is waiting." Then she leaned in and whispered so only I could hear, "No regrets, Clara."

As soon as she was out the door, Belle turned on me. "You can't possibly have thought this through."

"I've been doing nothing but thinking for months," I argued.

"You've done nothing but work and avoid reality. Now you're running back to the man who broke your heart!" No one would have guessed from looking at Belle that this slender blonde could raise such a ruckus. I, on the other hand, knew better. If I didn't calm her down now, we both might say things we regretted.

"I thought about him. I spent every night wishing he could be a different man," I said quietly, hoping the shift in volume would change the dynamic between us. "But I realized I don't want him to be different. I want him even with all the drama that comes with him. And he's trying to give me what I need in return."

"And what are you giving him?" she asked, lowering her voice to match mine.

"Everything," I admitted. I didn't need to go into details about our sex life, because she wouldn't understand. How could anyone but Alexander and I?

"I don't want to see him hurt you."

"I can't promise that I won't get hurt, but beautiful things can come from pain." My own hard-won liberation from my ex-boyfriend was proof of that. "I have to take the risk, because if I don't, I'll always regret it."

Belle's blue eyes grew as distant as the sky on a cloudy day. When she finally spoke, her words were hollow. "You're right, of course. Regret isn't something anyone should live with."

Her words twisted into me like a knife. We all lived with regrets. The only thing we could do was follow our hearts and trust the people we loved. Both of us knew from experience that meant risking heartache. I couldn't be certain if we were talking about Belle's past or my own. Although it occurred to me that we might not be talking about either.

"Do you hate me?" I didn't care what many people thought of me, but I did care about my relationship with Belle. She'd been my constant for the last four years. We'd seen each other through countless rough patches, and the thought of choosing between the two people I loved most in the world was unfathomable. I needed Alexander in my life, but I needed her, too.

Belle reached out and clasped my hand. "You're my sister. At least as close as I've got. I might not always like the choices you make, but I will always love you."

Tears pooled in my eyes and I did nothing to hold them back. They fell freely down my cheeks as I hugged my best friend. Within seconds, we'd both turned into a soggy mass of feelings in the middle of the kitchen. "Just because I won't be here doesn't mean I'm disappearing."

"I know," Belle whispered, but the sadness in her voice spoke another truth.

People changed when they fell in love. We both knew that. I just had to show her that I wouldn't let love change everything.

My mother's voice shrieked across the phone line. "You're living with him and I had to hear about it on the television!"

I pinched the bridge of my nose and took a deep breath. I couldn't exactly explain to her what had actually happened, especially now that I was actively moving in with him. Across my bedroom, Belle raised an eyebrow. There was no need to tell her who was on the phone.

"It just happened," I assured her, wondering how far I could stretch the truth before it became an outright lie. "I barely even realized it was happening."

Belle covered her mouth to smother a laugh. I couldn't blame her. It was the understatement of the century.

"When your father gets the news..." she trailed away in an attempt to add gravitas to the threat.

I seriously doubted my father would care that I'd moved

in with my boyfriend. He didn't subscribe to my mother's need to keep up appearances.

"Where is Dad?" I asked, trying to change the topic.

"He's gone on business until Tuesday." But she wasn't so easily swayed. "Do you have a date set?"

"A date for what?" I asked, then realization dawned on me. "A housewarming party? Yes, it's next week."

Now that was a lie, and a not terribly well-thought out one. She'd expect an invitation. Of course, just mentioning it was invitation enough to my mother, which meant that I now actually had to throw a party. All my fantasies of enjoying privacy with Alexander shattered around me. I had to hand it to Madeline. She could finagle an invite to any event, even fake ones.

"Send over the details. We'll be there," she spoke in the clipped tone I recognized from childhood. It usually preceded her telling me I was being obstinate. "But I'm talking about the other date."

"I really don't—"

"Don't be daft, Clara," she cut me off. "For the wedding!"

"The...wedding?" I blinked several times trying to process the question. Finally I sat down. Belle had stopped helping me sort through my wardrobe entirely and was now shamelessly eavesdropping. "Whose wedding?"

But I knew exactly whose wedding she meant. Trust my mother to pull out the ultimate guilt trip. If Alexander was going to go around making bold announcements like the one that had gotten me into this mess, maybe he should be the one to handle my mother. In fact, he might be the only one who could.

"You can't live with a man without a firm commitment, especially not a man like Alexander. The press will eat you alive." Her tone sank to a conspiratorial whisper. "And you can't sleep with him before the wedding! I think there's laws against it."

There probably had been at some point back in the Dark Ages, but I didn't tell her that. "I assure you that there's little to no sleeping going on."

"Clara!"

"I'll call you with the party details later this week." I hung up the phone before she could get in another word. I'd expected her to be shocked but I hadn't expected her to jump to this conclusion. Turning slowly to face Belle, I blew out a long-held breath. "I think my mother wants to go hat shopping for a wedding."

"Can you blame her?" Belle asked. "The hats at your wedding will be spectacular."

"We're not getting married." Heat flushed my cheeks. I'd barely had time to process being in a relationship with Alexander at all. Talk like this would only complicate things further. Not to mention that there was no way I was ready for marriage. Not because I wasn't certain of my feelings for Alexander, but because I still wasn't sure I wouldn't crack under the continued pressure of being in the public eye.

Belle bit her lip and gave me her best so-you-say-now stare.

"We aren't getting married!" I said more loudly.

"No," said a voice behind me, "we aren't."

I pivoted to find Alexander standing in my doorway. Burying my head in my hands, I moaned, "Where's a giant sinkhole when you need one?"

He immediately switched to business mode, as if bracing himself. Picking up the already packed bag on my bed like he hadn't heard a thing, he swung it over his shoulder. "We are picking up your toothbrush though."

"Yes," I said weakly, "and we're having a housewarming party next weekend."

He accepted this with a great deal more aplomb than I expected. Probably owing to the fact that a housewarming party seemed inconsequential in comparison to the sacrament of marriage. I couldn't blame him for that.

"Of course. Will you be much longer?" His voice was distant and my stomach flipped over. "My father called and would like to speak with me. No doubt, he also wishes to discuss the change in my circumstances."

"You could...invite him to the party." If I hadn't already been dreading throwing together a party, the thought of Alexander's father being there made it worse.

But my dedication to etiquette earned me a smile. "I'm afraid he's not wild about parties."

I refrained from openly celebrating this fact. "I have a few more things to track down. Half an hour?"

"I'll have Norris return and take you home." Then, as though to reassure me, he hooked his free arm around my waist and drew me against his lean, hard body. My breath caught and for a second I almost believed if I held it, I could make this moment last forever. His piercing blue eyes fixed on me. The comfortable weight of his arm around my waist. Slanting his lips over mine, he kissed me possessively. It was a sign of good things to come.

"I'll see you at home," he informed me before heading out.

Home. A few hours ago I'd thought of it as my haven. Now I was inviting controversy and judgment on myself by opening it to others for a silly housewarming party. Try as I might, I couldn't escape the fact that wedding or no, the honeymoon was over.

CHAPTER TWELVE

I'd forgotten what it was like to look forward to going to work. Having spent the last few months working myself to exhaustion, the office had become my refuge. I was surprised on Monday morning to find I still enjoyed my job. Few people could say that. Of course, after the weekend I'd spent with Alexander, the whole world felt new and brimming with possibility. I breezed past a newsstand on the way into the building, resisting the urge to read the headlines. Alexander's face greeted me from a few, making my pulse race.

I wasn't certain I would ever be accustomed to seeing my lover's face on the covers of magazines. I would never get used to seeing mine. But today I didn't care about their speculations and insinuations. A weekend in Alexander's bed had put things in perspective. Whatever sensational story they wanted to claim, we knew the truth. Not that the truth had been entirely easy to swallow. Alexander had revealed things to me that I was still trying to wrap my head around. I loved him regardless of his past, regardless of his darkness, but if I was being honest, his confession left me feeling curious. Who was this woman who had been his submissive? She had clearly been well-chosen because an Internet search had turned up no mention of Alexander's darker proclivities. Part of me felt guilty for even looking. Part of me felt jealous. Whoever she was, she'd shared something with him that I hadn't. I couldn't help thinking she'd been braver than me. All I wanted was the pleasure. She'd carried his pain for him.

Strolling across the lobby's marble floor, I quickened my pace to catch the lift just as the doors began to close. A petite hand shot out, prompting the doors to jerk back open.

"Thanks," I said breathlessly, smiling to discover my savior was Tori.

"No problem." She returned my grin, even as she pushed a folded tabloid into her bag. Her face was sheepish as she shrugged guiltily. "I promise I bought it to read about Isaac Blue."

There was something so artless about her confession that all I could do was laugh. "He's much more interesting than most of their other stories."

"Definitely," Tori agreed, a relieved look flashing across her face.

"We need to do lunch." I'd been avoiding her invitations for months. I'd been avoiding most people actually. Now it was time to rebuild bridges.

"Oh yes." She clapped her hands together. "This week. Wednesday? Thursday?"

"Either should be fine." A contented sigh slipped past my lips. Things were falling into place again. Alexander and I were discovering and rediscovering. We were building and rebuilding. His past was exactly that—his past. Mine too. We had a future to focus on, and there was still plenty to deal with, including planning a last-minute housewarming party.

"Good weekend?" Tori guessed, drawing me out of my thoughts.

"Pretty spectacular," I admitted. I couldn't help but notice that Tori's own glow rivaled my own. "It looks like you did as well."

"Yeah." She blushed deeply, shaking her head as if to clear her thoughts. "Isn't it funny how life can surprise you?"

"You can say that again." The lift doors slid open and Tori shot me one more giddy smile before she darted over to her cubicle.

My own desk was across the room, closer to my boss's office. I deposited my bag at my desk and went to check in about the week ahead. Popping my head into Bennett's office, I found him staring absent-mindedly at his computer. "Got a minute?"

He looked up, obviously startled that he was no longer alone. Waving me in, he turned his attention to the mess on his desk. "It's only Monday and already I'm completely disorganized."

"Did you have a nice weekend with the girls?" I no longer needed an explanation as to why my boss looked like he needed a holiday on Monday mornings. Keeping up with his twins was much more tiring than going to work every morning.

"They can't stop talking about you. I'm fairly certain they think you hung the moon. Apparently, I'm not nearly as posh when it comes to tea party etiquette," he said with a smile. Despite being obviously harried, his kind face seemed softer this morning, as if some of the edges it usually bore had been buffed away. "I can't thank you enough. I don't think I realized the healing power of a night out."

"I was happy to do it. Maybe next time the girls can stay over at my house. We have spare rooms." The invitation was out of my mouth before I'd considered what I was offering. Not that I wanted to take it back, but it was a bit surreal to remember how drastically my circumstances had changed over the course of a few days. I couldn't be sure that Alexander would enjoy having two energetic seven-year-olds bouncing around the house, but I'd wager he'd like being without me for a night even less if I offered to babysit at their house.

"Madness. A whole night without them? I wouldn't know what to do with myself." He leaned back in his chair, grinning like the Cheshire cat.

"Let me know," I said encouragingly. Bennett was used to people worrying about him, but all that concern seemed pointless if no one actually did anything to help.

"I will," he promised.

The conversation shifted to our new campaigns and where we needed to focus our energies this week. By the time I turned to leave, my to-do list had grown by several pages.

"Clara," Bennett called, stopping me in my tracks. "It's nice to see you happy again."

"I suppose the wind changed this weekend," I said, recalling a favorite childhood movie of mine.

"Word of advice. Don't waste time waiting for the wind to change in the future."

I arched an eyebrow at him. If I didn't know better, I'd say that he benefitted from more than just a night out. "Sounds like it changed for both of us."

"Okay, lecture over. Get to work already."

I grinned at him. "Whatever you say, boss."

Returning to my desk, I discovered a single red rose waiting for me. Snatching up the accompanying note, I ran my fingers over Alexander's seal. Popping it open, I drew out the card and read:

Poppet,

A single rose. Elegance and pain twisted into something beautiful. It reminded me of us.

A day will come when your entire job is to stay in bed with me all day. Until then I want to make certain you know that I'm thinking of you—thinking of running my tongue along your cunt, imagining how snugly you envelope my cock, recalling your face as you spill over.

Tonight,

X

Desire tightened across my belly as my body recalled the exquisite torture I'd experienced at Alexander's hands this weekend. He'd taken my request to explore into consideration, slowly introducing me to his more demanding tastes. It had only made me hungry for more. Now the memory of sucking him off with my hands bound behind my back resurfaced and an insistent throb began between my legs. I clamped them tightly shut. But even in my desire, I knew I wanted more than that. I wanted to lose myself to him. I'd glimpsed his darkness, lurking under his masculine dominance, and I craved it. Setting down the note, my fingers itched to delve under my skirt to seek relief. I restrained myself, but I was going to have to stop reading these at work or X was going to have to make himself available for lunch breaks.

I slid open my desk drawer where it would be safe from prying eyes. I'd barely opened this drawer in months, avoiding the other notes from him that I'd filed away before things had ended between us. Now I was delighted to add to the stack, except the notes weren't there. Frowning, I rummaged through the drawers contents. I must have taken them home. It was better that way. We were starting fresh. I'd have plenty more notes to secret away soon.

An hour later, I'd worked through half my to-do list with Alexander's note tucked safely in my desk. Every once in a while I'd open the drawer and run a finger over the broken wax seal, fantasizing about what tonight held for me. It gave me an idea, and a quick Internet search proved you really could get anything in London. I stopped by Bennett's office on my way out. "I'm going to run an errand and grab some lunch. Want anything?"

"Actually, I have plans." Bennett ran a hand over his curly brown hair nervously. "Is my tie straight?"

I nodded, wondering what had my boss so anxious. I hadn't asked much about his date when he'd returned home, but now I wondered if it had gone better than expected. Bennett wasn't the kind of man to wear ties or take lunch breaks. He was a workaholic. That only made me more hopeful that his lunch plans included someone special. Of course when you were in love, you wanted everyone else to be as well, I mused as I made my way toward the lift.

"Wednesday?" I called to Tori as we passed in the hall.

"Perfect! No break for me today." Her eyes darted to the pile of paperwork she was carrying to Bennett's office.

"I can grab you something," I offered.

She shook her head. "I'll be fine."

As I stepped out of the Peters & Clarkwell building, a black Rolls Royce immediately pulled up to the curb. Norris appeared at the other side and opened the back passenger door. I wasn't surprised to see him, but I wasn't happy about it either. If Alexander thought our new living arrangement included following my every move, he had another thing coming.

"No, thank you." I shook my head and pointed down the street. "I'm only going down the block to grab a few things."

"Mr. Cambridge insists," Norris said, crossing his arms over his chest. Physically, there was nothing particularly menacing about Alexander's guard, but I suspected that was the point. Still I wasn't afraid of him nor was I inclined to let Alexander's possessiveness affect my work day.

"And I refuse," I informed him. "You may tell him that."

Norris didn't press the matter. In fact, his face belied no reaction whatsoever. He simply returned to the driver's side. No doubt he would follow me. I couldn't blame him. He'd been given orders, which meant I'd have to deal with his employer directly if I didn't want a constant shadow.

For now I had things to do. The little stationary store I'd found online had already set aside my order. I inspected it with delight before having it packaged up. Outside, the world was glorious. The September air had the promising crispness of fall to it. Soon I would need warmer dresses and jackets. My mobile rang as I waited for my order at a popular food truck.

"Did you sense I was thinking about shopping?" I answered.

"It is one of the gifts of my people," Edward responded dryly. "But don't try to distract me. Rumor has it that Alexander is shacked up with a tart, and said tart didn't call me."

"Said tart has been deliciously preoccupied." It might have once bothered me to know what the rest of the Royal circle thought of me, now I no longer cared.

"So it's true then? My brother didn't break the hearts of women the world over to call your bluff. You actually moved in with him?"

Edward knew his brother well. Too well. Both had been taught to hide who they truly were, which I supposed made it harder for them to have secrets from each other. Of course, he'd seen through Alexander's publicity ploy. Edward was well versed in playing to a camera.

"Actually I could use your help. I might have panicked and told my mother we were having a housewarming party this weekend. Up for planning a party?" Between unpacking, work, and the constant need for physical connection between Alexander and me, I was more than a little worried about adding another thing to my plate.

"Of course. Consider it done."

"You're a lifesaver. I'll send over names and details." I paused before deciding to add, "Bring David."

"I'll ask." The sadness in his voice told me everything I needed to know. "Apparently actions don't always speak louder than words."

"You could always tell the world you're living with him," I suggested. "It will be a hell of a row, but the angry shag is fantastic."

"I think David would settle for holding hands in public."

"If you don't feel up to party planning—"

"No," he interrupted. "I could use the distraction. And Clara, I'm happy for you. Truly."

We hung up with plans to talk again in the morning. Juggling my purse, take-away, and Alexander's present, I almost wished I'd let Norris drive me. But I knew that was a slippery slope. If I was going to maintain a life outside our relationship, there had to be boundaries. Our passion was all-consuming, and I knew all too well how easily affection could turn to co-dependence. Sometimes I had the uneasy feeling I wanted him too much, especially after his admissions to me. My desire for him ignored boundaries in the bedroom. If I wasn't careful, there would be none in my life outside the home as well.

Shoving my bag's strap higher on my shoulder, I turned the corner and caught sight of my father across the street. I hadn't been avoiding him the past few months, unlike my mother. But he'd been busy, working hard on a new tech start-up that he thought could rival the success of partner.-com, the website that was responsible for my family's fortune. He had never accepted that he had one big idea in him. I didn't doubt that was where I got my work ethic—or my stubbornness.

Opening my mouth to call to him, the words died on my tongue as he caught a woman's arm and pulled her close. A woman who couldn't be older than me. A woman who laughed adoringly at him. A woman who was definitely not my mother. I couldn't tear my eyes away as he leaned in to kiss her. I was still frozen in place when he opened a cab door and disappeared inside. My gaze flickered up and I realized with horror that they'd just left the Kensington Grand Hotel.

I couldn't process what I'd seen. This time when I saw the Rolls idling nearby, I walked over and got in. Norris headed toward the building without direction from me, and I sat quietly, working through the haze of confusion clouding my brain. It was as if the world had shifted on its axis just slightly enough that no one else noticed, while still throwing me off balance. Suddenly my mother's strange behavior made sense to me. She had to know, or at least suspect. Late nights. New projects. Business trip. It was all code for an affair. Why hadn't I seen it before? Because I'd been too wrapped up in my own world to notice. But now I knew. There was no choice but to talk to my father about what I'd seen. I just needed to get him alone. Luckily I knew exactly where he would be this coming Sunday afternoon.

I FINISHED OUT THE DAY, trying to ignore the chaotic, negative feelings growing inside of me. I was angry with my father. I felt betrayed. And I was frustrated with Alexander for not trusting me to go into work alone. Was this how relationships went sour? Small lies and distrust. My parents had been in love when I was little. Then everything had changed. With money, I'd watched my mother become someone else. A person who was never content, who never had enough money or attention. I didn't blame her for my father's infidelity, but I suppose I wasn't surprised that he'd strayed either. Not that I thought he deserved a pass. Far from it.

But the thought that turned my stomach over, was wondering if I'd push Alexander away, too. I had my own set of neuroses. Was it just a matter of time before he found himself in the arms of someone who didn't come with all the baggage I did? That was why I'd wanted to maintain some independence—keep my job, walk to work, ride the tube. What happened if I became too dependent on him and he finally walked away?

I also knew now that he'd protected me from his more depraved tastes. My father had treated my mother with kid gloves, too, always desperate to protect her fragile spirit from the truth. Now he was hiding an affair.

I wasn't fragile and I didn't need protection.

By the time Norris pulled up in front of the house, I'd whipped myself into a mental frenzy. Bursting through the front door, I threw my bags on the floor. I needed to set the record straight immediately.

I found Alexander in the living room. His mouth curved into a wicked smile. "Hungry?"

I was famished, but there was no way I was telling him that. "I can feed myself."

"Poppet." His eyes narrowed as he stood. "I don't like your tone."

"And I don't like being followed around by a bloody babysitter all day. What's next? A personal bodyguard in the office?" The realization hit me that I sounded hysterical, but I ignored it.

"What I do is for your safety," he reminded me.

"Do you have a whole team following me?"

"Only Norris. When we were...apart, I had more than one detail. Now I would prefer if Norris handled your personal safety." He was choosing his words carefully, but that didn't make them any easier to swallow.

"And why's that?"

Alexander abandoned his bourbon on the console and

crossed to me. "Because he's the only one I trust with my family."

Another time those words might have softened me, but now they only made me angrier, reminding me of all I had to lose—if I'd ever had it all. "I'm not family. You don't love me, remember? I'm just the tart you're fucking."

"You will not speak about yourself in that way." His eyes flashed as he spoke.

"Or what? You'll punish me?" I was pushing his buttons now and I wasn't even sure why. Perhaps it was all the things left unknown. All the things left unsaid. All the dark corners we hadn't yet faced.

"Yes," he confirmed in a low voice. "I will allow no one to speak of you like that—not even you."

His words splintered my fury, but I held onto its pieces. I wanted to be angry. I didn't want to wind up like my mother and father, always walking on eggshells around each other. Thinking of my father made me wonder what it would be like to discover Alexander was sleeping with another woman. My stomach roiled at the thought. I couldn't handle it anymore. There would always be barriers between me and him, but some of them needed to be torn down. I was tired of wondering how far he might take me—of where the line stood. "Show me."

"Show you what?" He eyed me suspiciously.

"You want to punish me. Show me."

"No," he said immediately. "I don't need to do that anymore and I won't do it with you."

"But you will with someone else? Why? Because I'm some slut you're shagging?" I sensed the rage growing inside of him, saw it flickering in his eyes even as he tried to restrain himself. I'd lost control entirely though. There was only one objective—push him past the boundary he'd set for himself—for our relationship. I couldn't survive more secrets. "Isn't that what they think of me? Your family? Your friends? I know it's true. I'm nothing but an American whore. We both know it."

Alexander's hand shot out and grabbed my wrist. "Careful, poppet."

"I don't want to be careful, I want you to show me what you did to her. I want to know how far you've gone."

"And if I'm unwilling to go that far again?"

I saw the battle in his eyes. If what he claimed was true—that he no longer felt the desire to punish—what was he fighting?

But I was well past the point of reason, and part of me—the part of me that responded to his demanding sensuality—wanted to feel the pain.

"Do not mistake my reluctance to punish you as no longer having the capacity to punish," he warned me in a tone that sent chills trembling down my skin.

"We agreed to explore and right now it's killing me that another woman experienced something with you. I don't want there to be places you've gone without me."

"This isn't a place you want to visit, and it's not a place I wish to take you." He relinquished my wrist and stepped away, creating a buffer between our bodies that neither of us were accustomed to.

"I can't live knowing you've been more intimate with another woman."

He pressed his lips into a thin line, his eyes growing as dark as his tousled hair. "That wasn't intimacy."

"The pleasure and the pain, remember?"

"You've experienced pain, Clara." Alexander's words were measured. Apparently neither of us could let go of the past. "The two should be felt together. You aren't a natural submissive. Your body won't respond to true pain with pleasure. Not physical pain. Not punishment. At least not by my hands."

"How can I understand the balance without knowing each for what they are individually?"

But I was getting nowhere with him. I would have to entice him—make the impulse impossible to deny. My fingers trembled as I unzipped my pencil skirt and allowed it to drop to the floor. Alexander didn't move to stop me even when I shimmied out of my thong and turned my bare ass toward him.

"Show me," I demanded. "Or should I hurt myself. I'm healthy enough for, what did you call it? Self punishment?"

"Clara," he growled. "This is not a game."

"No, it isn't. It's a request. I'm asking you, X."

His hand cupped my ass and my eyes closed in expectation.

"You don't know what you're asking."

"I do."

"You can't know," he murmured, his lips dangerously close to my ear.

"I suppose not until you show me."

He lifted his hand, but I shook my head. "You've spanked me before. Whip me."

"I don't keep a room full of floggers," he said humorlessly. "All I have is my belt, but the strap..."

I blanched, momentarily losing my nerve, but I pushed away the fear. "Use the belt."

Alexander drew it slowly from his belt loops and coiled it around his hand. Between my legs, tension mounted, my sex swelling with macabre expectation even as fear closed my throat. I waited, but all he did was circle his prey, surveying me with untamed eyes.

"You will do this properly. There will be no crying out. You may cry—I expect you will—but you will remain silent. If you do not, I shall have to whip you more. Do you understand?"

I nodded even as tendrils of anxiety curled through my belly. For a moment, he watched me and I studied him. Both of us trying to determine exactly what we were starting. There was no sign of refusal in his body now. His broad shoulders were straight, his eyes cold and distant. This is what his submissive had experienced: a beautiful, unreachable man who longed for release.

"Clara, you may use your safe word." He paused, then added in a clipped tone, "I do hope you will."

His hand pressed against my back, directing me to bend over the console table. I folded over the edge, my ass presented to him, and took a deep breath.

"Ready?"

I steeled myself for the impact. A loud crack split the air as the leather belt made contact. Time seemed to stop, my mind unable to process the connection between the sound and the otherworldly pain seeding across my backside. I bit down a scream and pain lodged raw in my throat.

"One," Alexander said under his breath.

Clutching the table's edge, I braced myself for the next

impact. The following lash hit harder, or perhaps it only seemed harder because my skin still smarted from the first. Tears rolled down my cheeks. My nerves sang with agony even as my mind went numb, unable to process anything but the brutal pain.

"Two."

A sob escaped my lips.

"I told you to be silent." His voice sounded distant, but it broke as he continued, "Now you'll receive more."

I fought against the part of me that wanted to beg for him to stop. I needed to understand. I needed to experience it, but it was more difficult than I'd imagined and I'd only endured two lashes.

All sense of the world faded away. My only connection was that of leather and skin, sound and pain. I stiffened as he raised his arm causing him to still.

"End this, poppet."

He wanted me to use my safe word, but that was my last resort. I'd used it before and while it was meant to protect me, I'd seen how it had broken him. I shook my head.

The leather cracked across my skin and this time I screamed. My body went limp. I was no longer positioned artfully across the table. Instead it was holding me up.

There was no movement behind me. I opened my mouth.

"Three," I choked out. Sobs racked my body even as I clung to my resolve.

Alexander lifted the belt and I tensed, my body already conditioned to know what came next. The strap ripped through the air, whistling past my ear, and smacked across the table top.

He sank to his knees behind me. The belt buckle clattered against the wood floor, and then his arms were around my waist, his lips pressing light kisses along my tailbone.

"Brimstone," he whispered against my skin.

But I was too weak to respond, too overwhelmed by the emotions coursing through my veins. For a long time, we stayed in this position. I was afraid to move and Alexander continued to kiss me softly as though to reassure me.

Alexander lifted me into his arms, cradling me to his chest, and carried me upstairs. He stopped at the edge of the bed and lowered me to my feet.

"Lay on your stomach," he advised me.

I did as he suggested. It took considerable restraint not to touch my backside to see how badly it was injured. Alexander hovered over me for a moment, but he didn't speak again. He didn't touch me. Instead he crossed the bedroom and paused at the door. "Now you know that I'm a monster."

CHAPTER THIRTEEN

Seconds stretched into minutes as I waited for him to return, although I wasn't certain he would. This time when tears collected in my eyes, it had nothing to do with the pain lingering in my body.

I'd pushed him too far.

I'd pushed him away.

The tears fell freely. For my father's betrayal. For the mess I'd made of things. For hurting the man I loved.

Alexander's footsteps came closer until I sensed he'd returned. I didn't bother to turn my head to look at him. There was no way I could face him after what I'd done. The bed shifted as he sat down next to me. With light hands he carefully brushed my hair back from my face, freezing when he saw my tears.

He swallowed audibly and leaned to kiss my forehead. "I'm going to attend to your bottom. I don't want you to bruise."

His words were hollow, although they echoed with self-loathing. I wanted to stem my tears, knowing it only destroyed him more to see them. But I couldn't.

"This will be cold," he warned me as he laid something soft over my backside. A moment later the chill of ice seeped through the cloth.

It didn't matter. I was already numb, overwhelmed by our experience. Nothing mattered. Certainly not my physical comfort. Not when I'd forced Alexander to do something against his will. I barely processed it when his weight shifted and he spooned against me, his arms sliding under my stomach. He pulled me close, abandoning the ice pack and cocooning me with his warmth as he buried his face into my neck and whispered apologies. My eyelids grew heavy, my body overcome by the scene, and I slipped into sleep, knowing I was the one who needed to say I was sorry.

I woke feeling empty to discover Alexander absent from our bed. I sat up, forgetting about the belt, and winced as my weight shifted onto my rear. It wasn't bad, just a bit sore. The room was dark but light slanted through the open curtains and fell over a form at the foot of the bed. Moonlight sketched Alexander's masculine profile, highlighting his carved body. He'd undressed but he hadn't returned to my side. His head was in his hands as though his thoughts were a burden. Crawling across the mattress, I slipped my arms around him, pressing myself against his strong back. His hand knit through mine and we held each other in silence.

"You're not a monster," I whispered, knowing what he was thinking.

A sigh heaved through his body and he shook his head. "You're wrong. I was wrong. I knew it, but I did it anyway."

"Because I forced you to." That was the truth, and he needed to see it. I'd given him no other choice, given how recently I'd ran from him and the fragile state of our relationship.

"I lost control. It should never have happened." His grip on my hand tightened. "I'm sorry, Clara."

"I'm not," I murmured, letting him go. Scooting off the bed, I stood before him and tipped his chin up with my finger. "I was going crazy not knowing. Now I know."

The fire was gone from his eyes, extinguished by guilt. He squeezed them shut, unable to meet my gaze. "It will never happen again."

"X—"

"This isn't a negotiation," he cut me off. "This is my hard limit. I can't promise that I'll never hurt you again, but I will not inflict physical pain on you. If you ask again, I will refuse. Are we clear?"

I nodded, swallowing against the lump in my throat.

"Do you hate me?" he asked, opening his eyes to search mine.

Why couldn't he see that how I felt for him was the furthest thing from hate? My heart ached knowing that my words could never reassure him. Words could wound and destroy but they'd never be enough to heal or rebuild. There were so few words that could do that and they were words he couldn't speak or hear. With us, we could only show one another.

I took a step back as my fingers found the buttons of the blouse I still wore. My shirt fell to the floor and I unhooked my bra, shucking it from my breasts. Alexander watched with distant eyes that only barely sparked when I finally stood naked before him. He took my hand and pulled me close.

"Turn around," he ordered softly.

I hesitated, knowing why he wanted me to.

"Clara." His tone was rich with the unrepeated command.

Shifting my feet, I turned my back to him. A low, strangled growl rose in his throat, raising goose bumps along my arms. His fingers skimmed across the tender flesh, writing apologies across my skin.

"I can't make love to you," he confessed. "Not after this. I shouldn't be allowed to touch your body."

I swiveled in his embrace and shook my head. "I need this. My body needs this. No negotiations."

His hands dropped to his sides. If that was how we had to play it, so be it. He didn't stop me as I straddled him, sinking into his lap. Hooking an arm around his neck, I circled my hips slowly, knowing his body would respond even if he insisted on punishing himself.

"Touch me," I said in a soft voice. "I know what you can't say. I know what you think you've done to me. But you can show me how you feel. I need you inside me. No more walls. There are no secrets now. Just be with me."

His mouth caught mine. He kissed me like a drowning man gasping for air, his hand curving up to cradle my back. I continued to move against him, feeling him growing hard against my soft thigh as I lost myself to the surge of emotions flooding through me. He was the earth and the air. Fire and water. My whole world packaged into one perfectly flawed man. His free hand slid between my legs, but he didn't touch me; instead he freed his cock from the confines of his boxer briefs. The tip nestled against my swelling cleft and my hips shifted, urging it to find sanctuary. Our bodies joined together instinctually as we clung to one another. Alexander rocked me gently, his lips never leaving mine as he bore me toward the edge. We held each other as we climbed, no longer fighting the overwhelming deluge of thoughts and emotions that saturated our blood and trembled through our limbs.

There was no more need for apology. No need to speak words still unsaid. It was all laid bare. I knew him—his body, his mind, his heart—as I knew my own, and when I brimmed over, he crashed along with me. Neither of us let go as we came, clutching flesh and binding souls. We'd never let go again.

CHAPTER FOURTEEN

The waiter pulled out a chair, and I plastered a smile on my face as I settled into my seat. The one in my office was padded but there was no such luck at Greene's Tavern. The discomfort was minor and I was sure by the end of our meal, I wouldn't notice it all. It was likely to be outweighed by heavy, awkward conversation. The upscale restaurant was fairly quiet for a Tuesday afternoon, but I'd taken an early lunch. Madeline had insisted. If she noticed my cautious posture, she didn't comment.

"Thank you for taking the time to meet me," my mother said in a quiet voice as she closed her menu. She'd dressed the part today, clad in a deep gray dress suit with a set of pearls nestled over her elegant collarbone. Still despite the mature ensemble, we could have passed for sisters, thanks to her loosely styled hair and flawless skin. "I feel as though I haven't seen you in ages."

Weeks would be more precise but certainly not dramatic enough for her taste. "I apologize. I've been busy with the new job."

"Amongst other things." She didn't continue, and she didn't have to. I knew exactly what she was inferring.

There were a million lies I could tell her to soothe her bruised ego, but I wasn't interested in playing into that game. "Yes, amongst other things."

"It's really not appropriate for you to move in with a man and not tell your family," she lectured me. At least she was finally getting to the point.

"It happened quite suddenly," I reminded her. I knew that didn't matter to her. All she cared about was that she'd been left out. Never mind I'd had nothing to tell her or that she'd actually been one of the first people to know. If I didn't count the thousands of television viewers that had been privy to Alexander's ploy.

Her lips pursed into an unattractive pout even as she shrugged. "It's your life."

That had never been a fact she seemed capable of grasping. The waiter delivered us from further conversation, but I had no doubt it was only a momentary respite.

"It's good to see your appetite increasing," she noted when he disappeared with the menus and our orders. "I don't remember the last time you ordered that much food."

"I've been running more." I didn't add that my suddenly active sex life played a larger role in my hunger.

Her hazel eyes narrowed and she studied me for a moment, leaning against the table. "Are you pregnant?"

"Mother!" My shocked exclamation drew the attention of most of the room's patrons, but perhaps owing to its posh atmosphere, they turned quickly away.

"It's a reasonable question." She sipped at her vodka tonic. "You did move in with him rather quickly."

"No, it's not," I hissed. "This is the twenty-first century, so please stop planning my shotgun wedding. I'm not pregnant."

"I'm relieved to hear that." She abandoned her drink and turned the full force of her maternal gaze on me. "It would be scandalous."

"There are always plenty of scandals. No one would care if I was," I said dismissively, even though my stomach flipped. There would be many people who would care. One in particular. "A baby isn't in our plans."

"Yet."

I opened my mouth to protest, but she held up a hand. Part of me wanted to slump in my chair and cross my arms defensively. Something about the situation reminded me a bit too much of how I'd felt as a teenager living under her roof.

"There will be expectations, Clara. You can't shack up with the heir to the throne. It isn't done. The press—and much of your family and friends—expect an announcement of your intentions."

"Did I mention this is the twenty-first century?" I mumbled, reaching for my glass of wine.

"It might be for most of the world, but not for the Royal family. There is etiquette and protocol and expectations."

"I know that," I snapped, aware that my resentment stemmed primarily from the reminder of something I'd rather forget. "It's much too soon for us to consider marriage."

I meant it. I'd only recently graduated. I had a new job that I loved. There were a million reasons not to add the pressure of marriage into that equation. Not the least of which was that we'd only met a few months ago.

"Alexander will be expected to take on more responsibility soon. One of the duties will be to find a wife and produce the next heir," she informed me.

"I had no idea you were so invested in the monarchy."

"I'm invested in you." Warning colored her voice and I bit back another jibe.

"I am as well," I assured her instead. "Our relationship is very new. I don't think anyone expects us to plan a wedding yet."

"Regardless, it is something to be aware of. Your actions are under a microscope, Clara, and the attention is only going to increase."

I swallowed the remainder of my wine. She was right. I'd already experienced the scrutiny, and Alexander had only welcomed more into our lives with his announcement. There would be speculation. There might even be retaliation from King Albert himself, who Alexander had carefully cut out of all our conversations. Life outside Notting Hill was only going to get more complicated.

The waiter appeared, presenting each of us with a salad, and I stared at the plate, my appetite slipping away. I forced myself to pick up the fork. It would be all too easy to slip into old patterns, especially as I sensed that at any moment my life might slip out of control. I was determined not to let that happen.

Across the table my mother speared lettuce onto her fork and smiled congenially. "Tell me about your housewarming. I'm terribly excited for Saturday."

That made one of us.

. . .

"Could you?" I asked Alexander, gesturing to the zipper on the back of my black lace cocktail dress. He was only half dressed, his shirt still unbuttoned at the neck, no cuff links on his sleeves, but he turned and fingered the pull, gliding it closed. When he reached the top, he kissed my neck. It was the same cautious brand of affection he'd given me since Monday evening. "It feels strange to have you dress me."

But the joke failed to lighten the mood. Instead he offered me a tight smile and returned to buttoning his shirt. He reached for a tie, but I caught his hand. This evening our house would be filled with family and friends. That was enough to have my stomach doing somersaults. I wouldn't be able to handle this evening if something didn't shift between us. "You can't avoid touching me forever."

"I haven't avoided you," he said in a gruff voice, pulling away and reaching for a tie.

It was technically true. We'd spent every evening in bed together this week, healing what we'd damaged with gentle touches and hours of lovemaking. But it hadn't been enough. "Then fuck me."

"Now?" He raised an eyebrow. "Our guests arrive in twenty minutes."

"When has that ever stopped you? Or are you not up for the challenge?" I purred. I skimmed my hand over the front of his trousers, pleased to feel his cock twitch to life at my touch. "I'm not broken, X, and from the feel of this, you aren't either."

"There are things to be done," he reminded me.

But I didn't care about checking that the catering was properly set up or the vases were filled. I cared about the fact that I could feel closer to him than ever at the same time that he pushed me away. I only knew one way to fix it.

I gripped his erection and shook my head before releasing it and reaching for his tie. It slipped from his neck and I wound it loosely around my wrists. "Tonight you're going to wrap this around my hands until I can't pull your hair or claw your skin, and then you're going to fuck me until neither of us remembers why the hell we've wasted the last week tiptoeing around one another."

His eyes hooded, imagining what I'd suggested. "Is that so, poppet?"

I nodded, feeling encouraged and added, "But right now you're going to get down on your knees and fuck me with your tongue."

He didn't need further prodding. Something wild returned to his eyes as he dropped to the floor and shoved my skirt up and around my waist. A low growl rumbled from his throat when he saw my naked sex. "Naughty, poppet. You've forgotten your knickers."

"It seems silly to wear them with skirts if you're only going to rip them off." Although I didn't mind when he did. "You told me once that I should be ready to fuck anywhere, and I like to please you."

"That feeling is mutual." He leaned in and his breath tickled across my swollen sex. He stroked a long finger along the seam and a pang of longing shot through my core. "Your cunt needs attention."

"Yes," I hissed as his lips began to move along my hip.

Alexander's finger slipped inside my cleft, massaging me with deliberate, teasing strokes. "Is this what it needs?"

I shook my head. It wasn't enough. Not for me, and not

for him. I'd watched him going through the motions this week and I couldn't let it continue.

"It needs to be fucked so hard that I can't stand up afterward. It needs to remember that it belongs to you. It still does, doesn't it, X?" The playful tone faded from my voice as a terrible thought occurred to me. My voice trembled as I forced myself to ask: "Or do you not want it anymore?"

His hand stilled and his eyes flashed. An eternity passed and then his other hand settled over my belly. Without warning, he shoved me against the door. My legs parted for him without coaxing and his tongue was on me, filling me—fucking me—with a possessive fury. He drew back but only to nip my throbbing clit with his teeth. I cried out, my body already shaking with relief. I needed this—the dominance. I needed to belong to him as much as he needed to own me. Fingers worked roughly inside me as he sucked and tongued me until a shudder rolled through my skin and tightened my limbs. My hips bucked closer to his mouth, desperate for more. His mouth clamped over my sensitive bud and I exploded in a deluge of stars and light.

Alexander caught me as I swayed and held me upright even as he continued to lick across my trembling sex. "All night I'm going to taste you on my tongue. Do you know what that does to me? Tasting your cunt?"

He stood and pressed his body close to mine, brushing his feverish erection against my bare stomach. I whimpered, ready to feel it inside of me and grabbed for it.

"No." He stopped me. "Not yet. When I finally take you tonight, and I will, I'm going to fuck you so hard and for so long that you forget your own name. Never mind being able to walk."

A loud knock startled us a few inches apart. Our time was up, and I'd never wanted him so badly. Alexander pulled his tie back on, a familiar smirk playing across his lips as I struggled to find the strength to push my dress back down and re-clip my stockings to my garter.

"I missed that smug grin," I told him as I slipped on my heels.

"Poppet, I promise you'll be seeing more of it later." He cornered me, his body pressing mine flat against the wall. His rock hard cock jabbing me as he traced his lips down my jaw. "Do you still want to be fucked?"

"Yes," I breathed. The knocking had faded away along with the world. There was only him and the hungry ache building between my legs.

"Tonight I'm going to fuck you against the wall until you can't stand up, and then I'm going to take you to bed and ride you. Your body won't remember what it's like to not have my cock inside of it." He drew back, the smirk was gone but his eyes were on fire. Straightening his tie, he gestured toward the bedroom door. There was a party to attend and it took every ounce of self-control I had not to drop to my knees and beg him to take me on the spot. X was back and badder than ever. An evening of small talk followed by a night of debauchery?

Yes, please.

CHAPTER FIFTEEN

Edward's hands were on his hips when I tugged open our front door. I shot him a sheepish smile that clearly read *guilty-as-charged*, and he shook his head. Bustling past me with bags in hand, he headed straight for the kitchen. To my very pleasant surprise, David followed him. I didn't know David that well, but I couldn't help reaching out and pulling him into a hug. No one else in the world understood what it was like to be in love with a man like Alexander. It was time for David and me to get to know one another a little better.

"It's nice to see you," I said sincerely when I finally released him.

"Edward insisted that I should come." David ran a hand over his cropped hair, nervousness flashing across his dark features.

Alexander came up behind me, threading his arms around my waist as I shut the door. "You're always welcome in our home."

A thrill ran through my chest. I thought I was over hearing him say things like *our*. Apparently I was wrong. It somehow meant more when he said it to other people, as though he was laying claim to me—laying claim to my heart by giving it a home.

"When you're through being sappy, I could use a hand," Edward called.

"I'll go," I volunteered. "Why don't you show David around?" It couldn't hurt to encourage a relationship between Alexander and his brother's boyfriend, especially since David already felt like an outsider. He'd been given a place amongst the young circle of Royals thanks to Edward, but that welcome would surely be revoked if any of them learned the true nature of their relationship. It was completely unfair, but having met the Royal Brat Pack myself, I didn't find it surprising. They hadn't exactly tripped over themselves to embrace me.

In the kitchen, Edward was rearranging the caterer's trays. I folded my arms over my chest and waited for him to put me to work.

"Are you capable of corking some wine bottles or has Alex expended all your energy?" he asked, holding out a corkscrew.

"How dare you," I said with mock sincerity. "Do I look like that kind of girl?"

"You haven't looked in the mirror, have you?" He lowered his glasses and surveyed me. "I'd call this look *just shagged couture*."

I smoothed my hair, noting that there were a significant number of strands that had worked their way loose from the knot I'd styled earlier. I shrugged guiltily, although no part of me felt ashamed, and took the corkscrew. "A girl has her needs."

"And it looks as though they've been well met. But unless I'm wrong, your mother is going to be here any minute, along with about thirty other people."

We set to work, laying out trays in the kitchen and living room. I'd purposefully overestimated how much wine we would need for the evening. If all else failed, I wasn't against falling back on a little social lubrication.

Within minutes a steady stream of guests trickled in the front door, offering flowers and more wine. Many of them I knew, but Alexander stepped in and introduced me to the few guests that Edward had added to the list. Belle arrived, dragging a beleaguered Philip behind her. Her honey blonde hair spilled in soft waves over her shoulders. She caught me in a tight hug, and I pulled back to admire her fitted black turtleneck and knee-length white tutu. Only Belle could pull off such polar opposites. Not only did she make the outfit look good, she made it look classic.

"Can I get you a drink?" I asked, tugging her toward the kitchen.

"You can get Philip one," she grumbled. "It's as if he thinks a party will kill him."

I laughed. Belle's fiancé had a perpetual stick up his ass, and I'd love nothing better than to get him drunk and yank it out. Giving Belle a glass of wine seemed like a wiser course of action. I poured some chardonnay into two glasses and handed one to her.

"To your love nest." Belle clinked her wine glass against mine.

"And who is this?" Edward appeared at my side, shamelessly admiring Belle. I couldn't blame him. Anyone would be impressed by my best friend's style, no matter their sexual preferences.

Introducing the two of them, I was pleased that there was an instant connection between the two.

"You're the one stocking Clara's closet," Edward guessed.

Belle held up a manicured hand. "Someone has to. She has no idea how gorgeous she is. If I didn't, she'd always be in trainers and jeans."

"That is not fair," I said with a mock pout, spinning to show off my dress. "I picked this out."

"The student becomes the master," Edward said, approval in his voice as he studied the lacy number. "Of course, all the designers will want to dress you now."

"Me?" I asked, flabbergasted. Thanks to running I had a nice figure, but I was hardly a model.

"You are so delightfully innocent sometimes." He took my hand and spun me around once more. "They love to outfit the Royal family. Probably due to us always being on the cover of tabloids."

Heat rushed to my cheeks, and I shook my head. "I'm hardly a Royal."

"You're living with the next King of England. To them, it's a done deal." He spoke nonchalantly, and déjà vu washed over me. My mother felt the same way, but marriage wasn't in Alexander's vocabulary as far as I knew. I didn't even want to consider the possibility. Living together had been a big step for both of us, and I wasn't ready to complicate things any further between us.

"Regardless, you're high profile now." Belle rescued me with a sympathetic smile. "I'm sure more than a few boutiques would appreciate the opportunity."

"I put on the clothes I'm given." It was easier to be dismissive than to admit that they might be right. I didn't particularly like being on the cover of tabloids. No amount of pretty dresses was going to change that.

"Let's go shopping this week," Edward suggested eagerly. "I know a few people who would love to meet you. It's been a long while since they had a beautiful woman to dress. Not since Mother, really. Sarah was still too young."

He spoke of his late mother and sister much more easily than Alexander. He'd been much younger, of course. But maybe a shopping trip would help me fill in some of the gaps I had in my knowledge of Alexander's family. It was a subject I'd avoided, not wanting to cause him more pain or guilt than he already felt. Still, it was something that I needed to have a better grasp of.

"I have been meaning to clean out Tamara's." I'd never actually been to the shop, but I'd vowed to buy every dress there after a particularly nasty exchange with Pepper.

"I'll set it up." Edward pulled his phone from his pocket. It shouldn't surprise me that he had that kind of pull. He was the poster child for Royal style.

"Give her my regards," a caustic voice called from the hallway.

The voice grated across my skin and I took a swig from my glass before turning to face her. Pepper's tall silhouette filled the doorframe. She watched us with practiced disinterest, but no one would look at her and think she didn't care. Her blue satin dress hugged her slight curves and flat stomach, stopping too short for practicality. It was a wonder she could walk without her ass hanging out. Not that anyone was likely to complain if her smooth, toned thighs were any indication of her backside. She moved into the light, her dark lashes fluttering artfully as she strutted toward us.

"Not going to offer me a drink?" she pouted. It was a work of art really. It almost made me feel guilty, but I knew exactly who I was dealing with.

Alexander stepped into the kitchen, surveying the lot of us. "I don't remember you being on the list, Pepper."

He'd never bothered to even look at the guest list, opting to trust Edward and me with the preparations. I loved that he knew she would never have been invited almost as much as I loved him calling her out on crashing our party.

"It's fine. The more the merrier," I said, deciding that where Pepper was concerned I'd rather take the higher road. But only because it would piss her off.

Her eyes flashed, rewarding me for my unexpected stance. Alexander strode toward us and wrapped a possessive arm around my waist. Judging from the nauseated look that took up residence over her perfect features, she got the message.

"I suppose the party is in here," Jonathan Thompson, Alexander's fair-weather friend, said jovially as he joined us in the kitchen. "I hope you don't mind that I brought Pepper along. She wanted to see your new place."

Beside me Belle bristled, unable to hide her internal struggle. Jonathan was too handsome and too charming for his own good, which was exactly why Belle had fallen victim to him our second year of university. The brief tryst hadn't ended well, and there was nowhere in the world she wanted to be less than standing here casually making small talk with him. But before I could rescue her, Philip came to check on his missing fiancée. He stopped in his tracks when his gaze landed on Pepper and Jonathan standing in the cluster of people occupying the kitchen.

His Adam's apple visibly bobbed as he swallowed before nodding a greeting to the newcomers. He extended an arm to Belle, drawing her away from our group. She looked at me apologetically, but there was no need. I understood a jealous lover. I had one of my own. Of course, I'd always pegged Philip as aloof, not possessive. But there was no doubt as he led her into the living room that he wanted to take her away. I was more surprised that Belle had even told him about Jonathan. It wasn't a conquest she boasted of—not after he'd shown his true colors.

Having never had the occasion to host a party before, I was pleased to discover that as the hostess it was entirely acceptable for me to slip away on the auspices of finding more wine or showing a guest the loo. An hour into the celebration I'd perfected the art of finding the only unoccupied space of the house. Right now that place was the small sitting room off the main foyer. The guests were congregated around the kitchen and dining areas, spilling into the living room. Due to the exclusive guest list, and Alexander's lavish taste, there was more than enough space for everyone to fit comfortably, even those who were uninvited.

Pepper appeared in the room as if she knew I was silently wishing she hadn't shown her face. Sauntering into the room, she ran a finger along the back of a leather club chair. Her nose wrinkled as she brushed imaginary dust from her hands. "What a charming place you have here, Clara."

Apparently we were operating under the guise of civility this evening. I doubted that would last long. "It's mostly thanks to Alexander."

"I was under the impression that you'd been living here for some time." There was a single note of innocence in her voice. She was calling my bluff. "At least that's what Alex has told the press. I did think it was strange not to see you at a single event this summer."

"I think you saw quite enough of me in the country."

"Oh? That little show." Her shrewd eyes narrowed, but she couldn't quite hide her displeasure at my reminder.

She'd caught Alexander and me in an intimate moment, but I'd kept my mouth shut as she'd looked on. Alexander had no idea she'd seen him fucking me over a railing at his father's estate, but I relished knowing she'd been forced to witness it. The only way a girl like Pepper was going to get a clue was if one was handed to her.

"It's unfortunate no one was there to photograph that. Maybe if Alexander was shown what a classless whore you are, he'd come to his senses," she hissed, nostrils flaring. It was quite possibly the most unattractive she'd ever looked.

I wished I had a photograph of that.

"Sticks and stones, Pepper," I told her in a soft voice.

"You think you've won—" she began, but I cut her off.

"I have won. Look around, darling." I gestured to the room surrounding us. "I have him. All of him."

Pepper grimaced as if she smelled something rotten. "There are things you don't know about him. No one has all of him. You're a fool if you think that you do."

"This isn't a competition," I reminded her. "Not anymore, at least."

"I am so looking forward to wiping that smug look off your face. I hope I'm there when you see him for what he really is."

"For someone who claims to love him—"

"I am the only one who can love him," she snarled. "Because I'm the only one who can forgive him."

"There's nothing to forgive." I'd had enough of her special brand of insanity. Pushing past her, I started toward the party. Even a large group of people was better than being stuck with her for a moment longer.

"Once you know, you'll disagree." She paused, obviously relishing delivering her final attack. "Not even you are pathetic enough to forgive him."

PEPPER'S FINAL BARB STUCK, even as I tried to shake off our encounter. Unfortunately, this was my party, which meant there was no hope of being swallowed anonymously into the crowd. Everywhere I turned, I was pulled into small talk. I lost track of who was who. Later this week I would have to get Edward to give me a primer of exactly who had come this evening.

Looking around, I noted with dread that my family had finally made their appearance. Belle had them corralled near the hearth, but even she was only so much of a match for my mother. I crossed to them, stopping for a few brief exchanges with other guests. There was no point in putting this off. Madeline Bishop wanted her presence to be known. I could tell as much judging from the form-fitting silver gown that she'd chosen for a simple party. More than a few people cast interested glances in her direction. No doubt she was pleased as a peacock.

I'd nearly reached them when a welcome face popped out of the crowd, grinning at me. Bennett's curly, brown hair had been smoothed into compliance for the event, and for once, his tie was snugly in place. Alexander caught my eye from across the room, and I waved him over, eager to officially introduce him to my boss.

"You came," I said, not bothering to hide my happiness. The house was full of people that I hardly knew, so it was exciting to see someone I genuinely liked.

"I decided it was worth the small fortune to hire my nanny to stay for the evening." He leaned forward and hugged me. When we broke apart, Alexander lorded over us, his face unreadable as he scrutinized Bennett.

I straightened up. Did he always have to be so dominant around any man that showed me attention?

"We haven't met." Bennett held out his hand and Alexander shook it, although not altogether willingly. "Clara and I work together."

"Bennett is my boss," I interjected, placing emphasis on boss. It had the necessary softening effect on Alexander, who smiled graciously.

"It's a pleasure to meet Clara's co-workers. She enjoys her job," Alexander said with equanimity.

"I hope so." Bennett shot me a teasing look. "None of us would function without her." He waved at someone in the crowd and I glanced over my shoulder, shocked to see Tori making her way to us.

"Hi Clara!" The petite redhead practically vibrated with energy, her gaze darting in wonder at the crowd around her. "Your house is lovely and..." Her words died on her lips when she spotted Alexander.

No surprise there. He had that effect on people, especially people of the opposite gender. And tonight, thanks to his black three-piece suit, was no exception. His hand slipped into his pocket, revealing the vest under his open jacket. The suit's precise tailoring showed off his athletic figure, but only I'd had the pleasure of knowing exactly what was behind those buttons.

"This is Tori," I stepped in, uncertain when the girl would regain her ability to speak, even as I was on the verge of losing my self-control, too. I looked questioningly at Bennett. It had been kind of him to invite her, but then it dawned on me. "Oh, wait. Are you two...?"

My boss responded by drawing Tori's hand to his lips. She giggled girlishly at the open show of affection.

"This isn't public knowledge," he confessed to me.

"Your secret is safe with me," I reassured him.

Tori grinned sheepishly and everything clicked into place. No wonder Bennett had seemed so self-conscious at work last week. Not only did he have a new girlfriend, she worked steps away from his office. It wasn't hard to see what had brought the two together. Bennett deserved someone full of life, and Tori fit the bill perfectly.

Alexander leaned in to whisper in my ear, "Your mother requires your attention."

My joyful mood faded at the edges. When didn't she? Pointing my co-workers toward the drinks, I made my way to my parents and my younger sister, Lola. From the outside, Madeline and Harold Bishop looked exactly like a proper married couple, but I couldn't help noticing how they stood apart, not touching. Did my mother know about the affair? I couldn't imagine she would stand for it, but she had always been capable of selling the image of a perfect family.

"I apologize that we're late." There was an edge to her voice, even as my father embraced me.

"I was stuck at the office," he explained, tugging at the buttons of his blazer. "Splendid party."

It physically hurt to hug him right now, and I wasn't entirely sure that I hid the fact well. Swallowing, I forced a smile. "I'm so glad you could make it."

"As if we'd miss it," Lola said with meaning. My little sister fit right into the crowd of well-to-do Londoners gathered here tonight in her posh black sheath, and unlike me, she wouldn't miss the opportunity to network with the number of important people in attendance. We looked alike with our dark chestnut hair, but Lola was slender and petite. She gave off a polished air that made me jealous. In so many ways, she was a better match for Alexander. Lola could handle the expectations and the scrutiny. "Is that Edward?"

I followed her gaze and nodded. Edward was holding court with a large group, but David was nowhere in sight. I made a mental note to look for him when I was free of my mother's clutches.

"Alexander," my mother cooed as he neared us. She enveloped him in a hug that felt a bit too familiar, but Alexander, for his part, looked unperturbed.

"Lovely to see you again." He stepped to my side, placing a strong hand on the small of my back. The touch was reassuring and arousing at the same time. We'd spent the evening so far orbiting the room, coming close to contact but always being pulled away by some other force. His presence relaxed me, and I wished there'd be no need for separation again.

But I also needed to talk to my father about what I'd seen on the street earlier this week.

"Will you excuse us for a moment?" Alexander asked as if reading my mind. "There's an urgent matter requiring Clara's attention."

My mother opened her mouth to protest but thought better of it.

She already knew there was no sense in arguing with him. Alexander guided me into the back garden, which was mercifully empty. Edward and I had agreed that, given the autumn chill, it would be pointless to open the space to guests. That decision was now paying off, granting us a rare private moment amongst the bustle of celebration and well wishes. We stepped out of the light cast from the windows, and Alexander was on me. Hands pushed up my skirt, closing over the lace of my garter belt.

"Why are all these people here?" he breathed against my mouth. "I want to play."

Yes, please. There were people steps away from us, only separated by the *decidedly* un-soundproofed French doors. There wasn't time, but all rational reasons why we *couldn't vanished* as his mouth crushed into mine. I melted into him, carried away by the moment. His hand cupped my ass, squeezing the bare cheek. He hadn't touched me there in days and my body responded instantaneously with a surge of desire. It pooled in my core, overriding my concerns of getting caught. I could only think of filling the aching hunger building between my legs. Alexander circled his hips against mine, igniting a fire in my belly, as his erection rubbed me through his trousers. My hand slipped to the hard length and I fisted his cock through the fabric.

"You can't go back in there like this," I murmured as I stroked him.

"What do you have in mind, poppet?"

My lips twisted into a mischievous smile. "I owe you one."

I knelt before him, not caring that at any moment someone could decide to go for a smoke or step out for fresh air. I could only think of one thing. He didn't object as I unzipped his trousers and freed his cock. Silhouetted in moonlight, it rose flagrantly and unabashedly masculine against the smooth contours of his lower stomach. My own sex swelled as I ran my tongue over his broad crown. A groan rumbled into his throat as my mouth closed over his shaft. I swirled my tongue over his length, relishing the feel of velvet against my lips. Alexander's hand caught the knot at the back of my neck and pushed my head further down until he was buried in my mouth.

"I love watching you suck my cock," he growled. "I love knowing that you can't control yourself. There's a hundred people in our house and you need my cock in your mouth."

I moaned as I continued to suck, aroused as much by his dirty mouth as by the possibility currently pumping against my mouth.

"Poppet, I'm going to fuck your pretty little cunt so soon. Is it ready for me? Does it like it when you suck me off?" He ground against my lips as he spoke.

Nodding, I drew my mouth up his shaft and traced circles around its crest before taking him fully again. Alexander responded by pistoning his hips furiously, not holding back as he fucked my mouth. The ache in my center built to an unbearable pulse as he jetted against my throat. I didn't release him even as he surrendered himself to pleasure. I relished having this power over him, delighting in knowing I could make him lose control, even if only for a moment.

Alexander stilled and finally released his hold on my hair. Reaching down, he helped me to my feet, brushing off my stockings before tucking himself back into his trousers. After I passed a cursory inspection, he held out an arm. "After you."

"You're such a gentleman," I said dryly.

"I can be, poppet," he said in a low voice that made me quiver. "Later I'll show you how gentlemanly I can be."

"Another quick shag in the garden?" I asked hopefully.

"No, I'll need a much larger platform for my plans. A bed. The floor."

"We have grass," I pointed out.

"And ruin your dress?" His hand closed over the doorknob. "I really didn't bring you out here to seduce you."

"You can't help it, X," I teased as we stepped back inside the house. Spotting David paging through a book near the shelves, I kissed Alexander on the cheek. "Find you in a minute."

I approached David warily, not wanting to scare him off. I had so much in common with him, but we barely knew each other. Not that I could fault him for being skittish, considering he had to keep up the pretense of being nothing more to Edward than a close friend.

"Have you read it?" I asked him.

He flipped to the cover and shook his head. "I'm ashamed to say that I haven't read much since graduation."

"I'm guilty of that as well," I admitted.

"Have you seen Edward?" David's voice was low so that his question wouldn't be overheard.

I hadn't seen him since before I left with Alexander, but I sensed the anxiety rolling off David. I had firsthand experience with feeling left behind at a social event. Edward had asked David to come. He might have even begged, and now he was nowhere in sight. "He's probably upstairs." I tried to sound nonchalant, knowing I needed to distract him from his boyfriend's absence. "Have you seen the library?"

"No, but I'd like to." He seemed to understand that this was his chance to get away from the crowd. It would also be an opportunity for us to speak to one another privately.

I led him upstairs, pointing out the various rooms, and doing my best to be a decent hostess. David visibly relaxed as we continued down the hall.

"I should have expected him to behave like this," David confessed to me as my fingers closed over the library's doorknob.

"I won't make excuses for him." Even if I did understand why Edward acted the way he did. "He's missed you."

"He has a strange way of showing it."

"Affection is not second nature to Alexander either," I assured him.

"He can't keep his hands off you," David said pointedly.

I blushed, embarrassed that he'd noticed. "I think he's overcompensating."

"That must be nice."

I paused, holding the door cracked open. "I said I wouldn't make excuses for him, so I hope this doesn't sound like one. But Edward is protecting you. Alexander tends to do the same. If they only understood that it drove us bloody crazy, maybe they would stop."

This earned me a genuine smile. David's white teeth

flashed as he grinned. Then he shook his head. "You're right, of course. It doesn't make it any easier though."

"No, it doesn't," I agreed. I pushed the door open and flipped on the light. "This is a work in progress, so excuse..."

My words died on my lips as we stumbled upon Edward.

And Lola.

Edward and Lola *kissing*.

CHAPTER SIXTEEN

Edward's hands were up as if trying not to touch her, but there was no mistaking that their mouths were locked together. My mouth fell open as my gaze swiveled from the pair back to David. His jaw tensed and his dark eyes narrowed, but he didn't speak even as the couple startled apart. It took Edward considerably less time to process what was happening, and he immediately shoved Lola back.

"David—" he began, but his lover was already out the door.

"What the hell is going on?" I stormed.

Edward began to speak then thought better of it and darted out the door after David.

"What the hell, Lola?" I threw my hands up. David might not have seen what was going on here for what it truly was, but I had little doubt.

Lola adjusted her dress and shot me a haughty smile. "Edward was showing me the library."

"I don't remember your tonsils being on the official home tour." Anger shook through me. This was the last thing David needed to see. Not while Edward was still trying to win him back. "What were you thinking? Or did you bother to think at all?"

"Don't pull that card on me," she hissed. "I'm not a kid anymore and if I want to kiss—"

"Did you ever stop to think he didn't want to kiss you?" I asked her.

Lola looked as if I'd slapped her, a pained look flickering over her elegant features. "Is it so hard to imagine that someone like him might be attracted to me? I know you're so drunk on Alexander that you can't see straight, but honestly!"

"You don't think it was a little strange that he ran out after David?" My voice dropped to a conspiratorial whisper. It wasn't any of Lola's business, but she was my sister and I didn't like the idea of hurting her feelings. I also knew Edward's secret would be safe with her. Lola could be thoughtless, but she wasn't cruel.

"I..." Her words trailed away as her eyes popped open and she stared at me. "Oh."

"Oh, indeed." I sighed and threw an arm around her shoulder, tugging her into a loose hug. "Do you see why I was surprised?"

She nodded.

"And do you see why I was upset?"

Her head bobbed once but then it reversed. "No, actually."

"David and Edward have a complicated relationship. It's secret for obvious reasons," I explained. "Things have been rough for them lately."

"And I just cocked it up more." Her lips twisted ruefully.

She turned sad eyes on me. "Can you blame me for trying? He's handsome and his reputation—"

"No, I can't blame you," I interrupted. "Maybe exercise a little more prudence next time."

"Says my sister who kissed her boyfriend the first time they met and moved in with him months later," she said. Heaving a big sigh, she looked toward the door. "Maybe I should go and explain."

"Let them work it out," I advised. "But do me a favor and don't drag any more of the guests into dark corners."

We made our way downstairs only to discover the crowd had migrated toward the front door, shamelessly watching the fight taking place on my front stoop.

David's voice rose above the whispers of the audience. "What am I supposed to think exactly? You asked me to come here, and then I find you kissing some girl."

Next to me, Lola stiffened. No one knew who David was talking about, but that didn't stop her from feeling guilty.

"I wasn't kissing her. She was kissing me," Edward pleaded, taking a step closer to him. If they were aware that they were being watched, they didn't care.

I pushed my way through the crowd, but Alexander stopped me at the door. "Leave them."

"No, they wouldn't want—"

Alexander cut me off with a stern look. Maybe he wasn't worried, but that did nothing to allay my concerns.

"Why am I here, Edward?" David demanded. "To make you feel better? Because you feel you need to make some claim on me? Because I'm not here for the right reasons."

Behind me the whispers grew louder as the truth dawned on people. I should have been glad to have one less secret in this sordid family, but all I felt was a sickening pit forming in my stomach.

"Because I love you," Edward thundered. "Because I always want you with me."

"You have a funny way of—" David's response was cut short as Edward closed the gap between them and drew him into a rough kiss. It wasn't a tentative display of affection. It was a revelation—to the two of them as much as everyone watching them.

And then to my surprise someone began to applaud. Others joined in. When the two broke apart they stared, startled, as the entire house cheered them on. Edward, always present of mind, tilted his head in acknowledgement before giving his audience an encore.

As they returned, hand in hand, Alexander met them at the door, gathering them both into a hug.

"It's about time," he crowed, ruffling Edward's hair with brotherly affection. David looked too shocked to speak. Whether that was from the uncharacteristically warm response of Alexander or the exhibition itself, I couldn't say. My heart soared, as I took my own opportunity to whisper congratulations.

"I had an excellent example," Edward said with meaning. He clapped a hand on his older brother's shoulder, sharing a long look with him. All around us, people gathered to offer support and congratulations of their own. The only person hanging back was Pepper, who couldn't contain her aghast expression. Why hadn't I carried a camera this evening?

I pushed the wicked thought out of my mind only to spot my parents in the crowd.

One less secret for Alexander and Edward to carry, but I

was carrying a secret of my own. It burned through me. I'd been dreading seeing my father this evening, knowing that I couldn't avoid what I knew any longer. Maneuvering through the crush of people in the entry, I reached my father.

"Can I talk to you?" I called over the noise. "Alone?"

He raised an eyebrow, but I didn't bother to explain myself. Leading him toward the kitchen, I prepared myself for a confrontation. Rounding on him, I tried to stay calm.

"I saw you," I said in a low voice.

My father looked genuinely confused. "Where?"

"On the street, getting into a cab." I did my best to keep my emotions from overtaking my words, but they crept into my voice anyway. "I saw her."

"Clara, I'm not sure what you're accusing me of," he said, but I saw the truth in his eyes.

I shook my head, unable to hold my tears at bay. "Does Mom know?"

"I spend time with my colleagues, some of them are female." His tone switched to an unfamiliarly condescending tone. Even when I was young, he never spoke to me like this.

"Do you kiss them all?"

"Enough," my mother interrupted us. She strode into the room and took my father's hand. "This is none of your business, Clara."

"It's your business though." I didn't hide my disappointment. She had known, but how could she live with it? For how long had my fragile mother, who needed us to tiptoe around her feelings, been living with this betrayal?

"I don't need my daughter treating me like a child," she snapped.

"That's just it, Mom. I'm treating you like an adult," I countered. "Something none of us have done for far too long."

"I will not be spoken to like this!"

"Clara," my father interceded, "this is a misunderstanding."

But regardless of how she felt about my interference, my mother wasn't about to let his comment pass. "It might not be her business, Harold, but I won't have you lying to her either. I've known what you were up to for months. You could respect your family enough not to lie."

"I...I..." He stammered, unable to come up with a suitable response.

"This is a party," my mother hissed, returning to her attack on me. "How could you think this was an appropriate place to discuss a private matter? You've been avoiding us for months and then you attack—"

"I'm on your side," I stopped her.

"Are you?" she asked.

I balked, frustration and hurt overcoming me. How could she think I wasn't? And how could she choose to live like this?

"I don't expect you to understand the complexities of marriage, especially when you treat the subject so lightly." Her harsh attitude tore through me.

Lola stepped from the shadows and placed a hand on our mother's arm. "We should go."

"Yes, that seems like an excellent idea." I crossed my arms over my chest as though I could protect myself from the pain.

My mother allowed Lola to guide her toward the door.

"I'll call you," Lola promised over her shoulder.

I nodded once, not caring if she did or didn't. After

tonight I was going to hole up in my house and avoid the world. It was all too messy. My father shuffled his feet uncertainly.

"Clara—"

I held up a hand to stop him. Right now I didn't care what he had to say. My whole life I'd looked up to my father, but there was no smoothing this over. Someone had to show him that. He left, his shoulders slumping in resignation. I watched this as they left, wondering why it always felt easier to cling to a lie than to confront the truth.

Lies were always told out of necessity. To protect. To comfort. Lies were simply *easier*.

CHAPTER SEVENTEEN

The party was winding down, but I couldn't stomach another second of pretending everything was okay. Between Pepper's threat and my nuclear family's near implosion, I needed a second to collect myself. The second floor was quiet, offering the respite I desperately craved from the lingering crowd downstairs. Slipping into my bedroom, I kicked off my heels and sagged against the wall. The room was dark and silent. Two things I welcomed after the chaos of the evening. Soon everyone would leave and I would have Alexander to myself. My body yearned for the reassurance of his touch. No matter how complicated things had been between us of late, there was solace in his embrace. There always would be.

The door to the en suite creaked and I startled. Maybe I wasn't alone after all.

"Is someone there?" I called out. No response came and I felt silly.

Sinking down onto the bed, I unpinned my hair, allowing it to tumble free. I would have to return to the party, but I no longer needed to be perfectly presentable. The few remaining guests wouldn't even notice. A hand slipped over my shoulder and a cold shiver ran down my spine, freezing me in place.

I was in my own home with a dozen people I knew and trusted—and a few I knew and didn't trust—but I recognized the touch immediately. It was as unwelcome as the fear paralyzing me now.

"Hello Clara. Lovely party." Daniel's voice was low, matching the darkness of the room.

I made a decision before I could overthink it. Jumping from the bed, I ran toward the door and the safety of numbers. Daniel beat me there, slamming the door shut and twisting the lock. Turning he barred the door and I skidded to a stop. My heart raced ahead but I willed myself to be calm.

"You weren't invited," I said coldly. I didn't dare to take a step closer to him. Daniel had never been physically violent, but he also had never broken into my house before.

"Regrettably, you're right." He sauntered closer, forcing me to back up. "I'm certain it was an oversight."

I squared my shoulders and found my voice. "It wasn't."

"That's hardly complimentary. We were so close, or have you forgotten that?" He closed the space between us, and I discovered to my horror that he'd backed me right into the opposite wall.

"You need to leave before something unfortunate happens." But I knew the warning fell on deaf ears. Daniel confirmed this with a laugh. "What are you doing here?"

"Perhaps I came to offer my congratulations." He reached out and trailed a finger along my throat, undermining the false sincerity of his words.

My muscles tensed, revulsion rolling through me. No one but Alexander had touched me this intimately in nearly a year and my body rebelled against his unwanted advance. "Don't touch me."

Daniel's reaction was instantaneous. His hand flew to my neck, gripping it tightly in a strangle hold. "Is that what you say to him?" He hissed the words in my face, sending drops of spit across my skin.

I wrenched away, but his grip tightened, holding me in place and cutting off my air supply.

"It isn't, is it?" he continued. "I saw the messages he sent you. I have to admit I'm surprised. You were never a whore for me, Clara. I can see it now though. What a little slut you are."

What messages? The truth dawned on me in horrifying clarity. The notes missing from my desk. The stranger who had called Bennett asking about me. It was all connected to the man with his hands around my throat. I choked, sputtering for breath as rage and fear bubbled in my chest. Daniel's eyes narrowed, but he loosened his hold.

I choked, sputtering for breath as rage and fear bubbled in my chest. Daniel's eyes narrowed, but he loosened his hold on my neck.

"Let me go," I wheezed. My fingers clawed at him, but he'd left enough distance between our bodies that I could barely touch him. Kicking out, my stocking covered foot made contact with his thigh but it didn't faze him. Tears crept to my eyes. I should have kept my shoes on. I should have listened when Alexander had suggested stationing security on every floor.

"Stop making a fool of yourself. I'll let you go when I

choose to let you go," he growled, his hand crushing my windpipe harder. "A few more seconds and everything will go black, Clara. I'm not here to hurt you. I only want to ask you a few questions. Check in on you."

I went limp, placing undue faith in his promises.

"Good girl." He relaxed his grip again but didn't release me. "I'd rather thought I'd run into you earlier in London. I expected you to come to your senses, but it seems you found other things to come to instead."

How much longer before someone would realize I'd been gone too long? People would be leaving soon. There was no way Belle would go home without saying goodbye. Where was she? Where was Alexander? I didn't dare risk crying out. Not when Daniel had been so demonstrative of how far he was willing to take things.

"Are you fucking him?" Daniel asked, coldness coating his voice. In the moonlight his eyes were a black void that seemed to reflect his hate.

There was no way I was answering that. He'd accused me once of cheating at Oxford, and I had little doubt that he still thought he had a claim to me now.

"Are you fucking him?" he screamed.

I shook my head, knowing the truth would not set me free tonight.

"You lying bitch." His other hand struck my cheek. Stars exploded across my vision and I cried out, but he squeezed my throat, cutting off the scream.

Footsteps clicked through the hall outside the door and I cried out again, overjoyed when they sped up. The doorknob to the bedroom jiggled, then shook before the pounding began. "Clara?" Belle's voice shrieked through the locked door.

I took my best opportunity and yanked away from him, getting out one good scream before Daniel tackled me.

"Clara!" Everyone in the house had heard that scream. But as Daniel rolled me on my back and pressed his body against mine, I knew it was too late. He ground his hips against me as his hands closed over my throat again. I punched at his sides, aiming for the kidneys as I'd been taught in a self-defense class, but he was too strong. Stronger than he'd ever been when we dated, and I realized with a sinking feeling that he'd been training—preparing for this.

"Have you told him?" he asked as he throttled me. "About us? About the baby?"

I shook my head, confusion overcoming me as I struggled to breathe. There was no baby. Daniel knew that. He had to give me a chance—a chance to explain. But my thoughts jumbled and slipped away like sand through a sieve.

What did I need to tell him?

Why was I on my back?

Blackness crept into the corners of my eyes, seeping slowly across my vision. The unlit room grew darker. Somewhere in the distance a drum pounded. No, it was too erratic to be an instrument. It sounded like a storm—a cacophony of screaming and slamming.

A form slammed into Daniel, knocking him off of me. Air rushed back into my lungs and I gagged on the incoming oxygen, coughing as my hands flew to my liberated throat. Gentle hands helped me sit up. Belle's concerned face swam into view, and I latched onto her, holding her as a strange mix of fear and relief rolled wet down my cheeks.

"*Shh*," she soothed, but her efforts at calming me were undermined as Alexander and Daniel went crashing into the closet.

With each breath I took, the room came back to life around me until I could focus on the brawl happening only a few feet from me. Alexander's fist smashed into Daniel's nose. Blood spurted across his face, but Alexander didn't stop as he made hard contact with his jaw.

"Stop him," I implored Belle. "Alexander will kill him. Norris. We need Norris."

"Philip's gone after him. He drove your parents home." A hysterical edge colored her words as she spoke, and I realized this nightmare was far from over.

I yanked away from her and forced myself onto my feet. Stumbling forward I tried to push myself between the two men, but Alexander shoved me out of the way. The momentary distraction gave Daniel the window of opportunity he needed and his fist jabbed into Alexander's left kidney.

"Stop!" I screamed as they fell on each other, wrestling precariously close to the window. My cry scratched my throat, leaving it raw, but it had no effect.

As if on cue, Norris darted into the room and caught Daniel's arm, twisting it violently until there was a sickening crack. Daniel faltered, and Norris took the opportunity. Within seconds, my attacker was pinned to the floor. Alexander paced nearby, fury radiating off him like heat from an inferno. Daniel might have been incapacitated but he was far from safe. Fighting against a sudden wave of nausea, I made my way to Alexander. My arms threaded around him as I pressed myself against his back. I had to calm him down. Alexander stilled in my embrace, but his muscles were still tense. He was on alert, waiting for the slightest movement.

"Police are on the way," Philip announced from the doorway. He glanced around the room, choosing not to step inside.

"What the fuck is your name?" Alexander demanded.

A laugh bubbled from Daniel and turned into a cough as blood caught in his throat. Norris pushed his face to the side, so he wouldn't choke.

"It's Daniel," Belle said quietly.

Alexander stiffened in my embrace as realization dawned on him. "You came into my home which is enough of a reason for me to kill you." His voice was eerily calm as he spoke. "But that you dared to touch her means you're as good as dead."

"X!" My hold on him tightened. "No."

Alexander pulled away, agitation triumphing over my attempt to soothe him. "He attacked you. He desecrated our home."

"And he'll pay for that, because I will be pressing charges." I spoke to Daniel now. It was time for him to realize I wasn't the girl he used to demean and order around. Things had changed. I had changed.

"He doesn't deserve to walk out of here," Alexander seethed.

Norris tilted his head, regarding his employer before shaking his head. "I have this under control. Alexander, take Clara somewhere safe."

I tugged at Alexander's arm, as anxious to remove him from the situation as I was to be out of it myself. He didn't budge.

Daniel's eyes flickered around the room like a caged animal before they locked onto Alexander.

"Has she told you?" he wheezed. "Has she told you she was no innocent virgin when you met? I saw to that."

"Shut up," Alexander commanded. "I have no interest in anything you have to say."

"But I have such interesting things to tell you," Daniel pressed. "About the things I used to do to her. About how she used to beg for it. About our baby."

"Get him the fuck out of here," Alexander ordered Norris, who responded immediately, dragging Daniel to his feet.

But Daniel wasn't through yet. "Tell him how you murdered our baby, Clara. I wasn't good enough for her. She wouldn't even let me see her after she did it."

A silence fell over the rest of the room as he continued to babble on, sounding crazier with each passing second.

Norris shoved him toward the door, forcing him out of the room and down the stairs. Alexander followed him and I lunged for him. He held up a hand.

"I need to see to this. Belle will stay with you." Alexander brushed a finger softly across my jaw, the muscles in his own tensing as he really looked at me for the first time.

Then he was gone.

"Go with him," I begged Philip. "Make sure...make sure he doesn't do anything rash."

Philip bobbed his head and disappeared into the hall. I didn't have much confidence in his ability, or rather willingness, to step in based on his passive participation earlier, but I couldn't be certain that Norris's loyalty wouldn't be swayed in favor of retribution. I had no clue what Alexander was capable of, but I suspected he'd meant it when he had threatened to kill Daniel.

I looked to Belle and collapsed onto the floor. She was by my side in an instant, wrapping me in a warm embrace. There were no tears left. I'd cried them all. Now there was only the numbness overtaking me like that day on Portobello Road. I sucked in a breath as it hit me. I *had* seen Daniel that day.

"Clara, what is it? What's wrong?" Belle drew back, searching my face for signs that I was more injured than I'd let on.

"He knows where I live." My thoughts tumbled out unfiltered. I sounded hysterical. I probably was hysterical. That didn't matter. I just needed someone to hear me. "He's been following me. He's crazy."

"I think that's established," Belle reached up and touched my forehead as if expecting to discover I'd developed a fever.

"I saw him," I confessed in a low voice. "The first day I was here with Alexander. I thought it was my imagination or a coincidence."

"And you didn't tell Alexander?" she guessed.

"It upset me, but I dismissed it. Things were over between us. I had no reason to believe..." My words trailed away when I saw guilt flash across Belle's fair features.

"I saw him, too. Near the flat a few weeks ago. I should have known something was up."

"No," I stopped her. "Daniel was a first class asshole, but there was no reason to suspect he'd gone off the deep end."

"None?" she pushed.

I started to shake my head but then hesitated. "He called a few times after I broke things off. I hung up on him."

"He came to the hospital," she admitted in a small voice. "I made him go away."

I clapped a hand over my mouth, closing my eyes for a moment before I relaxed again. I'd been hospitalized for malnourishment, but at the time I'd feared it was something far worse. Daniel's obsessive behavior had driven me to unconsciously stop eating. I'd been so desperate to control anything in my life during that time. "He said he came. He told Alexander. Oh god—" a sob racked my chest —"he thinks I was pregnant."

"It doesn't matter what he thinks," Belle said firmly. "You weren't pregnant and Daniel is clearly delusional."

"I...I..." My eyes implored Belle. Would she understand? What would she think of me?

"Clara, you weren't pregnant." But this time her voice peaked on *pregnant*.

"I don't know," I confessed in a whisper.

"How can you not know?" Belle stared at me as though I'd sprouted a second head. No, it was worse than that. She looked at me like she didn't know me at all.

"They ran tests." The truth poured out. I hadn't known how much I'd been holding in. "When the doctor came in, he explained that I was very sick and they needed to monitor me while they ran fluids. I asked him—I asked him if they'd run a pregnancy test and he...hesitated."

"That doesn't mean anything," she said, but her eyes told another story.

"So I asked if there was a baby and he said no. I didn't ask more questions. I didn't want to be pregnant, so I let it go. Don't you see? Maybe Daniel found something out. Something I didn't even know and that's why he snapped."

"You're going to drive yourself crazy trying to guess why Daniel did this," Belle interjected. "But there's no rationalizing it."

"What if, though?" Couldn't she see that this changed everything? If Daniel had found out what I'd refused to learn myself, there would be no stopping Alexander from procuring that information. "What if I was? What if Alexander finds out? He'll think I lied."

"Then tell him the truth." Belle hesitated before giving me a reassuring squeeze. "Clara, I think you need to find out. You shouldn't live your life wondering about something like that."

She was right. I had to find out. Dread swirled through my stomach at the thought of revisiting past ghosts. Would it change anything if Daniel was telling the truth? Would it change how Alexander felt about me? Would it change me?

"Ghosts only haunt people who are scared to face them," Belle said softly.

A man cleared his throat and we both jumped before we saw Philip waiting silently at the door. "Clara should rest," he advised.

"I can't leave her alone." Belle's harsh rebuke caught me off guard. Was it possible I hadn't imagined the tension between them earlier?

"Alexander is finished. Daniel has been taken into custody, and I doubt Norris will budge from the front curb all night." This should have been reassuring, but coming from Philip, it came off as dismissive.

I forced a smile, not wanting to add additional strain to the situation. "I'm fine."

"Are you sure?" Belle asked, and I could tell she didn't buy my act.

"She will be," Alexander said, striding into the room. He offered a hand to Belle and she scrambled to her feet before he scooped me off mine. "A hot bath and a glass of wine. Norris sent for something to help you sleep."

"I don't want to sleep." I sounded like a petulant child, but now I understood why children fought the night. They knew that closing their eyes invited nightmares.

"You're safe, poppet," he whispered, pressing a reverent kiss to my forehead that seemed to wash away my fears.

Philip shuffled nervously, extending his arm to Belle.

Belle paused at the door. "Call me tomorrow."

"I promise." This time I would keep that promise. I could only imagine how hard it would have been to walk out of here if I was in her shoes. I didn't trust Philip to take care of her. I knew that now. And I very much doubted that she trusted Alexander. Given all we had been through, I didn't blame her.

Alexander didn't follow them downstairs. Instead he cradled me against him, whispering reassurances to me. From the foyer, Norris's reassuring baritone echoed as he showed them out.

"Norris has checked the house," Alexander informed me. "There's no sign of how he got in."

"Which means he walked right through the front door." I felt sick all over again. "This is why I hate parties."

But neither of us laughed at my weak attempt at a joke. Our privacy had been invaded before by hackers and paparazzi, but this was different. It shook through my skin and down into my marrow, contaminating my very being. I told myself I didn't know how far Daniel would have gone. It was easier in this instance to swallow my own lie than face the truth.

Alexander carried me to the bathroom where he lowered me to my feet, waiting to ensure I could stand. A few minutes later the tub had filled halfway with water and bubbles and he stepped around me. Brushing my hair over my shoulder, his fingers found my zipper. He tugged it down slowly, his lips kissing the back of my neck as he slipped the straps of my dress off. It fell, pooling at my feet. Unhooking my bra, he ran his hands over my breasts as he removed it. He continued, unclipping my garter belt and unrolling my stockings until I stood stripped before him. Vulnerability overcame me and I folded into him, fumbling for his buttons. I didn't want to be alone. Not for a moment. I met with no resistance as I undressed him. We faced each other, exposed and raw. Alexander lifted my hand to his lips and kissed the tip of each finger before gesturing for me to step into the bath.

I sank into the water and he followed. We settled against each other and I relaxed into him. My eyes closed as he soaped up my arms and back, washing away all but the memory of what had transpired this evening. Neither of us spoke for a long time, finding solace in the silence of each other's company.

"Clara." My name was a prayer on his lips. "I'm sorry."

My throat went raw, and I swallowed against fresh tears. "You did nothing wrong."

"I didn't protect you," he said in a strangled voice.

"You did protect me, X. I'm right here."

"When I came in and found you..." The thickness of his voice said what he couldn't.

I could barely process it myself. How must it have looked to him?

"What he said," Alexander continued, "about the baby—he assumed you hadn't told me. Why?"

Somewhere deep inside myself I found the last remnants of strength I had left. "I told you about the hospital, but I wasn't being entirely honest with you. Or myself."

I expected him to pull away or tense up. Instead he held me closer, giving me the last bit of strength I needed.

"I don't know if I was pregnant," I admitted. This time the confession came slowly as I tried to work through the muddle of emotions it provoked. "The doctor said there was no baby."

"Then you weren't pregnant." The relief in his voice stung.

"I don't know." Belle was right. I had to be honest with him about this. I had to face it myself. "I asked if there was a baby and the doctor said no, but he didn't answer when I asked if I had been pregnant and I didn't push him. I was too scared to know the truth."

"Would it change things for you if you had been?" he asked.

It was such a simple question, but one loaded with meaning. "Would it change things for you?"

He didn't answer and my heart sank.

"There's no baby now." It was the best—and only—answer I had. What-if's had nearly driven me crazy in the past. I was unwilling to go down that path again. "What's past is past."

"You don't want to know?"

"No," I said confidently, "and I don't want you to find out. I want everything about Daniel to be in my past."

"I can respect that."

Could he? Did he? "If I was pregnant once, how would that make you feel?"

"I'm the last person who can judge you," he reminded me in a gentle voice.

"It's not about judgment. How would you feel?" I wasn't sure why it was so important for me to know. Perhaps it was needing something concrete after being caught in an invisible web.

"It would worry me but not for the reason you think," he added quickly.

"For what reason?"

"If you had lost a baby, I would be concerned you might regret that. That you might want to have a child someday, which is something I can't give you."

"Oh." This was news to me. I'd never really considered having children. Not yet. But now I found this information difficult to digest. "I didn't know you couldn't—"

"*I can*, Clara, but I have no desire to."

Emotions trembled through me at this revelation. I was too young to consider children. It had always felt like a dream, something much too far away to touch. Discussing the possibility had the odd effect of bringing it nearly close enough to grasp.

"I should have told you this before," he said when I didn't speak.

"It's okay. I understand," I responded flatly, suddenly feeling as lifeless as the future now seemed.

"No, you don't. My children will be brought into a life of

duty. They will have no choice in their lives. They'll be born into a cage."

"X." My fingers knit through his as a fresh wave of grief passed over me. Was this what it was like for him? Living in constant mourning for the life he could never have? Would it be different if he was just an ordinary man?

"Don't feel sorry for me. It only means I'll never have to share you."

My throat constricted as it always did when he referenced a future that I only hoped to share with him. How could he say he didn't love me and still talk of a shared path forward? The contradictions gave me strength when they should have scared me away. Even now, discussing the hypothetical family we would never have was more real than a future without him. It didn't make any sense, but did love ever truly make sense?

Alexander traced the curve of my neck, giving me quiet to process my thoughts, and circled around the back of it to the other side. By the time he got there his body was wound tight as a wire. The severe shift in his body drew me back to the here and now—back to what had happened earlier tonight. I skimmed my fingers across the skin of my throat, battling against a sudden surge of fear. Although I couldn't see it, I could imagine what it looked like based on its tenderness.

"It's nothing," I said, hoping that I sounded reassuring.

But Alexander could see the damage, making it impossible for him to ignore. "He left marks on you. That is not *nothing.* You need to see a doctor."

"I'm fine." He might be right, but there was no way I was going to risk this leaking to the tabloids. It was the last thing we needed. The second an ambitious paparazzo found out about Daniel, he'd have a platform for his delusions. Alexander didn't need to suffer from any more scandals.

"Stop being a martyr," he commanded. "This body is mine. Or have you forgotten that? Tomorrow you're getting checked out. Our family doctor is discreet if that's what you're worried about."

That was primarily what concerned me. But there was more than that. I wanted—*needed*—to put this behind me as quickly as possible. Still, after everything that Alexander had been through this last week, I would agree to anything that appeased him. "Of course."

"I'd almost hoped you would fight me on it, poppet," he whispered in my ear, "so I could remind your body who it belonged to."

"In that case, do remind me." My breath caught as his hands moved to my breasts. He plumped them teasingly, his thumbs circling my nipples until they grew heavy, swollen with arousal.

"I promised to fuck you tonight." His words were hot on my neck as one of his hands slid lower. "But our plans have changed."

I sank against him, losing myself to the deliberate stroke of his finger over my aching sex. I didn't care what our plans were as long as they included more of this. "Hmm."

"Instead I'm going to take you to bed and make love to you until we forget this nightmare, but first I need to worship you." His hand snaked up my throat, abandoning my breasts, and capturing my jaw. He tilted it until our mouths met. The kiss was a slow burn, simmering with promise, as our lips moved slowly. We were rediscovering each other and I knew then that we couldn't forget what had happened. We could only move past it together. This was the first step.

I turned instinctively into him, no longer caring about the hand between my legs. I needed him—needed his body pressed against mine. My skin sang where it met his, reminding me that I was alive. In his embrace there was no danger. No fear. When he touched me, there was only a sense of belonging. Of returning home.

His hands lifted my ass up, placing me on the edge of the tub. I perched there, instantly missing the comforting contact, as he pushed onto his knees. Warm water lapped around my feet and moisture beaded down my skin.

"Are you cold?" he asked, dropping a kiss on my kneecap.

I shook my head. How could I be cold with him so near me? I was on fire for him, aware only of the delicious man between my legs.

"I'm going to make you feel better," he promised, running his hands up my thighs and urging them apart. "I'm going to take you where there is only this and you and me." His head lowered as he began to kiss down my navel and across my belly, pausing when he reached my apex. A finger grazed over my swollen seam, and I gasped with approval as he spread open my softness. Sinking down, his tongue stroked heat across my sex, slowly at first but building in urgency. My head fell back against the tile as I clutched the edge of the porcelain. I knew this wasn't about taking me. This was a gift. His mouth closed over my clit, tugging it gently between his teeth as he sucked hungrily. But I needed more. I needed to fall over the edge.

I needed to let go.

Alexander hooked an arm around my thigh, allowing me

to fist a hand in his hair. My fingers tangled in his damp locks as I drove him closer. I wanted more. More of his tongue. More of his mouth. More of the promises he made without words. The night faded into a beseeching melody that built to a crescendo that thundered through me, and I crashed along with it in a symphony of moans and shudders.

The head between my legs stilled, but Alexander lingered there, holding me to him and breathing me in.

I exhaled raggedly, tremors still ravaging my body, even as peace settled over me. I wasn't content though. I wouldn't be until there was no separation between us. Not until he was inside of me.

"Careful, poppet," he warned as I attempted to stand. "Allow me."

He pushed up, stepping out of the tub like a god being born from the water. It dripped off his hard, lean body, trickling along the carved ridges of his abdomen and across the chisel of his pelvic muscles. He opened a towel in invitation, not bothering to dry himself off. I stepped into it, drinking him in as he wrapped it around me. Reaching out as if to prove he was real, I skimmed my fingers down his chest, pausing on the rope-like scars that I once thought marred his body. I loved them now, because I loved everything about this man, even the shadows of the past that marked him still.

I carried my scars internally in places that I thought no one could touch. No one ever had until him.

Daniel had given me many of those scars, and he'd tried to give me new ones tonight, but Alexander was a balm to my soul, healing me with his touch. I ached for his medicine.

Alexander guided my hand away from my neck. I hadn't even realized what I was doing. My fingers had found his scars and traveled instinctually to the visible ones remaining on my own skin from the attack.

"I am the only man who will ever touch you again," he vowed.

There was a time when I would have fought against this assertion of dominance. Tonight I welcomed it, seeing it for what it was.

"Take me to bed," I murmured, "and make love to me."

I'd missed the significance of his words before, distracted by the insatiable whims of my body. Now as I repeated them back to him, the full force of their meaning roared through me. My eyes met his and there was no wall between us. We'd stripped it brick by brick. We'd torn it down.

Alexander held out his hand. A gesture I'd witnessed a hundred times before tonight, and yet, it was the first time. Dropping my towel, I took it. I had never experienced a moment as intimate as when our hands touched. He drew me close and kissed me deeply before lifting me and carrying me to the bedroom. Laying me onto the bed, he crept slowly over me until our bodies hovered parallel to each other's. His arms bracketed my torso, hooking around my shoulders. My heart pounded—a war drum calling for battle. I steeled myself as the emotions swept through me. His eyes reflected my struggle, torn, too, between certainty and fear. But something else shone from them—something unmistakable. It stole my breath and ached across my limbs.

"Clara, I...I—"

"It's okay," I murmured in reassurance.

"I tried to stop myself." His words rushed from him, uncontrolled. Uncontrollable. He searched my face for forgiveness I would never give him, because there was nothing to apologize for. "I tried to protect you, but I can't. I love you. God help me, I love you so much."

I arched into him, our lips colliding with the urgency of new lovers. Our love was born of fire, baptized with the flames of fear and longing, and in it we were made new. Two souls fused into something forbidden and inexorable as our bodies joined. We melted into one another, each discovering ourself in the other. When we found the edge, we shattered together in a torrent of cries and whispered promises. We clung to each other, entwined and inseparable, still and silent in our wonder until the ache of new love summoned our bodies together once more.

CHAPTER EIGHTEEN

It didn't seem to matter that Daniel was in jail, because except for work, I was on unofficial house arrest. Norris accompanied me to work and back home again. Alexander closed himself into rooms and held whispered conversations. Belle called constantly. Yet somehow the story hadn't reached the media. I took to wearing scarves and slouchy cashmere turtlenecks to hide the physical reminders of the attack. My life had been reduced to varying degrees of faking okay. Not everyone I trusted knew about the attack, and while I wanted to keep it that way, it was exhausting. Life outside my inner circle went on as normal while those inside it struggled for normalcy.

"I've taken the day off of work," I announced to Alexander on Wednesday morning.

He abandoned the kettle and circled me protectively from behind. "Are you feeling okay? I can cancel my meetings."

"Don't worry, X, I'm playing hooky. Edward set up a shopping trip with Belle." I popped a pod into the automatic coffee maker and hit the button. Shifting my weight, I leaned back against him, appreciating the warmth on the chilly autumn morning.

"Shopping," he repeated, as if it was a foreign concept.

"Does Norris do all of your shopping, too?" I asked with a laugh.

"No." He shook his head. "I don't think so. Clothes seem to appear."

"You must have a fairy godmother," I murmured. "I should thank her for making you look so good."

Alexander spun me around and bracketed me against the counter. His ink-black hair was tousled artfully, and I resisted the urge to run my hands through it. Judging from his navy three-piece suit, he had serious business to attend to today.

"You're what makes me look good," he said.

My heart sped up, sending blood rushing through me. Would this feeling ever fade? Or would I be blessed enough to be this wildly in love for the rest of my life? I couldn't imagine another moment passing by without him. I didn't want to.

I willed my excited body to calm. "What meetings do you have?"

"Boring ones," he said with a smirk. "Someone in Parliament. A late lunch with my father. Batman."

"Batman?"

"Checking to see if you were paying attention, poppet."

"I'm always paying attention to you, X." My fingers closed over the knot of his tie, straightening it before I caressed the red silk. I raised an eyebrow suggestively.

Alexander took a step forward, locking himself against me. "You're giving me ideas."

"That was my plan." My breath hitched as his fingers dug into my hips, gripping them tightly.

"You'd like me to take this tie off, wouldn't you?" He waited for me to nod. "And then what? Do you want me to cover your eyes so you won't know where my hands or teeth are? Where my cock is?"

A moan answered him.

"Or maybe I should strip you down and tie you to a chair? I could call into my meetings," he said silkily, "and watch you squirm while boring men discuss boring things."

Yes, please.

"Decisions. Decisions." He rubbed a finger over my lower lip, and my mouth parted to taste his skin. "Or maybe I'll take you to bed and tie your delicate ankles to your wrists so that your beautiful cunt is at the mercy of my fingers and tongue—and finally my cock. I could fuck you for hours, plunging in and out of you."

My body responded to the promise of his words, wanting to be at his mercy

"I choose all of the above," I whispered.

"Unfortunately, I can't cancel these meetings."

"Then we better make this quick," I whispered, tilting my lips closer to his.

Alexander's mouth slanted over mine, kissing me until I forgot about his carefully styled hair and the troubles waiting outside our front door.

NORRIS HANDED me off to Belle at the entrance to Tamara's Boutique. Despite knowing Daniel was in jail, it comforted me to have the trustworthy bodyguard escorting me. I knew, though, that hired muscle was only a Band-Aid fix. I had to rip it off and face the sting of fear that followed. I couldn't allow the past to destroy the fragile happiness Alexander and I had finally found. My best friend hugged me tightly.

"I've got her from here," she promised him.

"I won't be far." He patted the pocket of his blazer.

Sooner or later I'd want the freedom to come and go as I pleased. For now, my fear was too fresh to go un-bandaged.

The shop occupied a small space in Kensington, but there was no questioning that its clientele was posh. Heavy silk curtains draped the storefront windows, allowing light inside but granting privacy to its exclusive patrons. Plush rugs scattered the battered wooden floor that was typical of a shop of its age. There were very few dresses on display; rather the entire shop centered around a cluster of overstuffed lounge chairs and settees. Edward had already taken up residence in the center of one, and he stood in greeting as Belle and I arrived.

Despite it being a dress shop, there was no doubt he belonged here. Dressed in a striking blue oxford and gray trousers, he looked every bit the fashion genius I knew him to be. Edward adjusted his horn-rimmed glasses to peer at us. I'd opted for the comfort of a t-shirt and jeans, uncertain how many ensembles I'd be forced to try on, but Belle matched him tit-for-tat in style, clad in a flowing cashmere sweater paired with skin-tight leather pants and ankle boots.

"Ladies." He spread his hands in welcome.

Belle kissed his cheeks, taking both his offered hands as if they were already old friends. Then they both rounded on me.

"How are you?" Edward asked seriously. His blue eyes

shone with concern, making him look even more like his brother.

My eyes flashed to Belle for confirmation of what I already knew. She'd told him about the attack. "You two have gotten close."

"He knew something was up," she said, crossing her thin arms over her chest.

"When Norris calls to arrange a transfer of custody—and I'm quoting him here," Edward interjected, "it's hard not to realize something's happened. Don't be angry with her. I pushed her to tell me."

"I'm not angry. It's hard to explain. I don't mind you knowing, but I don't want you to worry," I said. "I'm fine really. Alexander is only being protective."

I plopped down onto a velvet divan with a sigh. Apparently there'd be no escape from the drama currently surrounding my personal life. It helped knowing that they were merely worried, but what I really needed was a break from the events of the prior weekend.

Edward cocked an eyebrow, suggesting he didn't buy it, but made no further comment.

"For a dress shop, there are very few gowns," I said, hastily trying to change the subject.

"We're here for a private showing," he informed me. Edward waited for Belle to sit before taking a chair for himself. "Tamara has all your measurements and she's arranged for an exclusive preview of her winter line."

"Ohhhh!" Belle's bright eyes widened in anticipation. "I hope you brought a blank check."

Edward waved off the comment. "Alexander has made all

the necessary arrangements. I'm under orders that you should take everything you like."

Somehow it didn't surprise me that my domineering lover had seen to this. He'd been extra protective the last few days, at times his behavior bordering on fanatical.

Tamara turned out to be a forty-something firecracker with more edge than most of the women half her age. She wore her platinum hair bobbed at the chin. Coupled with her chic wrap dress and knee-high boots, she could easily have passed for one of the models and not the designer herself.

"This must be Clara." She eyed me appraisingly and then smiled with approval. "You are going to look divine in my platinum evening gown."

I wasn't certain I'd have much of an occasion to wear something like that, but I nodded, finding myself eager to please her.

"The models will be out presently. Can I offer you a refreshment?" she asked. "Sparkling water? Champagne?"

"Coffee?" I asked hopefully, my American nerves winning out over my desire to appear posh.

She disappeared into the back room, leaving us to chat.

"How's David?" I asked Edward, who beamed at the mention of his boyfriend's name.

"No one has ever been so happy to be splashed on the cover of a tabloid," he admitted with a rueful grin. "Unfortunately, that's not a sentiment my father shares."

"Sod him," Belle said, earning an appreciative laugh from Edward.

"Indeed. It's incredible how much lighter I feel," he confessed. "I should have outed myself years ago."

"Hearts are broken all over England," I informed him. "The crown's most eligible bachelor has been caught."

"I think that you hold the honor of catching the most eligible bachelor. They're only sad that their consolation prize is already claimed."

I'd found myself checking the gossip site headlines the last few days, thrilled to discover that the majority were supportive. I'd even had to chuckle at the suggestion that it was just further proof that the old dinosaur of the monarchy still had some edge.

We fell into an easy rhythm, the conversation flowing as if we'd all known each other for years. For the first time since Alexander and I had reunited, my own burden lifted. My phone buzzed in my purse and I pulled it out, frowning to see Lola's name flashing on the screen.

It wasn't that I didn't want to talk to my sister. It was that Lola reserved phone calls for practical matters. She wasn't the type to phone simply for a quick chat.

"Hello," I answered, leaving Belle and Edward to debate which photo from TMI's ongoing coverage of his outing was the most flattering.

"Clara, I'm so glad I've caught you. Do you have a minute?" She spoke breathlessly and continued on before waiting for me to respond. "Mother wants to set up a family meeting."

It was refreshing not to be bombarded with more pitiful enquiries to how I was coping with Saturday's events. Alexander had managed to keep the media out of the situation through means I didn't question, but he had insisted on phoning my parents. Their lack of response told me that their own issues were far from resolved.

"She's insisting that we need to hire a PR consultant to handle the Daniel situation and..."

"And the affair?" I finished for her.

"You know Mother. She didn't come right out and say it, but yes. She's concerned with how a scandal might affect you," Lola confessed.

"Was this your idea?" I asked her bluntly. Lola was still at university but she'd already nearly finished her own PR degree. No one could question her ambition, but I also knew that she didn't see a family matter as a private concern. All she saw was the best way to spin.

"This was her idea." There was an edge to her voice now, and I backtracked.

"The only way Dad cheating on her is going to affect me is if he doesn't stop," I said in a flat voice. "I hardly see how his affair affects me in other ways."

"You're poised to marry the most powerful man in Britain."

I ignored the slight condescension. "There is a difference between dating and marrying, Lola."

"Don't shoot the messenger," she warned me. "Will you come if she sets it up?"

"I suppose." Not a bone in my body agreed with how my mother was handling the confirmation of my father's affair. The whole thing stank. What my parents needed to worry about was their marriage. Instead they were focused on their public personae. Not to mention the fact that Alexander wasn't going to like the idea of me speaking with a publicist.

"I'm making a few calls, but I'll send you the information as soon as I have it." She ended the call without a farewell and I dropped my phone back into my purse. Then dug it out and turned the ringer to silent.

"I take it that wasn't Alexander," Edward said.

"My mother wants to hire a publicist," I said pointedly, gratefully accepting a hot cup of coffee from Tamara. Belle laughed at the revelation and after a few moments I joined her.

"Alexander was right," Edward said thoughtfully. "You really will fit right in with the family."

"Is everyone planning my wedding?" I asked in dismay.

"No one but the whole of the free world," he assured me.

"I already told her that." Belle grinned smugly.

"Wipe that grin off your face, Annabelle Stuart." But her smile only widened at my warning.

"Don't pout. There's no pouting while shopping," Edward ordered as a statuesque blonde strutted into the room in a fitted navy blue dress that fell gracefully below the knee. She turned, showing off its boatneck collar and open back. The skirt seemed modest until I saw the slit in the back that allowed glimpses of her toned legs.

"You need that," Belle murmured.

"It's so..." I struggled to find the right words.

"Classic? Sexy? Timeless?" Edward offered, and I could only nod.

It was exactly the kind of thing I was expected to wear. I never would have picked it up off the rack, but seeing it on her... I ordered it on the spot. The next hour passed in a flurry of taffeta and linen and crepe. I lost count of the number of items that Edward and Belle insisted that I *had* to have, and I was all too willing to be swept into the glamour of it all. Belle and Edward left to find us a table for lunch while I finalized the bill.

When Tamara began to bring me shoes, I leaned down to whisper in her ear. "How much have I spent?"

"The bill is taken care of. Mr. Alexander insisted you not see it." She patted my arm and then handed me a pair of Louboutins. There was a convenient lack of price tag. "You're living a fairytale, Clara. Try to enjoy it."

But the problem with fairytales is that people only remembered the love story and forgot the twisted beasts and evil witches lurking in the shadows. Happily ever afters weren't easily won, they were fought for, and the oldest of these stories didn't often end prettily.

I slipped the pump onto my foot, admiring the sexy arch that curved into a sky-rise heel.

"You need those," a gruff voice said over my shoulder. My core clenched, the words splitting the world around me like lightening. Sudden. Powerful. Undeniable.

I spun in my seat and stretched my calf out so he could admire the expensive shoe.

He nodded at Tamara. "Wrap them up."

"I'm afraid I've been bad and bought too many dresses," I told him when Tamara had left us.

He bent down over my seat, propping his strong hands on its arms. "I understand that this shop offers private viewings. Perhaps you can show me."

"I'm expected at lunch," I reminded him, but the silky edge of longing crept into my voice.

"Choose one." It wasn't a request.

I ducked into the back room and found Tamara overseeing the packaging of my gowns and dresses and shoes.

Once upon a time, it might have embarrassed me to ask a stranger a question like this, but Alexander put fire in my veins, and I could only think of extinguishing it with his touch.

"Alexander is requesting to see one of my purchases," I explained to her. "He'd like a private showing."

This woman was far too sophisticated not to catch my meaning. But I had just purchased half of her winter line, so she tilted her head in approval. "Of course, love. Whatever His Highness wishes, we will see to."

Whatever His Highness wishes, I will see to, I corrected her silently.

"I'll let you choose what you want to show him." Tamara stepped away from the rack of dresses waiting to be boxed up and delivered to my house. It took only a moment for me to find the one I knew he would appreciate most.

"I told you that one would suit you."

She showed me to a back dressing room and pulled open the damask curtain, hanging the gown so I could change. "If you need help, I'll be around the corner. Out of sight."

I didn't miss the suggestiveness of her words. This was what life with Alexander would entail. Special privileges. Purchased privacy. And, I thought as the platinum silk dropped over my head, beautiful objects. I didn't need any of it, and yet my skin warmed thinking of how he could bring the world to its knees. Just as he'd brought me to mine.

The gown rippled across my tailbone, held up by two slender ropes that curved gracefully across my shoulders, leaving my back exposed. But its most scintillating feature was the slit that revealed my thigh to the point of indecency.

It was the kind of dress that required a very particular type of undergarment, or better yet, none at all.

"Clara," Tamara called from the other side of the curtain. "I've brought you some stockings and shoes. It won't do to have you only half-dressed."

I seriously doubted that Alexander would complain, but I took the items from her. The garter belt she passed me was impossibly delicate, a mere whisper of lace gliding over my skin as I hooked it over my hips. A seam ran up the back of the sheer stockings starting exactly at the back heel of the sequined Louboutins she'd brought me. There was a time when I wouldn't have dreamed of wearing this dress with these heels and so very little underwear. But now I saw my body through Alexander's eyes. He'd made me comfortable in my own skin.

Outside the dressing room, the shop felt deserted. Tamara and the models were nowhere to be seen. But even though I felt sexy, I was no way runway model. The thought of strutting into the showroom made me feel ridiculous, but as soon as I stepped in front of X, all the doubt vanished. He drank me in, fucking me with his eyes. His mouth twisted into a wicked smile that promised sin without apology. Alexander had been my greatest temptation from the moment we met, but our roles had reversed. Now I was the apple, and it was clear he wanted a bite.

My thigh slipped through the gown as I crossed to him, exposing the ribbon of my garters in invitation. I sashayed toward him and stopped just short of his reach to turn slowly around. Alexander lounged against the velvet divan, an arm draped casually over the edge and the other stroking the stubble on his strong jawline. He'd unbuttoned his jacket and loosened his tie, but even in this relaxed state, power radiated from him. Hours ago he'd been discussing politics with world leaders, preparing to take on the role of leading a country. Minutes ago he'd shut down an entire store, because he could. Now he tapped a finger on his lower lip, drawing my attention to his mouth. That was the true nature of his authority: his ability to simply exert his will on the world.

His extended his hand, hooking a finger in silent command. I stepped forward, finally close enough to touch him, but I refrained, waiting for his cue. The need to dominate had returned. It sparked in his eyes while the rest of his face remained passive and in control.

My center ached, wondering what exquisite torture he had planned for me even as I knew it would never be enough.

The back of his hand caressed across the bare space between stocking and silk, and I trembled at the contact. Bumps rippled along my flesh as my body reacted to his touch.

"I have half a mind to roll this off of you—" he fingered the band circling my thigh—"and tie you to this chair."

"Why don't you?" I murmured, shifting so that his hand slipped higher up my bare thigh.

Alexander's mouth twisted into a smirk and he drew back, leaving me unsatisfied. "I'm always ripping your clothes off, Clara. I think this time I'll leave them on."

"But how will you touch me?"

"Oh, I'll still touch you, poppet. Are you worried that I can't turn you on if I don't have you naked? If I can't brush my fingers over your bare nipples or see your lovely, naked cunt?" He leaned forward and cupped my breast through the gown's silk. "Do you think it will be a challenge for me to get your body to respond? Because it won't. Your body understands what I want from it—what I *expect* from it. Doesn't it?"

His thumb orbited the tips of my nipples until they pebbled against the fabric. The silk grazed across their sensitive furls until my breasts swelled under the gown.

"I can't decide," he said in a measured voice, "if I'll allow you to wear this dress out of our home. Everyone who looks at you will see your curves, and your body is so responsive, particularly your breasts. You won't be able to hide these. They demand attention, don't they?"

A moan slipped from my lips as he pinched my beaded nipples. The sting of pleasure shot through my body and rolled through my core.

"On the other hand," he continued, "part of me wants them to see my prize. I want them to admire your graceful body. I want them to lust after you—crave you. Because they can never have you. Why is that, poppet?"

"Because I'm yours," I breathed as shivers rippled across my skin.

"Good girl," he said in an approving tone. He abandoned my breasts and slid a hand between my legs, curving it possessively over my sex. Rubbing along the length of my slit, he coated his fingers in my arousal. "I'm going to reward you for knowing that, and I'm going to reward your body for knowing as well. I love when you well up at my touch—so wet and ready for me to fuck you."

My head swam as all the blood that usually helped me function rushed to pool in my swollen mound. It was agony and ecstasy blended into a heady cocktail, and I was intoxicated.

"I want you to ride me, Clara," he ordered me through the haze permeating my brain. Unbuckling his belt, he liberated his cock from the confines of his trousers. "I want to watch your gorgeous cunt sink onto me and then I want *you* to fuck *me*."

He gripped my hips and pulled me roughly onto his lap, tugging the gown's delicate silk aside so that I was on full display for him. I sank onto his length as he'd ordered me, slowly adjusting as his cock stretched my delicate entrance.

"Like that, poppet," he murmured, rubbing a thumb across my aching bud. My eyes locked with his, but then his gaze traveled down as I raised my hips up, allowing his shaft to nearly slip from the confines of my sex. His eyelids grew heavy, hooding with lust as I lowered myself bit by delicious bit and sheathed myself to the hilt. My ass circled against him and I savored the fullness piercing me through my very core.

"I love you," he groaned as I pressed myself harder against him.

His words were an aphrodisiac—the affirmation I'd long craved—and I dipped and rose, rolling my hips. I wanted more. I wanted to fuse with him. I wanted to bind my body to his until nothing could tear us apart again.

"I love you," he said once more and my speed increased, building to meet the strength of those three perfect words. My muscles coiled, tightening my limbs as my fingers fisted in his thick black hair. I clung to him, my hands tightening as I held on. Alexander's breathing grew ragged and his control slipped. His cock plunged into me, matching my pace and then urging me faster. Faster. Faster. We drove each other on, frantically seeking release. Teeth rasped my tender nipple and I burst, shattering against him as he continued to climb.

"I love when you fuck me," he grunted, thrusting hard into my quaking entrance and pushing me back into the race. My body burned, my center molten and inflamed. It was too much, but it was always too much—and never enough.

We moved with raw instinct, chasing each other toward the peak.

"Come," he ordered in a low voice and I splintered around him as he surged inside me, grinding out his climax with a growl that echoed through my bones.

Collapsing against him, I shook with new life. We stayed fixed to one another until the languid bliss seeped through my skin and made it possible for me to move. Alexander brushed a curl from my cheek and kissed the hollow of my neck.

"I might want you to continue this fashion show at home."

"That can be arranged," I promised him as I lifted myself carefully from his lap. His finger swept across my cunt, drawing the moisture of his release across its tip.

"I love knowing you're full of me." A familiar hunger reignited in his face as he spoke.

I wagged a finger at him, pushing onto wobbly legs. "I have a date."

"Lucky wankers." He grinned. "Until tonight."

Tonight couldn't come soon enough.

CHAPTER NINETEEN

The office hummed with energy the following morning, and after the night I'd spent with Alexander, so did I. Peeking inside Bennett's office, I spotted Tori perched on his desk. She clutched a notebook, but judging by the adoring look on his face, not much work was getting done.

I knocked on the door. "Am I interrupting?"

"No," Bennett said. They both looked rattled. It was rather adorable.

"I forgot to drop this report off to you on Tuesday." I crossed to his desk and handed him a file.

Tori grinned at me, her cheeks matching her red hair. She pushed off the desk. "I'll leave you two to discuss." She glanced at Bennett with obvious affection. It wouldn't be long before the rest of Peters & Clarkwell realized something was up between them. "And we'll continue this later."

He watched her leave, relaxing back into his chair with a sigh.

I couldn't help being a bit jealous. They were clearly still in the honeymoon stage of their relationship, but it was more than that. Despite trying to hide an office romance, things were simple for them. They could go on dates without worrying about paparazzi following their every move. No one was planning their wedding. Not yet. Although I couldn't help but wish things would become that serious for them. Then again, Bennett was a widower with two little girls. Maybe I only saw the romance of their situation and not all the complications. After all, relationships always looked easier from the outside.

"How was your day off?" he asked.

I hadn't bothered to lie to Bennett about my intentions. Since I'd started at the firm I hadn't used a single personal day or any of my vacation. "Fabulous."

It was an honest answer. Yesterday had felt closer to normal than any day since Alexander and I had worked things out. I'd found myself wishing that it was fresh start.

"You look tired." Bennett studied my face.

I choked back a laugh. There was a lot of stress in my life at the moment, but that wasn't why I looked tired. That was entirely due to my insatiable boyfriend.

"I checked and you still have all your vacation days," he continued. "Those expire at the end of the calendar year."

"I'm sure I'll use them over the holidays." Alexander's schedule had been full of meetings with visiting dignitaries and charity events. He had suggested that I accompany to him to these daytime appointments, but I'd been all too happy to remind him that I had a job.

"I'm holding you to that," he said pointedly. Bennett's brown eyes glanced out the door of his office. "I could use your help with something."

“Whatever you need, boss.” I lowered my voice to match his, immediately curious to why we were whispering.

“I’m taking Tori out on Friday,” he confessed. “We’ve mostly been hanging out at my house. She’s a saint with the girls. But I don’t know...I guess I want to be romantic.”

It would be impossible for him to be any cuter. I nodded for him to continue.

“Do guys still buy flowers?” he asked. “I’m out of practice at this, and I want to make her happy. As happy as she’s made me.”

“Yes, they do.” My voice grew thick, overcome with emotion. With all the crap going on in my life, I needed to see someone I cared about happy. “Tori seems like the kind of girl who would like tulips. Something different.”

Bennett scribbled the suggestion on his notepad. “Thanks, Clara. I keep waiting to mess this up.”

“You aren’t going to mess this up,” I promised him.

“I constantly screwed things up with my wife,” he admitted. “You realize all the things you never said after you lose someone. I don’t want to make that mistake again.”

I couldn’t form words. Losing Alexander felt like a distant possibility right now, but it was always there. The possibility. His scars proved how close I’d come once.

“I hope Alexander shows you how he feels,” Bennett said in a soft voice.

My mouth widened into a smile. The thought alone of Alexander—of how far we’d come together—vanquished the sadness creeping into my mood.

“What am I going to do without you?” Bennett asked thoughtfully.

I startled from my thoughts, laughing nervously. “I’m not going anywhere, unless you’re firing me.”

“I just assumed.”

Making assumptions seemed to be a common problem amongst my family and friends of late. “I’m not going anywhere.”

“Good,” he said with a smile, but it didn’t reach his eyes.

Bennett’s cautious smile stuck in my head as I made my way back to my desk. Everyone saw my life changing but me. Yes, I’d moved in with Alexander. Yes, we were wildly in love. But I hadn’t worked my way through a top university to catch a husband. I loved my job, which seemed to be hard for most people to grasp. A relationship with Alexander came with its own responsibilities. He’d begun to mention upcoming black tie dinners and charity fundraisers. I was certain my social calendar would be full soon. That didn’t mean I had to give up my career.

My worries faded when I saw the note sitting on my desk. I recognized the elegant scroll of my name. Snatching it up, I carefully broke the seal and pulled out a second envelope. This was new. My fingers trembled as I opened it to discover the schedule for an upcoming chartered flight.

The phone on my desk rang and I lunged for it. “Hello?”

“Pack light. You won’t need many clothes.”

I fell back against my chair, temporarily lost in the huskiness of his voice. “I didn’t know you still used the phone.”

“I missed your voice. I’ve been listening to oil negotiations all morning.”

The confession caught me off-guard. Alexander rarely called me. He preferred to express his desire in writing. “So we’re running away?”

"We need to get away." The line went silent, but then he continued. "I've already spoken to Bennett."

"You have?" No wonder my boss had mentioned my vacation days. I couldn't help but think this was simply a ploy to put more distance between me and Daniel. A completely unnecessary, extravagant ploy. "I'd prefer to handle my own schedule. I'm a professional, X."

"But you wouldn't have agreed to come."

"I still haven't agreed to come. It's not a good time to go away." There were a million reasons to say no him. Not the least of which was that he occasionally needed to hear it.

"Poppet." There was a trace of warning in his tone. "It's been arranged. I think you'll find Bennett as unwavering on this as I am."

I threw down the paper schedule. "Where are you taking me?"

"It's a surprise," he said. I could almost picture the smug satisfaction written across his face.

"No clues? Do I need a coat or a swimsuit?"

"I thought I was clear on that earlier. You won't need clothes. Not many, at least. I imagine you might want to wear something to the airfield." He paused, before adding. "Although I wouldn't mind watching you walk around in a bikini. Everything else will be taken care of."

"Got it. Bikini and toothbrush," I said dryly. "But this works both ways, X. If I'm going to spend the weekend mostly naked, you are too."

"You're bringing the only thing I need," he responded simply.

I swallowed hard at the thought of a weekend of Alexander's glorious body on full display.

"I'll be taking care of some things late this evening before we leave. Norris will stay at the house with you."

"Now you're being cruel," I pouted. "Putting naughty thoughts in my head and then not coming home."

"Antici...pation," he breathed.

I hung up the call, squirming in my seat. A mid-day call from Alexander was bound to be bad for my work ethic.

Alexander might not take no for an answer, but that wasn't going to stop me from giving Bennett grief. This time I strode into his office without knocking.

"Yes?" A smile twitched on his lips.

"I was going to tell Tori that you're a catch, but now I'm rethinking my stance," I informed him.

"You need a vacation before you work yourself to death," Bennett said, his face growing serious. "Remember what I said earlier? You're never going to regret missing a day of work, but you'll regret the happiness you don't take."

"I can be happy in London."

"It's going to rain here all weekend. Go be in the sun. I can put it on your to-do list if that'll help your guilt."

"I don't feel guilty," I argued. "I just don't need a vacation."

Bennett raised an eyebrow, and I realized that I had been shouting.

"Okay, maybe I do need one." I pinched my fingers together. "But just a short one."

"See you next week," he called as I bolted for the door, slightly embarrassed.

Tori caught me in the hall, carrying take away. "Have fun."

"Don't start," I warned her.

"You do realize most girls would kill to be swept away by a prince, right?"

She had me there. "Maybe. I hear you have plans of your own on Friday."

"I do." Her face lit up, a sign that Bennett wasn't the only one who was smitten. "Oh, there was a woman waiting for you in the lobby."

"For me?"

"Blonde. About our age," Tori confirmed.

There was no reason for Belle to visit me at work, except to grab lunch. Stopping by my desk, I grabbed my purse and headed downstairs. I knew I should call Norris and let him know I was planning to leave the building. But since I wasn't going out alone, I decided against it. As soon as the lift's doors slid open, I realized my mistake.

Blonde? Yes.

Belle? No.

Pepper turned and our eyes locked. I fought the urge to step back into the lift. Whatever reason she had for visiting me at work had to be a good one, relatively speaking. I sincerely doubted anything involving Pepper was good, but I couldn't wait to hear why she'd shown her haughty face here.

She leaned causally against the reception desk, tapping her polished fingernails relentlessly. Only Pepper would wear a leather mini-skirt and strappy platforms into an office building. I tugged at my sophisticated, but modest wrap dress, feeling overdressed in comparison. Every man who entered the lobby did a double take. It was almost comical to watch their heads swivel to stare at the leggy blonde.

Steeling myself, I approached her. She was up to no good. That much was apparent.

"Clara." She smiled warmly at me. "They've been phoning your desk."

"I was in a meeting," I said, playing along and allowing her to air kiss my cheeks in greeting. The last thing I needed was for someone to snap a picture of a catfight between me and Pepper Lockwood.

"Is there somewhere we can talk?" she asked.

I held up my purse. "I was on my way to pick up some lunch. Walk with me?"

From the outside no one would suspect how bitterly we loathed one another, but I felt it. Hate roared through me, and it was all I could do to keep a smile on my face as we stepped outside.

Norris exited the Rolls, which I assumed had been parked in front of the building since he'd taken me to work earlier this morning.

"Miss Bishop, do you need me to drive you?" he asked in an uncharacteristically clipped tone. Maybe I wasn't the only who despised Pepper.

"I'm fine," I reassured him. "We're popping around the corner to grab a bite."

He nodded and waited for us to continue. He'd only be a few steps behind us, which was probably more important for Pepper's safety than my own. I couldn't guarantee I wouldn't throttle her in the next twenty minutes.

"Alexander does keep a short leash on you," she noted. The false friendliness had faded from her voice even though she still wore a sickeningly sweet smile.

I let the comment slide, preferring to keep our interaction brief. "What do you want?"

"I was so looking forward to a nice chat. Do you really want to skip straight to business?"

"Nice chats are for friends and neighbors, not us." I wasn't interested in playing pretend with her. Pepper was a snake waiting to strike, and the less time I spent with her, the better.

"I wanted to give you a chance."

I raised an eyebrow. "A chance to what?"

"A chance to run," she said in a low voice. "We both know Alexander's duties lie elsewhere. Eventually he's going to toss you out with the rubbish. Why wait around to be hurt?"

"How thoughtful of you." I stopped in front of a small sandwich shop. "But you needn't concern yourself with Alexander or his duties."

"What can I say? I'm loyal to the monarchy." A wicked smile crept over her face. "I already warned you that I had information that could destroy him. Believe me, when I say it will destroy you, too."

"So let me see if I'm following you. I break up with him and this information goes away?" I clarified.

"Exactly."

I studied her for a moment. As ugly as she was on the inside, I couldn't deny she was beautiful. Most women would find it intimidating just being near her. Everything about her screamed sex, but I'd seen her tone down her sensual appeal in favor of fitting in with the aristocracy. She was all too willing to play the part of perfect consort to Alexander. Too bad that I wasn't about to let her. When we'd first met, she'd overwhelmed me, but now that I saw her overeagerness I only felt sorry for her.

"Do you think if I leave him, he'll run to you?" I asked her bluntly. "Let's be honest for a moment. I left him this summer. Did he seek you out? Did he come running into your arms?"

Pepper blinked, her prim nose tilting into the air. "You don't know Alexander at all. You don't know what he's capable of, and you don't know what he needs."

"I know that no matter how hard you try—no matter how often you throw yourself at his feet—he'll never need you."

She recoiled, visibly stung by my words, but Pepper wasn't the type to cry. Instead she simply walked away, pausing a few steps from me to toss one more threat in my direction. "Remember this moment, Clara. Remember the moment you destroyed him."

CHAPTER TWENTY

ALEXANDER

Clara's eyelids fluttered, and I wondered what she dreamed of. The steady vibration of the aircraft had lulled her to sleep nearly as soon as we'd taken off from the private airfield in London. Her cheeks flushed in her sleep, hair spilling across her face. She had never looked more delicate. My chest constricted at the reminder of her fragility. Clara was strong—emotionally, psychologically, but not physically. In the few seconds before I'd managed to pull Daniel from her, I'd glimpsed her one weakness and it had shaken me to the core. I'd been afraid to love her, afraid to allow myself to claim her body and soul. Every woman I'd ever loved had slipped through my fingers. I never saw my mother's smile one final time. Sarah's blood covered my hands as she died in my arms. I'd convinced myself that she would be safer if I always kept her at a distance. Then I would never have to face the prospect of losing her, too. But seeing her with Daniel's hands around her throat, the wall I'd erected between us crashed down. Losing her was an impossibility. In that moment, I was too selfish not to love her. It was why I couldn't allow her to go unprotected.

My thoughts returned to the exchange I'd shared with my father only yesterday. The crown would not offer her the same protective services it would employ if one of the monarchy was under threat. It hadn't surprised me, but it had disgusted me. Daniel might have been a threat from her past, but it was our high-profile relationship that had enabled him to track her down. And now he was free, thanks to an ambitious young barrister who paved the way for him to be bailed out. My own lawyers assured me he would be tried and sentenced, but that hardly mattered to me if he was allowed to walk the streets in the meantime.

The glass in my hand cracked, and I looked down in surprise to discover blood streaming from a cut on my palm. I hadn't realized I was squeezing it so tightly, and when I relaxed my grip the pieces shattered on the tray table. Clara startled, awoken by the sharp clink of glass fragments hitting the plastic.

"What..." Sleepiness faded from her voice when she saw. "Oh my god, are you okay?"

"An accident," I said dismissively.

"We should find a bandage. Where's the flight attendant?"

"I sent her to sit with the pilot," I informed her, maintaining a level head. I'd learned the importance of controlling my own reactions around Clara, knowing my mood too easily colored her empathetic spirit. "I didn't want her to disturb you."

Clara crossed to the storage units near the aircraft's door

and began to search them. Wrapping a napkin over my wound, I joined her.

"Here we are." She pulled a first aid kit out. "And look what else we have."

Next to it was a full box of condoms.

"I suppose they're okay if their clients join the mile-high club," she said with a giggle.

Her laughter in that moment was the sexiest sound I'd ever heard. There'd been far too little of it in the last few days. I had suspected that the farther we got from London, the more she'd return to me. And I needed her far away from London—from him. I needed to hear her laugh, needed to watch her face as I devoured her. Perhaps here I could finally show her how much I loved her. Fear had held me back for far too long, and now it tainted the time we shared together. This weekend would release us from that, even if only for a moment.

"Would you like to join that club?" I asked her, moving to press her against the cabin's walls.

"Yes," she said breathlessly, "but not while you're bleeding."

I stepped back, allowing her room to find the supplies she needed. Clara reached for my hand and gently cleaned the wound. I watched with silent awe as she dressed it and then pressed my palm to her lips.

"And a kiss to make it better," she whispered.

"I can think of other ways to make me feel better." Slipping my good hand under the waistband of her blue jeans, I fondled her cunt, pleased to discover she was ready for me.

"How much longer is this flight?" she asked with a moan as my fingers stroked her cleft.

"Not long enough." I withdrew my hand quickly and unbuttoned her pants, pushing them to her feet in one swift motion. My craving for her consumed me—not just her magnificent body but the whole of her. Inside her I found solace. The more that I accepted her love and allowed myself to feel my own, the more possessive I became of her. I'd wanted her since the moment fate threw us together, but now I knew that even as I claimed her body, she ruled my heart.

She posed no resistance as my compulsion took over. Instead her ass circled against me with a delicious willingness that made my cock push harder against my trousers. My fingers clutched her panties, twisting the thin elastic before ripping the flimsy fabric from her hips, exposing her lower half to me. Gripping her hips, I twisted her around, crushing her against the wall, as I unbuckled my fly. The pain in my hand faded as hungry desire overtook me, but I restrained myself, allowing it to build. Love for her washed over me, and I nudged against her soft folds. They parted to envelope my crown, and I paused. As much as my body demanded her, I wanted to draw out her pleasure by giving her the dominance she craved. The dominance she needed to be free. "This weekend, you will wear no clothes. I want your cunt naked and waiting for me at all times."

"I guess we won't be sightseeing." Longing tinged her words, and she wiggled her bare ass to welcome me.

My hand smacked against her left buttock with a satisfying whack that made my palm vibrate. The sting only turned me on more, making it more difficult not to sink inside of her. "You will strip as soon as the door locks behind us," I continued with my instructions, noting how she sagged against me. "And I will spend the weekend attending to you. Would you care to voice any further objections?"

She shook her head and I pushed inside her slippery sex another inch. Clara whimpered, and I watched as her soft pink entrance stretched over my cock.

"What do you need, poppet?" I asked her silkily.

"I need to be fucked." Her voice was small and pleading.

"And I'm here to give you what you need." I thrust into her, relishing the cry that escaped her lips as I filled her. My hips bucked, plunging my cock faster and deeper against the warm velvet of her channel. It welcomed me, pulsing and contracting as I continued to fuck her with long, powerful strokes. I wanted more. More of her. Clara naked and on her knees for me. Clara's lips wrapping warm around my cock. I'd spent the last week in a perpetual hell, worrying about her every moment we were apart. For the next few days I planned for us to be apart as little as possible. I wanted to devour her and fill her, draining away her fear and my own in the only way I knew. By being joined to her both body and soul.

"Come, my love," I ordered her as her breathing quickened to shallow pants. Her cries and whimpers were a broken symphony that urged me on until her body tensed and she fragmented against me. The tremors of her body drew forth my own, annihilating the control I held over my desire, and I burst inside her, clutching her hips as I found my release.

I held on until her shaking subsided and then carefully unsheathed my cock. Bending, I drew her pants up as she clung to the wall that supported her. Then I led her back to the seats. Gathering her in my lap, we nestled together as the plane shifted, carrying us to our final destination. A sense of wholeness washed over me as I held her. She'd shown me I was lost and then led me home, healing so many of my broken fragments. Now it was time to heal hers.

THE CAR DELIVERED us to the private chalet I'd procured for our use this weekend. The house was tucked against a snowy mountain, overlooking a serene ski resort. St. Moritz was largely unoccupied this time of year as the summer holidays had passed and the winter tourists hadn't yet arrived. Clara snuggled into the down coat I'd presented to her upon landing. Her hand rested over my bandaged one as she drank in the untouched beauty of the mountainside.

"Would you have preferred the beach?" I asked as she unfastened her safety belt.

"The only preference I have is to be with you," she answered. "The view is lovely."

"It is." My words were thick. My eyes had barely strayed from her since she'd woken on the flight.

"You're not looking," she accused, flushing under my gaze.

"I assure you that I am."

The fireplaces had been lit for our arrival as I'd requested.

"This place is incredible," Clara said as we entered, stepping aside to allow the driver to leave our bags by the door.

I'd chosen the location for its privacy, but I was glad that it pleased her. The front door opened to a large great room that boasted overstuffed sofas and thick fur rugs. Overhead a rustic chandelier glowed against the late afternoon light. Floor-to-ceiling windows offered an expansive view of the town below us. That view was the closest I planned to get to civilisation for the next three days. The weather in the Alps had begun to drop for the season, capping the mountaintops in snow. The forecast predicted storms over the course of the weekend that would keep us inside for the entirety of our too-brief holiday.

"The kitchen is fully stocked," I informed her. "We'll have no need to leave."

"Well, X, you've spirited me away to an isolated mountain lodge. What will you do with me?"

I answered her by locking the door. The bolt echoed in the quiet space with an ominous click. Clara spun to face me, eyes wide with anticipation. I held out my hand to her. She took it without trepidation. This weekend we would begin the work of healing the damage inflicted upon us. She needed to be shown that I would protect her, and I would do so by taking control until her body remembered that it was under my safekeeping. The Crown might not offer her security, but I would. And someday my name would be her protector as well.

"Do you remember our agreement?" I asked.

Her head tilted seductively and she drew back, dropping her coat behind her. It landed with a soft thud on the wooden floor. "I don't remember agreeing to anything. I remember being told."

"And do you have an objection? I seem to remember you being more than willing to agree to my demands."

"I have no objection," she said, removing her shoes. She stood and placed a hand over the button of her jeans. "But I have a request."

"I'm here to meet your needs," I assured her. My throat

constricted as she unfastened the button and shimmied the jeans over her shapely hips. It took effort to restrain myself as she revealed herself to me bit by bit. It always did.

My gaze fucked her body as she stripped, lingering over her full breasts and perfect nipples. Later I would take them in my mouth and suck them until she came. My tongue licked my lower lip, imagining I'd already claimed them.

She stepped forward, naked, and brushed a finger over my lips, calling me back to her. "Don't be gentle. Take me as you need me. Use my body. I want to feel it all with you."

"Sometimes I like to be gentle," I reminded her, choosing my words precisely. It was more difficult now that her cunt was bared and ready for me.

"I want it rough and slow and desperate and kind. I want you. *All* of you," she said huskily. She looked down and I sensed the confusion churning within her. The passion still overruled her. She was asking for me to take control. Her need tore through me, and I resisted the urge to take her on the spot and give her the answers she sought.

Clara had rebuilt me and yet she continued to offer more of herself. Her body. Her heart. She'd not only accepted me, she'd welcomed me despite the darkness and secrets that had tested our love. The gift of that overwhelmed me. It tested my restraint.

Placing a finger under her chin, I tipped her face back up to meet my gaze instead. "You're giving me your trust. I don't take that lightly. When I fuck you, Clara, and I will fuck you until you plead for me to stop, I'm not using you. I will never use you. When I fuck you, I'm setting you free. Do you want to be set free?"

"Yes, please," she whispered.

CHAPTER TWENTY-ONE

I waited on the bed as he had instructed, my face turned toward the wall. Candles flickered, casting the room in a romantic glow. Running my fingers over the soft down of the pillows, I resisted the pull of sleep as I listened to his preparations. The sharp scrape of fabric against wood. The creak of the floor surrounding the bed. I'd offered myself completely to him without clarifying what that would entail. But with each mysterious new noise, my pulse quickened in expectation. What had once frightened me now thrilled me, kindling my desire into a sensual blaze.

His hands and body could provide release from the nightmares that had plagued my life for the past week. I only had to trust him to set me free, and I trusted him entirely, ready to submit to his primal dominance. His declaration of love had liberated me and continued to, but the fear hadn't left his eyes since that terrible night. Here, with much needed distance, between us and London, we could finally give into the full weight of our feelings.

The mattress shifted under his weight as he sat beside me. A hum of longing vibrated through my body as his hand caressed my bare tailbone. My hips writhed in his direction only to be stopped by his firm hand. His words flashed through my mind. I would always come, but only when he said and tonight I suspected I would beg.

"I'm going to blindfold you," he spoke softly, rubbing my ass. "You'll understand why." Alexander lowered a scarf over my face, pausing to give me a chance to say no. I remained silent, and he tied it around my head, tightening the knot and obscuring my vision. His hand found mine and he pulled me up, guiding my feet to the floor. He walked behind me, one hand pressed to the small of my back. The small gesture of reassurance stifled the minute apprehension coursing through me. My hip bumped against the end of the bed and he stopped me, pressing my belly against the cool, wooden frame.

"Spread your legs." I did as he ordered, earning an approving "good girl." He lifted my arms over my head and began to wrap a silky rope around my wrists, tucking and weaving it until my feet arched. I was suspended, my toes clinging to the ground and supporting my weight. The rope brushed against my breasts as he circled my torso. He paused and I felt a knot cinch into place between my shoulders. He crossed my stomach, coiling it just tightly enough that it dug into my flesh. His arms wrapped around me and another knot cinched across my belly button before he dropped the remaining line to swing between my spread legs. My body molded to his artistry, each binding a master stroke.

Rope scraped against my left ankle, coiling tightly, as he

tugged it to secure it. He repeated the action, spreading my legs further and forcing me higher on my toes. My body ached, drawn wide. It was exhilarating, the slight pain of my bindings giving way to arousal. I hadn't been sure I could do this, but with each passing second, my body relaxed into the tension. For a moment, neither of us moved and I focused on his ragged breath. Then the sharp metallic click of a belt unfastening followed by the swish of leather against fabric. My limbs tightened, bracing for the sting until I heard the belt drop to the floor. But my release had been stifled by the memory of pain. Fabric thudded softly to the floor and then his heat radiated against my vulnerable skin. I wanted to press against him, and I pulled against my restraints.

"Relax," he commanded, he drew a finger down my lengthened spine. "You will know no fear at my hands, Clara. Only pleasure. I've taken the use of your hands, of your feet, but you still have your voice. Do you understand?"

I nodded, but he caught my hair and stopped the movement. "Use your voice. Tell me."

"I understand," I whispered.

"Tell me what you're thinking." He loosened his grip on my hair and sank his teeth into my shoulder.

I groaned, as pangs of pleasure shot through me, hardening my nipples against the coolness of the room. Without my sight, without my hands, my other senses heightened and flooded me with sensations. I could feel the air fluttering against my skin despite the lack breeze. My nostrils flared, inhaling the mingled scent of wax and flowers.

"Tell me," he repeated firmly as he pinched my nipple between his fingers. He twisted it, overwhelming my already saturated nerves.

"I want to p-p-please you," I stammered.

"This pleases me, poppet," he murmured, releasing my breast to fall heavily against the rope wrapped under it. "Seeing you trussed up, completely at my mercy—do you have any idea what this does to me? What it makes me want to do to you? Do you want to see?"

I started to bob my head but caught myself. "Yes."

The blindfold slipped off my head and I blinked, my eyes adjusting to the dim luminescence of firelight and candles.

"It's a pity you can't see the whole picture." Alexander moved to the corner of the bed, drinking in my reaction as I slowly looked up. A red rope hung, secured to a wooden beam that ran the width of the chalet's ceiling. It twisted into an intricate knot and then continued to my wrists. The silky rope spiraled in thick coils that held my arms over my head. My gaze traveled down to discover that it crossed over my chest, twisting under my breasts. I'd felt him do it, but seeing the bindings sent a surge of pleasure through me, undermining the exhaustion starting to creep into my weary limbs. The elegant knot tied at my belly was so intricate that I wondered how many times he'd done this before. Who else had been lucky enough to be under his complete dominion? I pushed the unpleasant thought out of my head. I could only catch a glimpse of the rope that fastened my ankles to the pillars of the bed.

Alexander's eyes were hooded with lust when I finally found him again. I devoured the sight of his carved body, my gaze landing on his erect cock. Heat flushed my cheeks as I became aware of my vulnerability to him. I wasn't embarrassed. I was on fire.

"You're so lovely with your rosy cheeks. It's making my

palms itch to turn your other cheeks pink." His words fell over me and I stiffened. "I will do as I please to your body unless you use your safe word."

I pressed my lips into a tight line, issuing an unspoken challenge. I'd told him I trusted him. I did trust him.

He returned to stand behind me and I longed to nudge my ass against him—to feel his hardness against my soft bottom. He chuckled at my pitiful attempts to move. His palm fondled the curve of my ass before it flew against it playfully. Alexander rubbed the spot before delivering another smack. He repeated the gesture, spanking and caressing away the sting until my bottom smarted with heat.

"Perfection." His mouth nuzzled against my ear. "Do you know why I wanted to tie you up? Because I want you to experience true release. I see you, clinging to the edge, waiting greedily for me to climax with you. You won't be able to do that tonight. Your body won't be able to fight me when I want it to come. I'm going to show you how much I love you —how sacred your body is to me. I'm going to make you scream and cry and claw at that rope and then I'm going to start all over again."

A whimper escaped my lips as he dropped between my legs. His knees hit the wooden floor and I moaned, anticipating him. He cupped my sex in his palm as his teeth nipped playfully at my sore cheeks. Then his hands parted me roughly. I barely had time to process this before his tongue plunged inside me. He fucked me with his mouth until my knees tried to buckle, but the restraints held tight. The sudden weakness in my legs shifted more of my weight onto my arms and I screamed, unraveling on Alexander's tongue. He continued to lick my swollen mound even as I cried for him to stop. I couldn't find my center, dangling between agony and elation. But just as my core began to clench, he pulled away. With one hand he supported my rear until I found my toes again. The arches of my feet throbbed, my calves smoldered with the effort of keeping me up, and my arms burned.

"I'm not done with you," he said wickedly. He stood and crossed the room, withdrawing a small bottle of oil from his bag. He took his time returning, obviously enjoying my pants and moans as my fingers twisted against the rope holding me overhead. I was lost to my role, overwhelmed by the scene unfolding around me, but desperate to submit to his demands at the same time. He'd turned me into a mewling, frantic creature and I loved it.

This time he pushed a finger into my pulsing hole. My body struggled against him and he slowed his movements until I calmed. He withdrew his hand and I heard the lid of the bottle flip open. I felt the oil glide across my seam all the way up until it coated my forbidden entrance. His fingers thrust inside me once more, curving and fucking me. And then his thumb pressed over the pucker of my ass and plunged inside. Alexander continued his ravishment, carefully preventing me from coming again.

"Do you mind when I touch you here?" He inserted his thumb deeper.

"More," I moaned. I could only think of being filled. I yearned to stretch myself until I broke.

"I'm not certain you want that." But his words were thick, and I knew he wanted to claim me there in the last avenue he'd yet to conquer.

"Fuck me," I pleaded. "Fuck me there."

His hand stilled, giving me a second to process what I was asking him to do. The lack of action only made it more enticing.

"Do you want me to fuck you?" He circled my tight pucker with his thumb.

"Yes. Oh god, yes. Take all of me and stop fucking asking," I snapped, losing patience.

But he backed away and I wanted to scream. To beg. My body was his to claim. Why wouldn't he do it?

"I'm going to release your legs," he told me and I swallowed against my frustration. I was a mass of frayed nerves and hopefulness.

The ropes on my ankles fell away and I tried to bend them, but I was still bound to the beam above me.

"I don't want to hurt you," he explained as his arms reached for the rope that held my hands. To my relief he only loosened it enough to allow my knees to flex. Alexander caressed my ass. "Ask for it. I need to know you consent to this."

"Fuck me there," I begged again. "Claim all of me."

"Bend your knees." Oil drizzled between my bare cheeks and then his thick crown pushed inside me. Fire ignited around the taut ring and I bit my lip. But the sting of my teeth did nothing to abate the agony. He hooked an arm around my waist, supporting my suspended body and relieving my tired arms. I was still under his total control, and he guided his cock in a little farther until the stretched muscles popped over his tip. My body's resistance to the unfamiliar intrusion diminished and bit-by-bit he entered me until I was full of him. My head fell to my arm and I sobbed against it.

Alexander stopped, allowing me to adjust to the new sensations. I knew he wouldn't continue without a sign that I wanted this. And I did. The tremors racking me did nothing to allay my desire to be possessed. The hand resting over my belly slid between my legs, capturing and rolling my clit with deft fingers. Exquisite pressure welled in my core, and I surrendered myself to his reign.

"Don't," I groaned, struggling to find words in my overcome state. "Don't...stop."

He drew back just enough to allow him to drive inside me, exercising restraint that I found baffling.

"More," I demanded, and he gave into his instincts, pounding against my ass. He held me firmly, grunting, as he thrust relentlessly, each stab of his cock searing through me. I was caught between pleasure and pain, but I felt the tension building to a frantic apex. I fractured in his arms, exploding in a deluge of screams that split the air around us.

"Fuck!" Heat flooded my insides as he released. There was no discomfort when the frenzy ended. He withdrew, running a finger down the seed he'd spilled upon his exit. "Now you're mine."

"Yes," I breathed, repeating it over and over, even as he undid the rope binding my wrists.

Alexander gathered me in his arms and carried me to the bed, soothing me with gentle shushes.

"I'm going to clean up," he said lightly. Yes, hygiene seemed like a good idea. The bathroom light flickered on as I lay quivering on top of the sheets. I'd been tested. I'd been loved. Alexander had taken me safely beyond my boundaries, giving me the most intense pleasure of my life. Yet, I still craved his touch as if it hadn't been enough. I would never have enough of him. When he returned, he pulled the blanket over me and slid in beside me. Then he made love to me, showing my body everything it meant to be his.

CHAPTER TWENTY-TWO

Alexander's side of the bed was empty when I awoke. I stretched, noting the delicious ache of my muscles. He'd taken me to the edge and bound me there, teasing and torturing, and my body remembered. The glow of the fireplace glinted off the silk rope that still hung in place near the foot of the bed. Sliding from under the covers, I padded barefoot to it and ran my fingers down its length. It was smooth and coarse. Binding and liberating. Wrapping it around my wrist, I replayed the scene from last night. The memories came in staccato bursts of pleasure then agony and finally exquisite release.

By the time I discovered Alexander sitting by the hearth of the great room, my body was practically vibrating with desire. I lingered, shyly, on the stairs, drinking in his strong, carved shoulders that gracefully met the sinewy shape of his back. This man—this god—was mine. The reality of that remained elusive, only becoming palpable through contact. I could not comprehend how out of the billions of people in the world, we had found one another. I stayed there for a long time, watching the light of the flames dance across his jet-black hair, until the pull of his presence lured me forward. It was then I realized we were bonded. Magnetically. Irresistibly. In a sea of people, I would always find him. We'd been brought together by an undeniable force that day at the club. Every moment in my life, every decision and mistake I'd made, had been carrying me toward him.

Alexander turned, his face obscured by darkness, and reached for me. I flew to him. Settling in his lap, I drew my legs up as he wrapped his arms around me.

"Couldn't sleep?" I asked.

He tucked a strand of hair behind my ear and kissed me. "I didn't want to wake you. I apologize for leaving you alone."

"No apology necessary. I think you screwed me into a coma." I traced the curve of his jaw.

"I should have checked on you." He shook his head, a familiar look of self-loathing flitting across his dark features. "Last night was intense. You shouldn't be alone."

"I'm fine," I said with emphasis. I hated when he questioned himself. There never seemed to be a way to convince him that I was as enthralled as he was. "Look at me, X. I'm happy. Truly. You make me happy."

"I try." His expression was pained and it tore through me.

"If you don't stop pouting, I'll have to spank you," I warned him

His hand slid to cup my ass and he smiled, albeit grudgingly. "That is my job, poppet."

"Then maybe you should get to work," I murmured, but the low growl of my stomach interrupted my attempt at seduction. Stupid bodily needs.

"I think I better feed you first," he said with a low chuckle.

I willed myself to stand up, and we made our way to the kitchen. Alexander opened the refrigerator and drew out a carton of milk. Within moments he had eggs and toast cooking. But his heavy mood remained, casting an unwanted shadow over the morning.

"You are seriously killing my buzz," I informed him, pushing myself onto the counter to watch him cook.

"We skipped dinner. That's unacceptable."

"I'm not going to break," I told him in a quiet voice. "I'm healthy, X. One meal isn't going to be my undoing."

"Still..." he let the thought trail away as he shoved a spatula through the skillet.

We lapsed into silence until he presented me with a full plate. Despite my best intentions, my hunger won out and I shoveled them down greedily, pleased to see a smile creep onto his lips. He needed to take care of me and I needed to be more open to that. Like most things, it would take time to accept that his concern wasn't a sign of perceived weakness on my part.

"I could get used to being fed every morning." I pushed my empty plate away and beamed at him. Small steps.

"I could get used to feeding you every morning," he said, but the words were heavy with a meaning that sent my heart racing.

"You'll have to if you're going to keep me up all night." But the joke didn't calm my frantic pulse.

"I'd like to keep you up every night," he continued. His eyes swept over me and stopped on my left hand, resting on the counter "There are expectations for me, Clara."

My speeding heart skipped and then plummeted into the pit of my stomach. We'd had this conversation before. It hadn't ended well.

"It seems that those expectations now include you." Alexander paused and cleared his throat. "Marriage was never something I wanted. It was merely another expectation."

"I know." I jumped in, trying to derail this train of conversation before it wrecked everything. "I don't expect it either. It's too soon—for both of us."

"Then you have no intention of marrying me? I gather you're just using me for my body." He grinned, but the smile was brittle.

"We're both young. I know your family has expectations and I know it's something we will have to face, but right now, I want to concentrate on me and you." I ignored the small voice inside me that reminded me there was a deadline on our relationship. Choosing to turn a blind eye to the fact that our separation was inevitable.

"I'm not certain you're understanding me." His tone was measured, but the fire of possession blazed in his eyes.

"I understand the world you live in," I whispered, "and I understand the world I live in. Right now I want to pretend that things can be different."

Alexander slid a hand under my bottom and lifted me into his arms. "Then understand this. Clara, you are my world."

Then he carried me to the bedroom and proved it was the truth.

. . .

His mood remained manic throughout the day, constantly shifting between passionate sensuality and dark despair. In the moments we made love, whether rough or tender, he was with me fully. But when we separated even for short periods of time he faded away into darkness. I sensed the struggle warring within him, but I didn't understand it. So I sought him out in the bedroom and on the stairs and across the bearskin rug by the fireplace. Each time I called him back to me, only to have him separated from me once more by the demons he wouldn't share.

And still I was happy. Whatever battle he was fighting drew us closer together. That much I knew. For now I could only stay by his side and let him wage the war. When at last my own reserves were depleted, I fell into a dreamless sleep, only to be woken by his gentle hands.

"Clara, you need to get dressed." The urgency of his request didn't match the careful prod of his touch.

"Why?" I murmured sleepily, rubbing my eyes, surprised to discover it was twilight outside the window.

"We have to leave," he informed me as he gathered the few personal items we'd left strewn around the room.

I sat up, clutching the sheet to my bare chest, and tried to process what he was saying. Leave? We'd only gotten here yesterday. "I thought we were here until Monday."

"I've been summoned back to London. The car will be here in a few minutes." He came to me and brushed a kiss over my forehead. "Dress warmly. The temperature has dropped."

Stumbling from the bed, I searched for my bag, which hadn't yet been carried away. I pulled a sweater over my head and found a pair of jeans. Panic would get me nowhere but that didn't stop my mind from producing an endless stream of theories on why we were suddenly being forced to return early. My thoughts flashed from Edward to Belle to the entire country itself and, of course, Daniel. What news would greet me when I stepped out the door? I didn't want to know.

Alexander reappeared in the room and collected my luggage without a word. I followed him, dread seeping into my bloodstream. But it wasn't until we were in the car, headed back to the airport that I was able to find my voice. "What's happened? Is it...Daniel?"

I needed to face the possibility that things had gone horribly wrong with his sentencing. It would be better to know, because then we could begin to deal with it.

"It's not Daniel." There was something not altogether honest in his answer, but he continued before I could question him. "There's been a development regarding the accident."

"The accident?" I repeated stupidly. Maybe it was the chaotic shift in circumstances, but I couldn't see where this was headed.

"My accident," he said in a low voice. "New information that changes things."

The accident had happened nearly eight years ago, but it still haunted him. What more ghosts could the press dredge up to torture him and his family?

"What information?" I asked.

"Someone is claiming drugs were involved." His answer was clipped, precise to the point of a knife's edge.

"I know there was drinking." I did my best to sound reassuring, hoping my lack of judgment would prevent him from shutting down. "Were there drugs? Were you high?"

"Not me." His mouth tightened as though he was trying to ignore a painful memory. "My sister."

I wasn't expecting that answer. "Sarah?"

"This person claims she was dosed with a date rape drug along with Sarah. She's telling anyone who will listen that the reason we crashed that night was because Sarah was driving."

No one knew what had happened that night. Alexander could barely recall the details himself. The media had sold the story that he had been driving, and he'd accepted the responsibility out of unwarranted guilt. But there was one thing we both knew: Sarah had been driving. And there were only two other people who had been present as that tragic night unfolded. I didn't need him to tell me who this source was, she'd already warned me this was coming. So it was no surprise when he continued.

"Pepper claims I drugged her, and that I'm the reason Sarah is dead," he said in a flat voice, his gaze never wavering from the rushing scenery outside the car window.

She hadn't lied to me. She was going to destroy him.

THE PLANE WAS WAITING at the airfield and we returned home to London swiftly. Each of us was lost to our thoughts even though Alexander's hand stayed tightly knitted through mine for the duration of the flight. This is what his world entailed. Emergency flights and strategy meetings. For the first time I truly saw how he fit into the complicated machinery of British politics. What I couldn't gauge was what lay in wait for us upon our return.

We exited the plane to discover two cars waiting at the private airfield. Norris stood in front of one, and Alexander dropped my hand, crossing to speak to him alone. Although they were only feet from me, the two kept their voices lowered. Alexander nodded in my direction and I had the sinking suspicion he was giving instructions on my handling. But if Alexander thought I could be induced to leave his side, he had another thing coming. We'd fought too hard to strip the barrier of lies and secrets that had stood between us. I wasn't about to let it be resurrected.

When Alexander broke from his conversation with Norris, a man I didn't recognize stepped forward. "Your father has instructed me to take you directly to him."

Alexander's eyes met mine and an unspoken question passed between us. He knew my answer. Extending an arm, he called me to his side.

"You father would prefer to speak to you alone," the man informed him, casting a cold look in my direction.

"There's no secrets between Clara and me. It's time he understood that." Alexander glared back at him.

The man gestured to the car, idling behind him, and we climbed inside. As the car carried us toward his father, I realized too late that I hadn't told Alexander about Pepper's visit to me at the office. I could have prevented this, and I hadn't. I'd been too blinded by my hatred of Pepper.

I was to blame for the coming storm, and worst of all, I'd allowed secrets to separate us once more.

CHAPTER TWENTY-THREE

I'd been to the palace before—as a tourist. Now I followed Alexander as we were led through private rooms that were definitely not a part of the official tour. Another time I might have marveled at the gaudy opulence surrounding me, but now the stately spaces seemed to narrow and constrict, as though the rooms themselves were living, breathing creatures closing in on their prey. Was this what the pressure of expectation felt like for Alexander?

Alexander burst through a set of French doors, and I followed at his heels. The room beyond the doors looked more like the set of a movie than a real office. Elegantly embroidered tapestries lined the papered walls and thick brocade curtains hung over the arched windows. His father, King Albert, stood with his back to us and hand resting on the mantelpiece. A few steps away, his mother sat with her hands folded primly in her lap, looking as if she'd been asked to sit for a new postage stamp. She didn't bother to look at us. Instead she maintained the careful posture she'd perfected over her years as Queen Mother.

"Grandmother." Alexander nodded curtly in her direction. "Father."

Albert didn't turn to address his son's greeting. "I asked to speak with you privately."

"I'm well aware of your wishes, but I have no secrets from Clara." Alexander stood, arms lowered, head held high in defiance, and in that moment, I fell in love with him all over again.

It was dangerous to do so, knowing that we were teetering toward the unknown. I'd kept important information from him and I had no idea how high a price I'd pay for that mistake.

"But you have secrets, Alexander." Albert spun to face him, his shrewd blue eyes narrowing as he looked at his eldest son.

"We all have secrets, particularly those of us with royal blood," Alexander reminded him.

"Not the kind of secrets that sell tabloids!" Albert exploded. "I've worked hard to protect this family from this sort of sensationalized drivel. So I will ask you once: is this true?"

A piece of my heart fractured at his question. My own family had their fair share of secrets and practiced lies. I'd watched my mother and father pretend at their marriage for far too long, but there wasn't a piece of me that doubted we loved each other. Even my family protected its members from pain and suffering, and when we'd finally been forced to face what we'd avoided, that love always won out. My parents had stood by me when I'd gotten sick. My mother and father hadn't denied the affair even when they shut me out. But for the first time I saw what it was like to be born into a family that prized duty over affection and prioritized obligation over understanding. I longed to shield Alexander from his father—to release him from the shackles of the life he'd been born into.

"You know as much as I do about that night," Alexander responded evenly. There was a weariness to his voice, born from years of speaking and never being heard.

"Then explain to me why that bitch is claiming she can prove she was given gamma-hydroxybutyric acid that night." Albert crossed the room in long strides, stopping inches from Alexander. Father and son stared each other down, unblinking.

"Bitch?" Alexander repeated ruefully. "Weren't you the one who suggested I marry her?"

The room spun and I locked my knees to keep myself from stumbling. Alexander had assured me that he had no interest in Pepper, but he'd also warned me of his father's expectations. The thought that she'd been deemed a more suitable match for him stung like a slap across the face.

"This isn't a time for your childish jokes. Will you laugh when the inquest begins?"

"Inquest? Will you really let it come to that?" Alexander circled his father, regaining the upper hand. "It might reveal more of the kind of secrets that sell tabloids."

"Do not threaten me," Albert growled, shoving a finger into his son's chest. "I'm your king and commander."

"And my father, right?" Alexander challenged. He ran a hand through his messy black hair and glanced away. "Because your concern is for me. Your concern is for your son. But no, let's not play games. You've always been too busy to be my father."

"You have no appreciation for the complexities of my life. I rue the day you have to take on this role, and I weep for this country that you are the best I can give them," he spat out.

My feet carried me forward before I realized what I was doing, but before I could step between them, Alexander held up a hand to stop me. This was his battle. I only wished he wouldn't fight it alone.

"Do you think I want to take your place? That I want this? A life of privilege in exchange for my freedom?" Alexander asked.

"And that is why you are my greatest disappointment." Albert moved to a cart and uncorked a crystal decanter. He poured the amber liquid into a glass and swirled it once before taking a swallow. "The situation is being dealt with. For the time being, Miss Lockwood seems to only be available to members of the press. I'm certain she'll make an exception for you."

"And not for you?" his son asked. "Was I part of the arrangement? Would she forgive you for wasting the last two years of her life fucking you if she could have me instead? A crown for her silence?"

My mouth fell open in shock, but behind us, the Queen Mother cried sharply. "Alexander!"

He ignored her, opting to pour his own drink.

"That is a private matter." But Albert didn't deny it.

Looking around the room, I realized that I was the only one who hadn't known how deep Pepper's ties to the Royal family were. The thought of Albert and her made me physically ill. Suddenly I understood why Alexander treated

Pepper with such disdain. But how much power could Albert exert over his son? Was it possible he would force the marriage to make the current nastiness go away?

"Regardless," Albert continued, apparently unfazed, "arrangements will be made. This story will go away. I'm certain once Pepper is satisfied that we have an understanding, she'll be more than happy to deny it. But we can't let this get any further. Right now it's merely ugly gossip. She hasn't given an on-camera interview, which gives us time to contain her."

"You'd have me marry her to shut her up?" Alexander asked, incredulity coating his words. He shook his head. "I'm not interested in your hand-me-downs. Or is that your plan? Have me marry her to keep her close so that she can continue to be your mistress?"

"I don't like what you're insinuating."

"I don't like what you're suggesting. "

"This isn't a suggestion." Albert's fist cracked against the wall, sending a shower of dusty plaster to the floor. "This is a demand. Consider this the first of many sacrifices you'll make in the name of this country. She's a natural choice for you. The right age. Close ties to the family. And impeccable breeding."

"I'm not a horse you put out to stud," Alexander warned in a gruff voice. "I've made my choice."

"I don't know why you're under the impression that you have the right to make a choice, but if you're insinuating that you've chosen this American slut, then perhaps I should reconsider whether Edward would be a better fit for the crown."

"You will speak respectfully of Clara or this conversation ends!"

"You're so intoxicated with her that you can't see the damage you've caused this family. It's time for you to start accepting your role. Or..." Albert trailed off menacingly.

"*Or what?* It must be killing you," Alexander said. "To have to choose between your greatest disappointment or your openly gay son. Well, in case you haven't noticed, neither of us are interested in meeting your demands."

"Mother," Albert turned to Mary, "please take Clara into the sitting room, so I can speak freely with my son."

I winced at the way he snarled *my son*. If he wasn't speaking freely now, I wasn't certain I wanted to be here when he unleashed the full fury of his opinion. But there was no way I was going anywhere, especially with her. I'd had the privilege of attending brunch with her once when Alexander had taken me to his family's country estate for the weekend. It had been enough one-on-one time to last me the rest of my life.

"Clara, stay," Alexander warned me as his grandmother rose from her seat. "We're nearly finished here."

"We are nowhere near finished, and we won't be until you understand that you will defuse this situation." Albert stepped closer to his son. The two were so very different. Alexander had inherited his mother's dark hair and striking features. His father's pale skin and graying hair made him look sickly in comparison. But seeing the two of them locked in a battle of wills, there was no denying the power radiating from father and son. Neither would back down tonight. That much was clear. What wasn't clear was who would win in the long run.

"This affair of yours is becoming a national embarrassment," Albert hissed. "Neither I nor this country will stand for it to continue."

"Affairs are secrets. My relationship with Clara isn't something I hide, and I don't give a damn what you or this country thinks of it! Your blood runs through my veins whether you like it or not. I will be king whether you like it or not." Alexander strode toward me, grabbing my hand roughly. "And I will be with Clara whether you like it or not."

Albert's lip curled into a foul sneer. "We shall see."

"We shall," Alexander repeated.

He whipped around, leading me from the room. Alexander walked so swiftly that he practically dragged me behind him, and I quickened my pace to keep up with him. As we entered a darkened hall, I released his hand, forcing him to stop and face me.

I was no longer his secret, but I had one of my own and I couldn't carry its weight any longer.

"I have to tell you something." My heart pounded a drumbeat in my chest. I ignored it, forcing the confession out in a tangle of words and apologies. "Pepper came to me before we left for St. Moritz. She warned me that she had information that could destroy you, and I didn't believe her."

Alexander stared at me in stony silence.

I gulped as raw fear rose in my throat but continued, "She gave me a chance to stop her, and I didn't take it. This is all my fault."

"What did she ask of you?" he asked in a low voice that chilled my blood.

"She wanted a trade of sorts. She said if I left you, she she wouldn't destroy you." Tears rolled fat and hot down my cheeks. "I was too selfish to protect you."

Alexander was next to me in a flash. His hand cupped my chin, raising my tear-stained face to his. "*I* protect *you.* Where was Norris? She should never have been allowed near you."

"I sent him away," I admitted. "I thought I could handle her."

"No one can handle a feral bitch like Pepper. I'm not angry with you, poppet." He wiped a tear from my wet lashes with the pad of his thumb. "I am angry that I was not made aware of the situation. Although I doubt anyone could have expected this based on a few vague threats and ultimatums. I will have to speak to Norris."

"Don't," I pleaded. "He did nothing wrong. I messed up."

"Be that as it may, I don't want you to have further contact with her."

"I won't now that I know how crazy she is," I said.

His face was cast in shadow, but the doubt that flickered over it was unmistakable.

"She...is...crazy," I repeated in a strangled voice. Every bit of me ached for the reassurance that Alexander had spoken honestly earlier—that there were no lies between us now.

"I didn't drug her. I don't find unconscious women arousing."

But he was leaving something out, purposefully withholding his thoughts from me. I wasn't going to force the issue, not while he was still processing this new information.

"There's more," I said, but I pressed my index finger to his lips as his mouth opened. "Tell me when you're ready."

"I need to be sure, and then I will tell you everything,

poppet. No more secrets. No walls between us." He kissed the back of my hand then clutched it in his own. "Tonight, though, I want to take you home."

"I'll go wherever you lead," I promised, knowing with absolute certainty that I meant it.

CHAPTER TWENTY-FOUR

The street was quiet as the Rolls pulled up in front of our gate. Alexander exited the car with express directions for me to remain inside. I waited, longing to be inside and behind the wrought iron fence that separated our private world from the public one forcefully encroaching upon us. When he finally opened my door and offered his hand, I was all too eager to take it.

"Norris will get the bags," he said quietly, "and I'll be right behind you."

He'd been silent for much of the ride home, and I didn't know if he was stewing over his furious exchange with his father or trying to fit recent events together. All I knew was that we were home. Unlatching the gate, I stepped onto the paving stones that formed a welcoming path to my front door. Movement caught my eye and I startled, falling back against the latch. My fingers closed over it, instinct telling me to run, until a familiar face appeared in the darkness.

"What are you doing here?" I asked, still breathless from the scare.

"I came to speak to Alexander. I imagine he's expecting me."

At that moment, Alexander came through the gateway and froze. His gaze grew icy as it locked on his old friend's face.

"Jonathan," he said coldly.

Slowly, a piece of the puzzle I'd been trying to fit together clicked into place, but the larger image was still obscured. I looked to Alexander and back to Jonathan, trying to read the unspoken thoughts that played across both their handsome faces.

"You shouldn't have come," Alexander continued.

"I had to," Jonathan interrupted. "I need to explain what happened—"

"Your presence here is all the explanation I require. Leave," Alexander commanded in a low voice. Jonathan shook his head and a growl rumbled through Alexander.

I stepped back, cloaking myself in the shadows of the garden. I wanted to fade into the night so neither of them would recall my being here. Luckily they only saw each other. The air surrounding us thickened into a palpable tension. I could draw my hands through it, slice it open, and still not damage the heaviness of the atmosphere. It warned of violence and blood as much as the brutal hatred emanating from Alexander's body. I took solace in the fact that Norris was nearby. I would be no match for these two if, or rather when, this came to blows.

"It wasn't what you assume." Jonathan stepped closer, shoving his hands nervously in the pockets of his wool coat. "It was innocent."

"Nothing that happened that night was innocent,"

Alexander roared. His words shattered through the night and echoed in the silence. A few houses down, a porch light flickered on.

But I didn't move to quiet them. What was passing between them was unstoppable. They were somewhere else entirely, caught in a web of the past that only confrontation would free them from. I could only watch the fallout.

"Pepper wanted it. It wasn't much. Just enough to loosen her up." Jonathan's voice rose, desperate to be heard. He shook his blond head. "I should have said no. She was just a kid."

"And Sarah?" Alexander snarled. "Did she want it, too?"

"I swear to god I didn't give any to Sarah. If she took some, it wasn't mine. They shouldn't have even been there that night. They were underage." Jonathan rambled on, only making himself sound guiltier. He was single-handedly signing his own death certificate.

The picture grew clearer until I could see all the pieces—the dozens of mistakes fitting together to form a tragic story. There had been drugs that night, but it hadn't been Alexander providing them. I'd known that, but I hadn't understood how Sarah had taken them. Now I knew. Jonathan had made a mistake, and it had cost an innocent girl her life.

"Did you know?" Alexander closed the space between them and grabbed Jonathan's collar. "When we left that night, did you know that Sarah was drugged?"

A wave of shame washed over Jonathan's features. "I suspected."

Alexander shoved him to the ground and lorded over him, hands curling into fists. The fury rolled off of him and my own terror rose into my chest, making it hard to breathe. I had no clue how far Alexander could take things or how much his blood called for revenge. I'd never been frightened of him before, but now he terrified me. Stepping from the shadows, I placed my body between the men.

"You don't—"

Alexander's sharp look silenced me. "This doesn't concern you, Clara."

"Everything you do—everything you feel and endure—concerns me," I said softly. "Don't chase the past, X. Let it go."

"Letting go is for mistakes. This wasn't a mistake, it was cold-blooded and cowardly." He pushed me away, crouching down so that his face was inches from Jonathan. "There is a time for forgiveness. This is not that time."

He gripped Jonathan's collar, dragging him to his feet. Alexander released him only long enough to strike the first blow to his friend's stomach. It caught Jonathan hard and he sucked at air he couldn't capture. But his response was immediate, his own fist flying to crack across Alexander's left cheek. I fell back as they struggled, torn between crying for help and running. Jonathan was no match for Alexander's strength, not when it was coupled with unconstrained rage. His hands closed over Jonathan's neck, who fought back, clawing at Alexander, desperate for air. Jonathan's face clouded as his fingers slackened, dropping to Alexander's chest.

"Enough!" The cry ripped through me, and I threw my weight against Alexander. It wasn't much of a fight, but it was enough to make him lose his grip.

Jonathan stumbled back. Gasping and sputtering, he collapsed to his knees.

"Not like this," I pleaded with Alexander. "He isn't worth it."

"She was worth it," he growled. "But you're right. This piece of shit isn't."

He rounded on Jonathan. "Get the fuck out. I never want to see your face again."

I clutched Alexander, restraining him the best I could while whispering soothingly to him. It had no effect. His body remained rigid and on edge even as Jonathan got to his feet and staggered to the gate.

Jonathan paused and turned to face Alexander, his knuckles white as he gripped the latch. "For what it's worth, I'm sorry."

Alexander didn't look at him, but his response sent a chill racing down my spine. "It's worth very little."

Some things could be forgiven. Some mistakes left in the past. This could never be forgotten. It would never be forgiven. Jonathan seemed to sense this, his eyes closing briefly, before he left the gate swinging behind him.

I entwined my arm around Alexander's, encouraging him toward the door, but he didn't move. He wrenched away, picked up the bags that lay scattered across the path and walked inside. I let the silence of the night envelop me, finding cold comfort in the contours of branches and the outlines of houses. Nothing felt real, as though the world had been erased down to the barest sketch, leaving me to exist in the shades of murky gray it cast.

This wasn't something I could fix. Jonathan's mistake

couldn't simply be shrugged off. It had shattered too many lives, and its revelation had only reopened the wounds Alexander carried within him. I could only love him through it, leading the way through the darkness that had been cast over us once more.

Norris came to the gate, drawing a surprised gasp from my lips. "Where were you? He almost...he almost..."

My emotions overwhelmed me and I fought hard against the tears threatening to spill over. How many times could I cry tonight? Things weren't a mess. This went above that. Albert wouldn't stop until he'd forced Alexander and me apart. With each passing second, the world cast more judgment upon him. How long before he cracked? How long before the past broke our love again?

"I protect Alexander," Norris said. He took my arm gently and guided me toward the house. "But he will always fight his own battles."

"How do I get him to stop?" I asked, my voice barely a whisper. "How do I show him he doesn't have to fight anymore?"

Norris smiled sadly. "You already know the answer to that, Miss Bishop. You've been healing him since the day he met you, but wounds like these take time to mend."

"We're running out of time." It ached to say it, to acknowledge that it was hard. As each buried secret came to light, it became more difficult. It was harder to find my way through the ghostly haze of mistakes that clouded our love.

"Love doesn't run on clocks," he said. He patted my hand, opening the door and waiting for me to step through. I watched him leave, contemplating his wise words. Since I'd fallen for Alexander, I'd been obsessed with the deadline that seemed to accompany our relationship. It had felt like a ticking bomb running on a timer I couldn't see. Maybe Norris was right, though; my love for Alexander couldn't be wiped away by past mistakes. It hadn't faltered when confronted with threats or lies or gossip. The only person that could let him slip away was me.

And I wasn't about to let that happen.

Alexander's athletic frame filled the doorway, and I looked to him, finding strength in that knowledge. I went to him, but just as I'd almost reached him, he pulled away.

"I can't. I'm sorry. I can't."

His words fell across me like a blow and I caught myself against the wall. I couldn't allow him to pull away, not now. Not when he needed me.

"Then let me," I said softly. "Let me protect you tonight."

"No one can protect me from this," he said harshly. His hands closed over the jacket he'd left strewn across the stair's railing. He whipped it around him, shrugging into it and headed for the door.

Deep inside me I found the strength to step between him and the door. "Don't chase ghosts. Stay here. Stay with me."

"I want to, but there's no point in pretending any longer, Clara. We both knew this day would come."

"Only if we let it," I whispered, but my words were lost to the darkness that consumed him. It had taken hold, preventing him from finding the light that would guide him back to me.

"I promised to protect you." Alexander's eyes flashed as he spoke and a familiar dread grew tendrils in my belly. "I will always do so. You are the air I breathe, Clara. The one good and true thing in my life. I understand now what protecting you means."

I understood, too. His words tugged at the fragile scars that held my heart together, and I felt it fracture and splinter along the fault lines I thought had healed. I had thought once that the pain of losing him would make me stronger. But this pain echoed though me, shredding me to the bone. With each breath I took, my chest contracted until I couldn't find the air I sought.

"No." I forced the word past my dry lips.

Alexander found me. His hand caught the back of my neck and brought my lips to his. It was a gentle kiss, the usual hunger absent, and yet more passionate for the bittersweet sorrow it tasted of. My lips parted in welcome, calling him to me as he searched for an answer without knowing the question. I answered with love. It washed over me and found him. A low hum built between us, but before I could mold my body to his, he broke away from me.

I didn't try to stop him when he opened the door. Alexander looked back at me, his eyes dull and distant.

"Come back to me," I commanded him.

"I'll try. I promise I'll try." And then he was gone.

Our bed felt too large. I curled into a ball, tucking my knees against my chest, but I felt his absence as acutely as I'd felt his presence. No tears came. There were simply none left to cry. Each breath felt like an act of faith as though the next would bring proof that life would go on, and when sleep welcomed me into its comforting embrace, I allowed myself to slip away. Minutes passed. Hours passed. Night became my friend.

And then I was no longer alone. I found him in my dreams, awakening to discover the weight of his body against mine. Alexander pulled me to him. His arms enveloped me, calling me out of the darkness. His fingers found my breasts, massaging my nipples until they throbbed painfully from the arousal of his touch, and I arched into him. I needed to feel his skin on mine—to know he was flesh and blood. The heat of his body scorched through me and I twisted in his embrace.

"I couldn't stay away," he murmured against my neck. "I need you, poppet."

The words hung between us, our mutual need building. I crushed my lips to his hungrily. Our tongues tangled along with our bodies as we struggled for more contact. Want devoured and consumed us, and no matter how forcefully we pressed together, it wasn't enough to subdue our longing. Alexander flipped me to my stomach and licked the length of my spine before standing and pulling my hips to the edge of the bed.

A primal rumble vibrated through his chest, and he grasped my ass with strong hands, yanking me to him until I hovered over his cock. His thick crown jabbed against my swollen cleft. I ached for him, not only physically but emotionally. I couldn't exorcise the ghosts of his past, but I could hold them at bay. I submitted to his will, rolling my hips and coating his tip with my wetness. Alexander needed control over his life. That was impossible, but I was prepared to give him control over me.

"Take me," I pleaded. "Take what you need, X."

He slammed into me with a force that stole my breath, sheathing his cock to the root. A whimper spilled from my lips.

"That's right. I want to hear you," he ordered, rolling his hips savagely. My hands fisted in the sheets and I held on as he plunged inside me again. Deep. Impossibly deep. My brain switched off, lost to his needs and the visceral reactions of my body. Every movement vibrated through my skin: a flick of the wrist, his fingers digging into the flesh of my hips, the pulse of his cock inside me.

"Don't stop," I begged. In that moment I needed him as much as he needed me. I needed the reassurance of his dominance. My body yearned to submit to him, desperate to be freed and to free.

His cock thrust into me, carrying me off my feet. I dangled off the bed, my body pinned to Alexander as he pumped relentlessly inside me. He was my center. My core. I was his sanctuary. His home.

"Fuck," he cried, burying his shaft to the hilt as he erupted. A hand hooked around me as he released and pinched my clit, splintering me and I burst against him, crying his name.

My body slackened, my channel still pulsing around him. He stayed behind me for a moment, tracing the curve of my tailbone before he withdrew his cock. The emptiness yawned through me, and as if he sensed it, he clasped me against him, urging me back onto the bed. Alexander propped himself against the headboard and reached for me. His blue eyes had calmed, but the desire for connection was palpable between us. I crawled over him, lowering myself gently toward his lap as he directed his still rigid shaft toward my tender entrance.

He cradled my back as I sank onto him. His cock pierced me to the core and I moaned as I clung to him. We didn't move. We only held each other as our breathing returned to normal.

When Alexander finally spoke, his words numbed me. "This isn't going to be easy."

"It never has been," I said cautiously. Part of me wanted to run before it was too late, but his hold on me was too strong. I was his willing captive and he was my ruler.

"My father has asked me to attend meetings out of country."

My blood ran cold. Alexander was being sent away again, coerced into exile for a crime he didn't commit. The distance didn't terrify me nearly as much as the possibility that he would return to me broken—that we'd be forced to once again pick up the pieces.

"How long?" I asked, focusing on the details so I wouldn't have to cope with the reality.

"Days. Weeks. I don't know," he admitted.

I traced the lines of his face, committing them to memory, already feeling the gaping weight of separation. It was worse not knowing how long we would be kept apart, which made this time more precious. *Love doesn't run on clocks*, I reminded myself. It was easier to believe that while we were together. But right now he didn't need my fear, he needed my faith. Entwined together, I had no doubt that we could overcome this, too.

Alexander stared into my eyes, and I met his gaze, unflinching. There were a million things we needed to say to one another before this trial began. A million decisions that needed to be made. But I couldn't find the words, so I swiveled my hips and rolled my sex against his hard groin, communicating in the only way I knew. He answered, rocking into me, driving us together. Our bodies spoke for us, and as my limbs contracted and I spilled over, he found the only answer we needed.

"I love you, Clara."

CHAPTER TWENTY-FIVE

My eyes landed on the calendar pinned to the wall above my desk. Two weeks. There were letters from him punctuated by long bouts of silence. The only constant was a single red rose delivered to work each morning with a two word note penned by the florist.

For Monday.

For Tuesday.

For Wednesday.

I tried to shrug off this morning's missing rose. I told myself the florist was sick.

I took to following the news of his travels to fill in the gaps. The one contact I could count on was the pictures that appeared in the daily papers and online. But even as he continued his exile, the rumors swirled around him. Pepper wouldn't be silenced. She sought out anyone who would listen and plenty of people were eager to lend her an ear. Today found her plastered on the homepage of the London Guardian, calling for the inquest Alexander's family was desperate to avoid. I knew the truth about what happened that evening, but I also knew it would be impossible to prove his innocence if it came to an investigation. Jonathan hadn't come forward yet with his version of events. It seemed unlikely he ever would.

I tapped my keyboard, vanquishing her face from my screen. I couldn't blame her for making a mistake that night. I'd made plenty of my own. But I could blame her for trying to ruin Alexander now.

I dialed his number absently, not realizing who I was calling until it was too late to chicken out.

"Miss Bishop," Edward answered brightly. "You're alive."

"I've been busy with work." A child could see past my lie, but Edward was too much the gentleman to call me on it.

"I miss you."

His confession caught me off-guard, and I realized that I missed him, too. Not simply because he was a tangible connection to the piece of me that was absent, but because I needed a friend. I'd fallen too easily into my old habits, trying to work through the time I was forced to spend without Alexander. "Me, too. Have you heard anything?" I forced the question across my dry tongue, feeling a slight twinge of guilt for asking. I didn't want Edward to think he was only a source of information.

"Pepper refuses to speak to any member of the Royal family," Edward sighed. His frustration with the situation mirrored my own.

So, Pepper preferred to spread her toxic version of events to the media instead of facing those she was accusing. It hurt that I had to find this out from someone other than Alexander

"Are you okay? I could meet you for lunch." Edward broke the silence that had overtaken the call.

"No, I'm fine, but let's get together this weekend. I could use the company," I admitted.

"I'll clear my schedule. We can watch sappy movies and drink too much wine."

I smiled. It was the mark of a true friend that despite his current happiness, he was willing to drown my sorrows with me. "It's a date."

"Clara," he said, his voice filling with concern, "if you need me, I'm here. Anytime. Any place."

"I know," I whispered. It was hard to stay strong when someone else recognized my weakness, but giving in now would only mean Albert had succeeded in breaking my resolve.

I hung up the phone and stared at the wall. I'd stayed out of things as Alexander had wished, allowing him to handle the private matters that threatened to destroy our relationship. That had to end. Right now.

Standing, I made my way to Bennett's office. I braced myself, half expecting to interrupt a tender moment between him and Tori, but he was alone. He glanced up from his desk and his eyes narrowed in concern as he waved me inside. I took a seat, squirming anxiously.

"Spit it out," Bennett ordered.

"I want to take a long lunch."

Bennett paused, obviously confused by my request. "Of course," he agreed slowly. "You don't have to ask. I'm fairly certain you've worked through enough lunch hours to earn a week long lunch break if you wanted."

"I know," I said quickly, "but I might not come back."

"Ever?" His brown eyes crinkled at the edges with barely contained laughter.

I relaxed a little and shook my head. "Today. There's someone I need to see, and I'm not sure it's going to be easy."

"Take the time you need." Bennett leaned forward in his chair. "I don't want to pry. I know you have a lot going on right now, but you know what you're doing, right?"

I nodded, knowing it was a lie. I had no idea what I was doing. This was about instinct.

"I'll see you this afternoon then." He settled back to his work.

As I left the office, I made the phone call. Belle picked up on the first ring.

"I need some backup," I told her before she had a chance to say hello.

"Tell me where to meet you."

I rattled off the address I'd found online. She didn't ask any questions.

I had friends and it was time I stopped avoiding them. Strength alone wasn't going to see me through this, but I knew they could.

I ARRIVED IN KENSINGTON, after giving the temporary bodyguard Alexander had left the slip. Belle had obviously taken the concept of backup to the *n*th degree. She was clad in tight black leggings and an oversized black sweater with her blonde hair knotted tightly at the back of her neck.

"You look like you're about to commit espionage," I said with a laugh.

"Hmph." She eyed me over a pair of wide-rimmed black sunglasses. "First you call and ask for backup, then you send me to a random address. I came prepared for anything."

"Then let's go, James Bond." But before I could take a step toward the door, she caught my wrist, stopping me in my tracks.

"What's up, Clara? Why am I here?" she asked.

No matter my answer, I knew she was one hundred percent on my side. There was no reason to keep it from her any longer. "So you can stop me if I try to kill her."

"Who?" Belle yelped.

"Pepper Spray," I answered, my eyes darting to the door.

"Do you think that's a good idea? One paparazzi shot and you're going to be on every news feed in the country."

My lips twisted into a rueful smile. "That's what I'm counting on."

I knocked on the door. Belle flanked me, putting on her best tough girl act, which was surpassingly effective. I may not have always made good choices in men, but my taste in best friends was unerring. No one answered and my resolve faltered. I hadn't come all this way to not get this done. My fist banged against the door. It cracked open and two familiar eyes peeked out at me, rounding into circles when they saw the cause of the disturbance.

"We need to talk." I pushed open the door before she could slam it shut in my face.

"How did you find me?" she asked, shock flitting across her perfect face.

"I have my sources." I didn't tell her that it didn't take a genius to know she'd have gone to the closest relative she had in the London area. The girl lived to be plastered across tabloid covers. She should know that her private life was anything but. If she didn't know, she did now.

Pepper crossed her thin arms over her chest, her eyes

darting nervously to Belle. I definitely owed my best friend a drink later. "I have nothing to say to you."

"That's fine." I crossed the length of the foyer and picked up a picture frame. In the photo Pepper was smiling with her arms wrapped around an older version of herself. I hated to admit that if she took after her aunt, she'd be stunning even in her forties. "I'm not interested in what you have to say. I came here to explain how this is going to work."

Her eyes narrowed to slits. "If you think I'm interested in making a deal with you now—"

"The time for deals has passed. I don't operate like they do." Planting my hands on my hips, I glared at her. "Starting right now, you have no connection to Alexander or his family. You will not go near them. You will not talk about them. You will not sell their stories to the tabloids."

"And why am I going to do that? You're nothing to them. I don't have to listen to you," she hissed.

"Because I'm pretty sure that your father wouldn't be pleased to find out his daughter has been fucking the king," I spat back. Belle's cool composure slipped at this bombshell and she slid her sunglasses off, her mouth hanging open in surprise.

The color drained from her fake-baked skin. "You wouldn't."

I'd found her edge, now I only had to fray it.

"Try. Me." I annunciated each word clearly, not wanting either of them to go over her vapid head. "Do you know what I do at Peters & Clarkwell? I write press releases. Now, I've never written a story to send to a tabloid, but I'm going to guess it's not all that different."

Pepper clutched the strand of pearls draping elegantly around her neck. "This is blackmail."

"I know. I got the idea from you," I pointed out. Was it possible for her to be any more stupid? It was a wonder she'd come up with the idea in the first place. "I've already thought of a few headlines to suggest. *Salt and Pepper: The King's Much Younger Mistress.*"

"Oh, I like that," Belle interjected smugly. "Definitely gets that May/December romance vibe across."

"But is it sensational enough?" I asked her, pretending to ignore the growing horror on Pepper's face. "What about: *How Long Has Sarah's Best Friend Been Shagging The King?*"

Belle tapped a finger thoughtfully on her chin. "Less clever, but more to the point. Honestly, I don't think you can go wrong with either one."

"And they'll need more than one," I pointed out. "I don't think any paper is going to want to pass this story up."

"Get out," Pepper shrieked. She flew to the door and threw it open.

"Not until we have an understanding that you will leave this family alone. Your relationship with them died with Sarah," I said coldly.

Pepper fumed as Belle and I sauntered past her and out the door.

"You'll never be one of them," she called after me.

I showed her exactly how much I cared about that with a casual flip of my middle finger.

As soon as we were around the corner, Belle bombarded me. "What the hell was that? Is it true? And what the hell have you done with my best friend?"

"It's true," I said with a shrug. "She should have seen it coming."

"Seen what coming?"

"Me," I murmured fiercely. "She should have known that I protect what belongs *to me*."

WE GRABBED a bite on the way back to the office after I discovered that revenge made a girl hungry. I felt lighter than I had since Switzerland. Confronting Pepper had reaffirmed my faith that I was strong enough to see both myself and Alexander through this mess. If she'd taken my threat seriously, she'd fade from the media spotlight along with the demands for an inquest into Sarah's death. Now I just needed him to come home.

When I finally returned to work, Tori's head popped up over the top of my cubicle. "Your phone has been ringing off the hook."

"I'm sorry." I checked my desk for messages, but found none.

"As soon as anyone answers, they hang up," she informed me. "Someone only wants to talk to you."

Tori's voice grew faint as panic roared through my blood, drowning out everything but fear. Daniel knew where I worked. He'd been here before. With the chaos surrounding Alexander, I'd chosen to avoid any further news about my ex-boyfriend's upcoming trial. If he'd been released, I would have been informed. As long as he was behind bars, I was safe. But I couldn't ignore the chill Tori's information produced. I had no proof that Daniel had called her before, just a gut instinct that the mysterious calls I'd received this summer were from him. I hadn't known to be scared then, I knew better than to not be now.

My desk phone rang shrilly and Tori tilted her head toward it before disappearing back to her own work. I reached for it, fingers fumbling as I lifted the receiver. He'd hung up on my co-workers, because he wanted to talk to me.

"Hello?"

"Clara." The voice on the other end sent warmth flooding through me. It turned to fire in my veins.

"God, X." I exhaled with relief, but the sensation was short-lived. "Have you been calling me this afternoon?"

"Yes," he confirmed.

"Normal people would have left a message instead of hanging up on whoever answered." Why was I lecturing him? Who cared if he hung up on every person in my building? Hearing him had closed some of the distance between us.

"I'm hardly your average guy," he said dryly.

"Never said you were, X."

I relaxed into my chair, relishing the banter almost as much as the sound of his voice.

"Norris will pick you up after work."

I sat up straight and clutched the phone. Norris had gone with Alexander. If Norris was picking me up...

"He'll be there at half past five," he continued when I didn't respond.

"You're home?" I whispered the question, afraid to hope that it could be true.

"Yes," he answered.

"Will I see you?"

"Yes. There are matters to...discuss. I apologize I can't

talk right now." He said something in a muffled voice and I realized he'd covered the speaker.

I chose to believe that the distance echoing in his voice was the result of distraction. He was traveling. There would be people around him. But I couldn't quite sell that story to myself. Still it was too painful to consider the alternative.

"I'll be waiting," I said, but he had already hung up.

CHAPTER TWENTY-SIX

Leaving London proper in the evening was always a gamble. My heart sank when I exited Peters & Clarkwell to discover cars packed in tight rows down the street. The sleek black Rolls-Royce edged through the standstill traffic and roared to the curb. I rushed to slide into the back seat, not waiting for Norris to get out and open the door. How I'd made it through the last few hours of work without going crazy, I would never know. I didn't want to stay in limbo a second longer. As soon as I shut the door, Norris steered us swiftly into an opening in the traffic jam.

I left the privacy glass down, preferring not to be alone right now. Not much of a talker, Norris' silent presence was better than nothing. But I couldn't escape the onslaught of what-if's swirling through my mind. My thoughts jumbled together, making it impossible to seize on one and fully think it through. Instead, I was trapped with flashes of memory and half-cooked theories. I'd gone into survival mode, not allowing myself to reach a logical hypothesis on what was about to happen. Instinct told me to protect myself, to brace for the worst, even as confusion churned in my stomach. I'd gone into my separation with Alexander clinging to the faith that we would come out on the other side together. I'd held to that belief for as long as possible. Some days it was easier than others. Today wasn't one of those days. I was certain of one thing:

I loved him.

More than I had yesterday or the day before that. Less than I would tomorrow. My love for Alexander had only grown during our time apart, and it was stronger than my doubt. If Alexander was lost, I would find him. If he was broken, I would fix him. We would fix each other. There was no alternative. There never was with love. Giving up just wasn't an option. Not anymore. Not without giving up on him. I saw Alexander for who he was. I loved him for the man he wanted to be and the man he would become. I was all in.

Norris glanced over his shoulder. "I'm going to cut through Westminster and see if I can avoid A501."

"Okay." I couldn't care less what route we took. Part of me wanted to tell him to speed up or hop out of the car and jump on the tube. The other part dreaded the oncoming storm. A longer car ride simply gave me more time to prepare for battle. Fate could have her way with my journey, but I'd made up my mind about my own destiny. Alexander wanted to push me away out of a misplaced need to protect me. But the only way I'd ever truly feel safe again was by his side. Alexander's absence had shown me that he was my other half; being apart from him felt as though I'd been cleaved in two. Half of my body, half of my heart, half of my soul, had been torn away from me. He completed me, and I wasn't about to let him go, not without a fight.

Parliament came into view through the front windshield. It filled the space ahead, already glowing with evening spotlights. Big Ben rose beside it. I had no interest in them, though. Instead my gaze flickered out my own window to a relatively new addition to the borough: the Westminster Royal. My heart lurched as I gazed at the windows of the top floor. It felt like an eternity had passed since I'd agreed to meet Alexander there. So many things had changed even though all around me were timeless reminders of the past. For a moment I wished time had reversed and Norris was taking me there. I wished I could loop my memories and live within them. It would be so much easier than fighting.

But it wouldn't be real.

Instead of cutting through Westminster, the car banked left to cross the bridge. I leaned forward, peering over the driver's seat. "This really is the long way home."

"Alexander asked me to make a stop," Norris said, offering no further information. It was one thing to not be talkative, it was another thing altogether to be cryptic.

Outside the window, the River Thames blurred along with the swarms of tourists taking photos along the famous Westminster Bridge. The speed of the car wiped away their expressions as we passed, making the external world appear as muddled as I felt inside. Ahead of us a number of cars had stopped, taking up both sides of the bridge. We slowed as we approached before Norris finally braked entirely. I scooted to the left side of the seat and rolled down my window, trying to get a glimpse of why we were suddenly stuck. There were no emergency crews or medics nearby, only clusters of excited tourists and security guards.

Private security guards.

I'd just processed that information when Norris unbuckled his seat belt and exited the vehicle. He opened the back door and helped me out of the car. Smoothing my pencil skirt, I searched the crowd for signs of Alexander, but he was nowhere to be seen. I buttoned my wool coat against the crisp autumn air. I lifted my hair from under the collar, trying to make myself look presentable. I hadn't seen Alexander for weeks and I was in work clothes. At least my Alexander McQueen coat flared elegantly at the waist, lending a feminine edge to my ensemble. I didn't think to grab my purse.

Turning to Norris, I raised an eyebrow. "Why am I here?"

His answering smile caught me off-guard. Norris was a subtle man, favoring restraint in conversation and emotions. But right now, he didn't bother to hide his feelings. It was a strange mix of joy and anxiety and confidence. He motioned toward the stone steps that led to the attractions that lined the river's southern bank. My gaze followed the gesture, surprised to see that the sea of tourists had parted into neat lines on either side of the stairs. Strangers snapped photos as I approached, and I fumbled for the railing. My apprehension turned to confusion when I spotted two familiar faces watching me from the landing that led to the next flight of stairs.

Edward beamed at me, standing hand in hand with David. I focused on reaching them, knowing they had answers. But when I stepped in front of them, Edward produced a single rose from behind his back.

"For today," he said softly.

My eyes smarted. I didn't quite understand what was happening yet even though my heart raced in my chest, trying to explain what I couldn't grasp. Alexander hadn't forgotten to send a rose. He'd known he was coming home and arranged this...this...That was what I couldn't process. What was this?

I looked to David, hoping for another clue. His mouth twitched as he glanced quickly at Edward before revealing another crimson rose. "For tomorrow."

Tears broke free and trickled down my cheeks. I accepted the flowers and a crushing hug from each of them. Every few steps another person would step forward and offer me a rose.

"For Thursday!" A woman exclaimed, thrusting a rose into my hand.

"For Friday."

For October. For November. For Christmas morning. It was hard to wipe away the tears clinging to my lashes with an arm full of roses, but I continued, laughing and crying. My nose began to run. No doubt it was beet red. I probably looked a fright, and I couldn't care less. Nearly tripping on the last step of the second flight of stairs, I shifted the roses in my arms to free a hand. There was no way I was ruining this moment by falling and breaking my neck. Someone lifted the roses from my arms, and I whipped around to find Belle behind me. I didn't need a mirror to see what my tear-stained face looked like, because Belle was crying as hard as I was. I folded my arms around her, love flooding through me. When we finally broke apart, she handed me a tissue. I dabbed and blotted until she gave me a firm nod of approval.

"You knew about this when you met me this afternoon," I accused.

She smiled smugly and shrugged her shoulders. "Everyone knows to call me for backup."

"Will you hold those for me?" I asked. Something told me there were more roses coming my way.

"Always," she promised. "I'm always here for you."

Her reminder only made me cry harder. Belle playfully shoved me toward the final flight of steps. "He's waiting for you."

I continued, surprised to see my parents mid-way down the steps. They handed me a rose together.

"For the hard times," my mother whispered.

In that moment, I didn't care about my father's betrayal or how my mother had handled it. No matter what happened, they'd be there for me. In their own twisted way, of course.

Lola smiled up at me from the next step, offering me another lovely stem. "For past mistakes."

I didn't recognize any of the people who lined the path that led along the riverbank. They were strangers, but they all held roses, guiding me toward my future. Lights twinkled in the trees, casting a dreamy glow as dusk faded to moonlight. A few handed me their roses as I passed, others simply cast them to the ground to line my path with beauty. A little girl broke free from her mother and toddled over to me. She held a rose up to me, and I crouched down to accept it.

"Luf," she said with a sweet baby lisp.

I tucked her pigtail over her shoulder and I gave her a hug.

For love.

All of this for love.

Straightening back up, I noted that the London Eye had stopped spinning. The towering ferris wheel ran constantly during tourist hours, but now it was still. I zeroed in on it, barely processing the rest of the well-wishers or the flashes of camera phones. At the ramp where a line of passengers should be, I found a man in a dark suit. He inclined his head and I spotted the earpiece he wore. Unhooking the rope that barred the VIP entrance to the popular attraction, he stepped aside. I climbed the stairs slowly, my pulse pounding so quickly that I trembled.

At the base of the wheel, a single passenger capsule waited with Alexander inside. His dark suit was cut to display his athletic form, although the sleeves strained against his biceps. Looking closer, I gasped. It was the exact suit he'd worn the day we met, down to the loose tie and unbuttoned collar. Our eyes met and his mouth curved into a wicked smile that sent heat rushing to my cheeks.

"Quite the gesture, X," I called as I approached him.

"I have one more rose for you," he said, but he didn't move to give it to me. Instead he waited for me to enter the passenger capsule. Behind me the door slid shut and I startled, pivoting around to discover the glass pod had begun to move, slowly rotating toward the stars. For a second I lost myself to the stunning view of nighttime London glittering against the mirrored backdrop of the Thames. When I turned back to Alexander, he was no longer standing.

I clapped a hand over my mouth. His palm cupped the blossom of a rose and nestled in the velvet petals was a ring. Like Alexander, it was nothing like I might have dreamed of as a little girl. Dozens of tiny diamonds circled a flawless and fiery ruby. The brilliant lights shining in from outside the pod glinted through it, making it blaze with undeniable beauty.

"For always," Alexander promised. "Marry me, Clara."

It wasn't a question, even though he was on one knee.

Even kneeling, Alexander couldn't restrain his dominant nature. My emotions warred within me, overwhelming me. I wanted to slip the ring on my finger. I wanted to run away. I wanted to cry and kiss him and say yes. I wanted to slap some sense into him.

"I...I..." I didn't know which side would win out.

"I suspected as much. You're always overthinking things, poppet." Alexander got to his feet and took my hand. "When will you learn to do as I tell you?"

"I'd say I've been an excellent student regarding that in the bedroom." I sucked in a breath and searched for strength. I'd come here, prepared to fight for him, but I wasn't ready for this. "But not so much outside of it."

"That's exactly why we're here," Alexander confessed. "I have you trapped for the next thirty minutes."

"We're in a glass capsule," I reminded him.

"It would be too easy to seduce you." He drew me against him, and I shuddered at the pleasure of touching him again. My reaction didn't go unnoticed. Alexander cocked an eyebrow as if to say *see what I mean?*

"So what is your plan?" I asked. My heart fluttered as my eyes darted between his perfect face and the ring he still held in offering.

"To convince you to become my wife." He slanted his head and captured my lips. It wasn't the hungry, barely restrained kiss we usually shared. This one was gentle and filled with unspoken promises. When he drew back, I resisted the urge to drag his mouth back to mine. He might not be trying to seduce me into a yes, but if I didn't get control over my body, that was exactly what would happen.

He took a gentlemanly step away, giving our bodies

enough space to allow us to focus. Alexander placed the flower and ring into his jacket pocket. Then crooked his finger, tempting me closer.

Regardless of what decision I made, it had been far too long since he'd held me. I went to his arms without question. He spun me around, so that I looked out over London. Enfolding me in his arms, he whispered into my ear.

"All of this. Yours."

A stranger might have confused his softly-spoken words, thinking that he was tempting me. But I heard the brittle edge in his voice. It wasn't a temptation, it was a warning. Choosing Alexander meant choosing duty over freedom. Marrying him meant giving up the life I'd planned on for one of inconceivable responsibility. If I became his wife, every moment of my life would be scrutinized and dissected from the clothes I wore to the events I attended. I'd had a taste of that life. The vultures had descended prematurely to pick me apart, and I couldn't claim to bear no scars.

"It's selfish of me to ask you this," he continued. "I have few choices in life. Duty binds me to this country, and I know I'm asking you to bind yourself, too. But there is one choice I *can make*. I can choose you, and I will choose you—above all else—for the rest of my life."

I stared out over the water as the wheel reached its apex and began its descent down. Choices were one thing I had an abundance of. I could choose my career. My friends. I could choose to get on a plane and start over. I could choose any man I wished.

And I knew my decision was already made.

I chose Alexander, even at the expense of all else.

"Yes," I murmured.

Alexander stilled, his arms tightening around my waist.

"Yes," I said more loudly. This time there was no doubting my answer. Alexander released my waist and stepped between me and the capsule's curved glass. He drew the ring from his pocket and slipped it over my trembling finger. Certainty washed over me as its weight settled against my skin. It belonged there. It always had. Alexander kissed the hand that now wore his ring.

"Yes, yes, yes." The answer tumbled from me, each acceptance more certain than the last.

Alexander scooped me off my feet and swung me around. "I'd never experienced joy until the first time I kissed you."

"Then kiss me again," I breathed. He set me on the rail that ran the perimeter of the capsule, wedging himself between my legs, which wrapped possessively around him. Alexander tipped my chin up and kissed me deeply. His hand settled on the back of my neck, cradling my head tenderly. His movements were slow with adoration.

He broke this kiss, nuzzling his nose against my cheek. "You have no idea how difficult it is to not take you on the spot."

"People in glass capsules should probably keep their pants on." I grinned widely at him.

"Then I hope you don't have plans this evening," he said dryly.

"I have plans every night for the rest of my life," I whispered. His response was swift and urgent. Fingers tangled in my hair, tugging it to give him better access to my mouth. My hands clenched his lapels as I pressed myself against him. The hunger between us grew greater as we held our bodies in check.

"Show's not over," Alexander murmured against my lips. He set me on my feet, and I realized the wheel had nearly completed its rotation. We were back where we started, and yet, we were only just beginning. A giggle bubbled through me and I caught Alexander's hand as the spinning stopped.

"Show?" I repeated breathlessly.

"I've been forced to share you with the world since the day I met you," he said, bringing my hand up to his lips as the capsule's door opened to dozens of camera flashes. "This was one moment I wanted to share. I wanted everyone to know that Clara Bishop chose me."

"I'll always choose you." I couldn't imagine anyone taking his place. In that moment, there was only Alexander, but I couldn't help winking at him. "What if I'd said no?"

"I knew you wouldn't." His shoulders straightened, and he winked back. How did he make cockiness so damn sexy? He led me off the London Eye and toward the throng of people awaiting us. Lifting my left hand for everyone to see, he shouted, "She said yes!"

The crowd erupted in cheers, but I hardly noticed as Alexander kissed me again, sealing our promise as the world looked on.

CHAPTER TWENTY-SEVEN

We spent the next hour exchanging hugs with the family and friends Alexander had invited to participate in his audacious proposal. Belle kept grabbing my hand to inspect the ring. My mother was already planning the wedding. Edward seemed keen to help her. When Alexander finally extricated us from the small crowd of well-wishers, I was more than ready to be alone with him.

"Take me home, and take me to bed," I murmured as he helped me into the back of the car.

Alexander slid in beside me. "Try to stop me."

I climbed into his lap, lingering in the bliss of this evening's euphoria. Since I'd made my decision, I'd been shown again and again that it was the right one. Marrying Alexander and accepting the responsibilities that came with wedding the heir to the throne was going to be difficult, but I no longer wanted easy. Not if it meant being without him.

He fingered the ring I wore and then smiled boyishly. It was unusual. So unlike the dominant, powerful man that had enthralled me since the day we met.

"This was my mother's," he admitted.

"Oh," I gasped. I saw the ring in a whole new light now.

"She gave it to me before she died." Alexander didn't speak of his mother often, but when he did, sadness always colored his words. Tonight the sorrow in his voice sounded bittersweet. "She would have liked you. My mother was beautiful and headstrong. She matched my father in every way. She was the only one who challenged him. You remind me of her."

It was lot to live up to, but I swallowed my fear. "I love it. I love you."

"I know it might seem like a bit much," he added hastily. "If you'd rather have something else."

I snatched my hand back. "You'll have to pry it off my cold, dead finger."

"That won't be necessary," he said with a laugh. Alexander could be distant. He could be domineering. Every facet of his personality aroused me. But when he allowed himself to be happy, I melted.

Alexander brushed a kiss along my hairline. "When..." he trailed away, his eyes glued to something outside the window. "Fuck."

"What?" I asked, afraid to turn around. Maybe someday I would be accustomed to the bad news that seemed to always nip at the heels of our happiness. Today wasn't that day.

"We have company," he said through gritted teeth. He drew back, stuffing his shirt into his waistband and running a hand through his hair to tame it. Then he assisted me in tugging my skirt back into place. He tucked my hair behind my ears and kissed me softly. The hunger that had ached through me moments before roared back to life and my hands reached to clutch him to me. Alexander loosened my grip and shook his head apologetically.

My eyes flashed to see exactly who had just made their way to the top of my shit list. There wasn't a single person in our lives who didn't know he had just proposed. If I was going to have to constantly field unexpected visitors, a change of address might be in order. A number of black sedans lined the street in front of our house. Apparently the no parking signs didn't apply to them. As we drove closer, I caught sight of at least a dozen men, dotting the gate, garden and front door. I couldn't see the rear garden, but I suspected there were men standing guard there. Every light in the house was on, and the front door stood open.

"A security sweep?" I asked, confused. Had something happened while he was traveling? Or perhaps it was standard procedure after a member of the royal family returned home from an extended trip.

"Undoubtedly." Alexander's lower lip curled with disgust. "One can't be too cautious when the king comes to call."

"K-k-king?" I tripped over the word, unable to process what he was suggesting.

"My father's come to pay us a visit."

As soon as Norris parked the car, Alexander was out the door. He bent and offered his hand, but as soon as I took it, he began to drag me toward the house. A few of the guards moved to stop us but stood down when they recognized him. I smiled awkwardly at them, wondering if it was against protocol to offer them a beverage. After my last encounter with Alexander's father, I'd be happy to find any excuse to avoid being in the same room as him. Alexander didn't give me the chance to escape the impromptu meeting, though. We found Albert in the living room, drinking a glass of wine. He'd settled comfortably on leather wingback chair next to the fireplace. I did my best to look unfazed at his unexpected presence, taking off my coat and laying it over the back of the sofa. But I was rattled. Albert had shown no interest in our life in Notting Hill up to this point, except to demand we discontinue our living situation—and our relationship. It couldn't be a coincidence that tonight he'd finally sought out our home.

"Come to congratulate us?" Alexander asked him stonily.

"Congratulations on your little spectacle," Albert said with a sneer. He sipped the thin red wine, shaking his head. "I didn't think you had it in you."

Alexander glared at him. "Careful, father. That almost sounded like a compliment."

"I assure you it's not." Albert abandoned the wine glass on an end table and steepled his fingers thoughtfully. "Perhaps I underestimated you."

I needed to let this conversation sink in. Of course Albert would come. Alexander had not only involved my family and his tonight, but members of the adoring public. It had all been a charade to endear us to the people. Make the ultimate romantic gesture so we couldn't break up without their hearts being broken along with mine. Alexander hadn't been proposing to me. He'd called his father's bluff, staging the whole proposal, inviting the world to watch so his father couldn't deny our relationship any longer. My words stuck in my throat, catching on the tears mounting there. It had all been a ploy.

"You said it was a show," I said aloud.

The two men ceased bickering and looked at me. Albert frowned. "What is she prattling on about?"

"It was all a show," I repeated, looking to Albert and stepping closer to him. "To undermine you."

It might as well be me to tell him the truth. Maybe then I could take back some of the control the lie had cost me. I closed my eyes, hoping that when I opened them, the scene would fade away. That I was trapped in a dream. That none of this was real.

Albert snatched my hand, ripping me back to reality. It was all true. This was happening.

"Did you have to give her your mother's engagement ring?" His jaw tensed from displeasure. "I think that's what they call overselling *it*."

"This isn't a charade," Alexander said in a low voice. "Yes, I purposefully proposed to Clara publicly. But it wasn't to hurt you. I did it because I wanted my choice to be known, so there would be no question in anyone's mind who I plan to marry."

A flicker of hope ignited in my chest, but I held my breath, refusing to fuel it. Regardless of his intentions, the idea that his proposal had been plotted to garner media attention didn't sit well with me. How many more of my life's private moments would be made into a spectacle for publicity?

"There are protocols," Albert hissed. "Protocols you blatantly ignored—"

"Fuck your protocols!"

"You have a responsibility to—"

"I have a responsibility to myself," Alexander stopped him with a raised hand. "To her."

"And to this country," his father reminded him. Albert tugged open his top collar button. "There are bigger issues at play than your little romance."

"This isn't the seventeenth century. I'm not taking a wife for political reasons."

"Not everything centers around the impulses of your knob." Albert studied his son for a moment before grabbing my arm and dragging me between them. "Does she know about your unsavory tastes? Does she know why you were sent away?"

"I keep nothing from Clara."

There was no point in arguing with the king over this. He'd made up his mind up his eldest son years ago, sending him away to war to avoid facing him.

Albert dropped my arm, looking at me in disgust. "If I had known these twisted impulses were more than a temporary phase, I would have ordered you to the front line."

Alexander opened his mouth to speak, but I'd had enough.

"Get out," I demanded. Crossing to the door, I swung it open. "Get the fuck out of my house."

Both men stared at me, before Albert recovered himself. "You do not presume to give me orders."

"I do presume," I informed him. "I did not invite you into my house. Now I'm telling you to leave."

"At least you have some fire in you." Albert eyed me coldly as he backed out of the door. "Consider this your welcome to the family."

A ritualistic sacrifice would have been more welcoming. I slammed the door shut behind him as my body began to shake. Albert had damaged my resolve, and I was cracking.

Our relationship was built on eggshells and when it finally broke me, I knew that all the king's horses and the king's men wouldn't be able to put me back together. Rounding on Alexander, I tugged his ring from my finger and held it out to him. Alexander stared at it in horror, the pain on his face reflecting the agony I felt. "Take it."

"What are you doing?" he asked in a thick voice.

"Take it," I pleaded as tears pricked my eyes. If this was all a ruse, I needed to put a stop to it now

He reached out and curled my fingers over the ring. "This is yours. It's my promise to you—one I intend to keep."

I forced myself to ask a question I wasn't certain I wanted the answer to. "Why did you ask me to marry you?"

"Because I love you."

Alexander closed the distance between us. He pressed his palms to the door, circling my torso. He had me trapped. I wanted to push him away, to free myself of the heady effect of his physical nearness. I couldn't trust my body not to betray me into believing anything he had to say.

"I deserve the truth. If you only asked me to marry you because you wanted to get back at your father—"

"This has nothing to do with my father!" he exploded.

"Then explain it to me, X," I pleaded, my voice barely registering above a whisper. My gaze found the floor. I dared to hope—to believe that I could have my happily ever after. I'd been swept away by the prince, carried away with tender promises. Life wasn't that simple.

Alexander drew the ring from my clasped palm and slipped it onto my finger.

"I'll marry you tomorrow, Clara. Our secret. If that's what will reassure you. I asked you to marry me because I want you to be my wife. I don't care what anyone else thinks. My father. The tabloids." He paused, cupping my chin to redirect my downward gaze up to his. "Say the word and I'll make this official tonight."

I turned my face into his palm, relishing the warmth of his strong hand. "Sorry. Your father tends to make me crazy."

"He does that to all of his children," Alexander reminded me. "You're already fitting in, poppet."

"Even if we ran away together tonight, there would still be a wedding."

"A wedding falls squarely into the duty I warned you of earlier." Sadness flashed across his face before he forced a smile. "If you've changed your mind, I will understand."

"No. I haven't changed my mind," I murmured. Despite Albert's intrusion and the pressure of his hate-filled demands, I knew with absolute certainty that I'd made the right choice. Alexander and I belonged together. I ran my hand over his vest, my fingers vibrating up his toned stack of abs even through the thick fabric, and paused over his heart. "This is mine."

My hand dropped lower, gripping his hardening cock through his trousers. "And this is mine."

"You're getting quite possessive." Alexander groaned as I unzipped his fly and grasped his hot shaft. He bunched my skirt over my hips, revealing my stockings and garter belt. He brushed a finger across the lace of my thong.

"I am," I agreed, stroking his length with my fist while my other hand pushed his pants to the floor. "You belong to me, but right now, I want to be claimed."

The tip of his finger wriggled along my wet panties.

Alexander caught my wrist, wrenching it off his stiff cock, and twisted it behind my back. I didn't fight when he repeated the action with my other hand. His strong arms bracketed me, restricting my movement. He pulled my trapped wrists down, forcing my torso to arch. He met my curving body with hunger, his teeth catching my left nipple through my shirt and sucking it into his mouth. His tongue flicked over its tip, circling the sensitive bud until it pebbled, swollen and tender. His mouth widened, claiming more of my breast. Tension pooled in my core, and I bucked against his groin. My swelling sex brushed his crown. The lace between us scratched as his velvety tip dragged along my seam, sending a tremor of ecstasy through my throbbing center.

But he wouldn't allow me to be so easily satisfied. Releasing my wrists, he hoisted me into his arms and carried me to our bed. He kissed me slow and he kissed me hard until I was senseless with desire. When he laid me on top of the sheets, I watched, lust building into a frantic pulse, as he stripped himself of his jacket. His vest followed. Then his shirt. He stood before me, flagrantly masculine and still indescribably beautiful.

I couldn't comprehend that we had forever. Forever to explore each other's bodies. Forever to find the answers we sought together. Forever to express our love. The idea stole my breath. He was mine. Always.

And I wanted forever to start right fucking now. My fingers fumbled with my own buttons, but he stooped, gripping the silky fabric, and wrenched it open. Buttons scattered across the bed and floor. Alexander shoved the thin shirt off my shoulders, wrestling it past my arms as we tangled together and my breasts fell into his hot palms, heavy with arousal.

"I need to taste you. I've thought about your body every day we've been apart," he said gruffly. My head fell back as he descended down my torso, licking and sucking every inch of my soft flesh he could reach. His hands massaged my breasts, kneading them as he continued his ravenous descent until he reached my bikini line. He nudged my thighs open with his chin, the slight scruff of his five o'clock shadow grazing the delicate skin and making me giggle.

"You like that, poppet?" He caressed his face against my inner thigh, and the tickling sensation shifted to a craving that took control of my body. I writhed closer to him. His hands abandoned my breasts. Alexander shoved the flimsy lace covering my sex to the side. "I missed your cunt. I'm going to spend the rest of my life worshipping it. Has it missed me?"

I moaned a yes as he pressed a tender kiss to me. My legs fell open in invitation and he accepted, thrusting his tongue between my folds and hitting my pulsing clit. I cried out, resisting the urge to clamp my legs against his head and hold him there all night. There was no need for force, because he was in no hurry, which he demonstrated by lapping my silky wetness with slow, deliberate strokes.

How had I survived without his touch for so long? I deserved some type of a medal. A girl shouldn't go cold turkey from a man like Alexander. I planned to tell him so when...My thoughts fell away as he hooked a finger inside me, discovering uncharted territory. I never wanted him to stop. My limbs tensed, clinging to the edge, disinclined to fall over it. This was the man I loved. This was the man I would marry. The thought nearly annihilated me, but I gripped the sheets and hung on. I willed time to stop, but it sped up as his skillful tongue pushed me closer to the brink. He milked me, massaging the spot with increasing urgency as his mouth closed over my clit with bursts of suction that liquefied the last of my body's stubborn resistance. I dissolved into quivers and spasms as the most powerful orgasm of my life rocked through me.

My body still quaked as he scooped me against him and flipped me over so that I covered him. His thumb caught my chin, directing my eyes to his and guiding me back to him through the hazy bliss permeating my brain. "I want you to ride me," he ordered. "I want to watch my cock slip inside your body."

I ignored the sensitive soreness thrumming between my legs and knelt over him. Lowering carefully, I impaled myself on his cock inch-by-inch, my cleft stretching to accommodate his considerable girth. I gasped as his crest knocked against my womb. He'd never been this deep inside me before and I wanted more. I wanted all of him. My hips rolled, circling the shaft buried to my core. I lifted my ass so that he could see, then slammed back down. His fingers dug into the flesh of my hips, encouraging me as I fucked him.

Rocking slowly, I ascended his cock again. I leaned back, gripping the sheets as I savored the sensation of gliding up his slick rod.

"Let go," he commanded. "Show me how beautiful you are when you come undone on my cock."

I unraveled over him, baring myself to him as promises spilled from my lips. I was his. I needed him to know that but pleasure washed away my words and I was pulled out by his powerful current, drowning in our love. We collapsed together, limbs entwined, neither willing to tear their eyes from the other. We'd fought for our love. We had dismissed the objections of his family and buried the ghosts of our pasts.

I pressed my face to his throat, counting the beats of his heart—*my* heart in *his* body. And in the privacy of our bed, he lifted my chin and asked me the question he'd posed hours earlier. "Will you spend the rest of your life with me?"

The gesture stole my breath. There was no pageantry. No show for the tabloids. It was raw and real and meant more than dozens of roses and fancy words.

My answer hadn't changed. It never would. But this was our sacred exchange—the vows that no one saw. The ones we would cling to in happiness and trouble.

"I will."

CHAPTER TWENTY-EIGHT

Rain fell in slants across the seedy pocket of Tower Bridge. Cautious tourists had abandoned the area before nightfall, warned away by overly anxious guide books. Ethan preferred it that way. The less people privy to his nighttime activities, the better.

He checked his watch, noting with annoyance that his contact was late. His instructions were clear, though. He was to wait. His boss's customer had paid a pretty sum for the brown-paper-wrapped package tucked inside his jacket.

Scumbags always paid well.

Footsteps fell in the alley behind him, and Ethan turned slowly, not wanting to spook the approaching man. A guy who was in business with the DeAngelo family had to be unhinged. Between the dark and the hood obscuring his face, Ethan couldn't get a good look at him.

"I'm expecting a delivery," the man said.

"Daniel?" Ethan breathed a sigh of relief. It was his contact and not some kid looking for an easy mark. The stranger didn't remove his hood as Ethan passed the package to him.

"This should take care of the cost." Daniel handed a thick envelope to Ethan, who pocketed it quickly in his leather jacket.

He was glad to be rid of it. It was one more debt paid to the mob boss who currently pulled his strings. Ethan didn't ask why the man wanted the gun. He could guess. Knowing would only add to the burden he carried from his illicit dealings.

They parted without exchanging false farewells. One man eager to forget that he'd been a party to coming violence. The other eager to finally strike.

ACKNOWLEDGMENTS

There are so many people to thank for helping me to see this book into the world. Continuing this book wouldn't have been possible without the love and support of my husband. Thank you for your endless patience as I plot and cry, cry and plot. Thank you for getting kids to school and reminding me to eat. And most of all thank you for enduring hours of sexual frustration to offer me notes and edits. That journalism major *did* pay off!

My deepest gratitude belongs to Tamara Mataya for lending her incomparable eye to my pages and for adding all those sexy u's and s's in Alexander's chapters. You've made this book better in every way.

Thanks to Bethany Hagen for fixing all the little things and always keeping better track of my characters than me. I'll cover your ass anytime.

Laurelin Paige, I'm glad you're as turned on by business as I am. Thank you for always finding time to read and for all the advice and support in this venture.

Thank you to Melanie Harlow and Kayti McGee for keeping it real and cheering this SCB on.

Seriously, you have no idea how much I love you all. After cuddling with my sexy mankat, you ladies are my first thought every morning. Always.

A big thanks to the girls of FYW for taking on this baby smut writer and answering all her silly questions. You all are my inspiration.

To Lauren Blakely, Melody Grace, and K.A. Linde for dinner, drinks, and strategy—and many, many PMs thereafter. I owe you drinks.

I would be going crazy without you, E.M. Thank you for believing I could pull this off despite the dozens of 3 a.m. emails. I couldn't ask for a better partner in crime. Move back.

My apologies to Lindsey. I'm glad you didn't chuck Command Me into the Atlantic Ocean. Thank you for riding my ass to the finish line. I hope you didn't mind spending so much time with Alexander. I love you, bitch.

To Tara and the team at Draft2Digital for putting up with all my emails and for being the best in the industry.

Thank you Vania, Chandler, and VLC Productions for the amazingly perfect cover art. I can't wait to see how you steam up the camera lens next month for Crown Me's cover. I'm already eying the lingerie!

My gratitude to Cait Greer for formatting even on a moment's notice. Thank you!

A special thanks to Trish Mint and the Schmexy Girls for their stamp of approval, shenanigans, and all around hilarity. Thank you to Angie McLain and Fan Girl Book Blog for letting me quote you. You have no idea what that meant to me. To Summer's Book Blog for being early to the Alexander train. And to all the bloggers who love and support authors, you make all the difference. Your passion inspires me. Thank you for doing what you do!

And to the readers—your notes, your comments and your support give me the strength to keep going when I wonder if I should give up. This story is for you, and I hope to give you many more. Thank you for reading. I love you.

ABOUT THE AUTHOR

Geneva Lee is the *New York Times*, *USA Today*, and internationally bestselling author of twenty novels with varying amounts of kissing. Her bestselling Royals Saga has sold over three million copies worldwide. She is the co-owner of Away With Words, a destination bookstore in Poulsbo, Washington. When she isn't traveling, she can usually be found writing, reading, or buying another pair of shoes.

Connect with Geneva Lee at:
www.GenevaLee.com

Made in the USA
Middletown, DE
21 August 2024

59537678R00187